Ragtime for the Rockies

Ragtime for the Rockies

Karl A. Lamb

To order additional copies of this book, contact:
Xlibris Corporation
1-888-795-4274
www.Xlibris.com
Orders@Xlibris.com
120583

Chapter 1

A S THE FORD MODEL T left the concrete highway to enter a bumpy farm road, Ruby held the picnic basket tightly between her feet, protecting it from bounces. She hoped the lunch she prepared would match the grandeur of the picnic site as described by Owen, her husband. They had been married for nearly six weeks; she still worried that some dish she prepared might not please him, although he was yet to complain. Ruby sensed the picnic was perhaps a final celebration of their honeymoon, for Owen's long vacation was ending.

Owen drove the Model T along the edge of a melon field. Suddenly he turned sharply, eased the car across a ditch, and stopped with its radiator nearly touching one wire of a four-strand barbed wire fence. Before Ruby could express her surprise, Owen set the brake, jumped down to the ground, and took three side steps along the fence. It had to be some kind of gate, but Ruby did not understand how it could work.

Owen stopped beside a thick fence post connected to a thinner post by wire loops at its top and bottom. Owen pulled the upper loop off the end of the thin post. With tension released, the four barbed wires connected to the next thick post went limp. Owen lifted the post out of the lower loop to open the gate, trotted back to the car, drove it through, dismounted again, fastened the gate shut, and again climbed into the Model T.

He grinned at Ruby. "We're almost there."

Ruby confessed, "I didn't know you could get through the fence that way."

"Some ladies who don't understand how that's done have lived on farms all their lives. They depend on the menfolk because we have special skills." He grinned.

Ruby realized the gate's design was simple. *I think of myself as a modern woman. I voted in 1924, stared at by hostile men. I voted because I was old enough, but before then, women had not even been allowed to vote. I sure won't wait for a*

1

man to open a gate. If I share responsibility for running the country, I should share simple tasks that may have been considered man's work.

Owen stopped in a small grassy field. Ruby stepped down into the grass, causing crickets to jump away from her boots. When she turned to get the basket, Owen had already hoisted it out of the car. He stepped around the radiator and took Ruby's hand.

As they strolled on, Ruby was grateful she didn't need to guide a skirt though the tall grass. She was wearing jodhpurs, as she always did for picnics and as many other occasions as possible. Nobody worried much about her wearing pants when it looked like she was ready to mount a horse. *I don't have to tell them the horse is in Illinois.*

Ruby looked through cottonwood trees toward the riverbank and beyond the river to rolling hills, with the sharp peaks of the Rocky Mountains in the far distance, outlined against the clear blue sky. Ruby drew her breath in sharply. She stood quietly, and Owen paused beside her. She seemed incapable of movement, as if she had discovered a master's landscape painting on a museum wall.

Finally she spoke. "Owen, this is unbelievable. It's so beautiful."

"This is just the first glimpse," Owen said. "Come see the rest of it."

Owen led Ruby through the trees to a miniature meadow on the riverbank. Ruby stopped by a clump of wildflowers with trumpet-shaped blue blossoms that shaded into purple, with white centers.

"Look, Owen! Columbines!" She sank to her knees beside the flowers. "They'll make a perfect centerpiece." She looked up, puzzled. "They grow in the high mountains. How did they get planted down here?"

Owen chuckled. "I think you can thank some passing bird."

Ruby giggled, amused by the image, and glanced up at the pure blue sky; but there were no birds in view. She spread the tablecloth beside the blossoms to form their table, took the basket from Owen, and placed it between them. Sitting side by side, they looked past the flowers and over the river to the mountains.

Ruby tore her eyes away from the distant peaks to glance at her husband. His curly light brown hair was usually untidy, counteracting the severe look of his eyeglasses with their horn rims and round lenses. He had grown up in view of these mountains but claimed he didn't really appreciate them until he saw Ruby's joy in them.

Smiling, he took her hand and suggested she look back at the river. It was wide and shallow, made up of several streams flowing down the twenty-yard width of the riverbed. They heard the sound of water rushing over rocks, and looked upstream to find water pathways beneath a bridge that spanned the river. The midday sun was relentless in the clear sky, but its force was broken by the shade of the cottonwoods and a mild breeze that came off the river.

Owen asked if it was time to eat. Ruby turned away from the view and unpacked dishes from the basket, uncovered them, and arranged them between herself and her husband.

*　*　*

When he finished his third piece of chicken and Ruby had lost count of his potato salad helpings, Owen sighed. Ruby recognized a signal of satisfaction. Then he looked toward snowcapped Longs Peak thrusting above its neighbors in the sharp profile of the mountain range.

"The peak is real clear today." He reached out and cupped the air. He drew it slowly back and turned the palm upward, as though presenting the mountain as a gift.

Ruby took the bait. "Can we go to the mountains again? Tomorrow?" She touched his hand.

"Sure. Get some gas and a tire-patch kit, and Lizzie will be ready to go. We'd better, while we have a chance. Next week I'll be teaching."

Ruby watched Owen turn toward her and look into her eyes. As he reached a hand toward her bright chestnut hair, her breath quickened, but they heard young voices. Three boys, ten or eleven years old, were walking single file along the riverbank, stepping from stone to stone when there was no gravel at the water's edge. As Owen and Ruby turned their attention to the potential intruders, the boys slowed their pace to peer through the fence and conduct an inspection. Owen shook his head, causing his glasses to slide down his nose, and glared at the boys over the top of the lenses. They hastened around a clump of bushes and were gone.

Ruby grinned. "Were you practicing the evil eye, to keep order in the classroom? Those boys could be your new students. Couldn't you call them up here to get acquainted?"

"No, they'd run like the devil if I hollered at them. Anyway, they're too young for high school, and they don't have George Lydell's permission to be on this property. They weren't about to ask us for an invitation to climb through the fence. I must have looked mean to them—they didn't hang around."

"At first I thought the one who was leading had to belong here. The Lydell boy would have recognized you, so they had to be neighbors. Tell me about the Lydells."

"They have two sons. I'll have the older boy, Ronald, in class. His younger brother is only four. I called on them to see about Ronald's research project on irrigating sugar beets. Ronald didn't have much to say. But the parents,

George and Susan, are real friendly. They showed me around the place, and I asked about this stand of cottonwoods with the view. George Lydell said we can come in anytime, long as we keep the gate shut. Say, are you going to eat that potato salad?"

Ruby laughed. It felt good to have her cooking enjoyed. She handed her plate, empty except for a few forkfuls of salad, to Owen.

The gentle breeze combined with their partners' nearness to increase the sense of intimacy. Ruby glanced back through the trees at the Ford, the honeymoon wagon. Certainly not elegant, but paid for. The rush of the river below was overlaid by the droning of cicadas coming from the melon field behind the cottonwoods.

"Sweetheart," Owen said, "this place reminds me of a hymn that I've heard dozens of times. You probably know it too. My sister claimed I couldn't carry a tune in a bucket, and she probably told the truth. But I'm going to try." Owen hummed a note, as if tuning his voice, and the words tumbled out.

> *Shall we gather at the river, where bright angel feet have trod?*
> *With its crystal tide forever flowing by the throne of God?*

Owen's face flushed. He was off the tune by the fourth note. But he had to know Ruby's smile was not mocking. Her clear voice began the chorus, and he followed along gratefully.

> *Yes, we'll gather at the river, the beautiful, the beautiful river;*
> *Gather with the saints at the river that flows by the throne of God.*

Satisfied that Owen now possessed the tune, Ruby sang the closing notes in harmony. Below them, the river rushed on.

"You got me out of a real pickle," Owen said. "I was killing that grand old tune. And I don't really think the South Platte flows by the throne of God. It only goes to Nebraska."

Ruby smiled. "I'm sure people in Nebraska claim it's God's country." Owen grinned in return. Ruby continued, "But it can't be God's country. No mountains."

"When you were growing up in Illinois, there weren't any mountains."

"I didn't know what I'd missed until I found them. First in Nevada, then here, and then Wyoming!"

Ruby thought their honeymoon, camping in Yellowstone National Park, was exactly what she wanted. She had come from Illinois to attend college, then fell in love with the Rocky Mountains—and Owen. Glad she found him, along with her mountains. *My cup of happiness runneth over.* When Owen leaned over to taste her lips, Ruby's heartbeat quickened. She hugged his shoulders and whispered, "It's time to go home."

Ruby packed the leftovers in the picnic basket. Owen folded the tablecloth and stowed it with the basket in the Ford. He reached across the seat to set the spark and the throttle, then went forward to the crank. He hooked his left forefinger into the wire loop of the choke and spun the crank with his right hand. The engine came to life with the second spin.

After both were settled in their seats, Owen released the brake and depressed the low gear pedal. The car climbed easily to the trail running along the melon field, which led them to the four-strand barbed wire fence on the boundary of the property.

Ruby laid her hand on Owen's arm. "You sit still," she said. "I'll get the gate."

"Do you understand how it works?"

"We won't know until I try."

Ruby jumped down and marched to the spot where two fence posts stood close together. She carefully pulled up the wire loop binding the thick post to the thinner one, freeing the thin post. Lifting the thinner post out of a loop on the ground, she pulled on it to keep the four wires untangled, and opened the gate by carrying it in a six-foot arc. After Owen drove through, Ruby carried the post back and replaced it in the wire loops to fasten the gate, then climbed back into the Model T.

Owen grinned at her. "I guess I can't claim that skill is special any longer."

"I saw you do it when we drove in. Did you think I wasn't paying attention?"

Owen made no further comment. Ruby considered her next step. *I will have him teach me how to crank this beast and then drive it. He doesn't need it to go to work. I could travel all day, all by myself, if I need to.*

Owen eased the car through a shallow ditch and onto the gravel of the county road. He shifted into high, and the Model T rattled along the uneven surface, making conversation difficult. Before long they reached an intersection, and turned onto the highway that connected Denver to the south with Greeley to the north.

Traveling more swiftly on concrete, they passed the ruins of the old fur trappers' fort and entered Platteville from the south. Crossing the town boundary, the highway turned into Main Street, a broad thoroughfare dappled by the shade of elm trees arching overhead. Soon they passed the Platteville Consolidated Schools, a single block containing grade school, high school, and playgrounds.

Owen turned sharply to enter an alley, pulled into a backyard, and stopped by a small house with shingle walls painted brown. It was obviously built to house the hired man when the large house beyond was a farmhouse. In forty years, the town grew three streets beyond, absorbing most of the farm's land. Selling the land enriched the farmer and made the hired man's house available for rent. Its proximity to the schools made it attractive for teachers.

Owen turned off the Ford's engine and waved his hand grandly toward the little house. "Welcome to our little brown home in the West!"

* * *

Ruby stepped down from the Ford and walked through the unlocked door. It opened directly into the combined living and dining room, which, with a kitchen and bath, made up the house. She deposited the picnic basket in the kitchen and entered the living room.

There were two doors in the wall. The first was a walk-in closet that Ruby entered to hang up her sweater. The second door concealed a brass double bed fully made up that, when needed, would swing out of its closet and fold down to the floor.

When Ruby came out, Owen had swung the bed mechanism out of its resting place. Instead of lowering the bed to the floor, he put his arms around Ruby and whispered, "Hello, sweetheart."

Ruby had meant the promise implied by her "time to go home" whisper, but Owen seemed awfully eager. Should she, for the first time ever, resist an advance by her groom? Before she could speak, a harsh bell rang out. It was the telephone installed in the kitchen the day before. One long ring and two shorts.

Ruby pushed against her husband's chest, saying, "That's our ring! It's our first call!"

"Let it ring! If it's important, they'll call back."

"Our number hasn't even been listed yet. Somebody found it out, so this call must be important." She slipped away, took the few steps into the kitchen, placed the receiver against her ear, and greeted the caller, who identified himself in a deep male voice.

She felt a thrill when she confirmed her own identity as Mrs. Owen Mattison. She answered the second question, "Yes, he's right here." As her husband came into the kitchen and reached for the receiver, she said, "It's a Mr. Arthur Stark."

Owen's conversation was one-sided. There were a "Yes, sir"; a "That will be fine, sir"; and "I will see you then. Thank you, sir." As he replaced the receiver in its hook on the wall, Owen told Ruby, "Stark's son, Matthew, will be in my Vo Ag class. I was supposed to call at their place on Monday to see about his project. Stark says that something came up, he can't meet me then. So I'll go out there tomorrow, although I don't normally make calls on a Saturday."

"But we were going to the mountains tomorrow."

"I know. I'm sorry, but I didn't think I could refuse. Arthur Stark is a member of the school board, and it only has three members."

* * *

Arthur Stark, a sturdy man in his late forties, replaced the telephone receiver on its hook and set the instrument down on the desk. He left his farm office and went to the kitchen, where his wife was drying dishes by the sink. "Thanks, Martha, for reminding me about Mattison. I called. He'll come at the same time tomorrow, so I can go to Greeley on Monday."

Martha set down the plate she was drying, and turned to her husband. "So you're determined to go to a Klan luncheon. You know they'll pressure you to join."

"Like I told you, Charley Vesser invited me. I've known Charley for years, and I respect him. His reasons for joining the Klan will be worth listening to."

"So you aren't going to keep away from it."

"No. See, this modern outfit does a lot more than ride around scaring darkies. They say the Klan runs Denver, especially the police department, and the Klan provides the only enforcement Prohibition gets down in Pueblo."

"I've heard that. But Arthur, you aren't the sheriff."

"No, but I'm a father. And something has to be done about how loose things have gotten. Women are wearing skirts up to their knees! They keep inventing outrageous dances to go with that jazz. Do you want your daughter to look like one of those flappers?"

Martha abandoned the lunch dishes and sat down at the kitchen table. "Irene is a pretty level-headed girl. She's smart enough to go to college, where she'll experiment with fashions. We should let her do some of it while she's still in high school."

When Stark spoke, the heat had gone out of his voice. "I doubt that. If we can't have decency at home, where can we find it?"

Martha shook her head. "You haven't been paying attention in church, to see what women are wearing nowadays. You'd better come in the next time the temperance union meets here, and see what even *they* are wearing."

"Don't tell me the Platteville chapter of the WCTU has turned into a bunch of flappers!" Arthur Stark laughed at his sudden vision.

Martha did not seem amused. "Hardly. But they've given up floor-length skirts. Come and see for yourself."

7

* * *

Owen guided the Model T through Platteville and onto the county road. He saw the Stark dairy farm from a quarter mile away. The round brick silo rose at the end of the light tan milking barn, which looked freshly painted. Other outbuildings were the same fresh color. The two-story white farmhouse was nestled in a stand of cottonwoods.

Cattle were gathered toward the far end of a lush pasture that stretched along the roadside. Their hides were colored a rich tan, with some light markings, and the animals were more compact than some other breeds. *Jerseys.* Still rattling along the road, Owen felt at home. His father bred and milked Jerseys. Yes, Holsteins, with their large black and white flanks, would look out of place. The buildings were painted to match the cattle.

Owen shifted into low gear as he turned to pass between the tan brick gateposts. A short driveway led to the house, which had a screened porch along its front wall. Owen stopped beneath a tree, set the brake, and walked toward the door.

It opened, and a woman wearing an apron over her housedress came out. "Mr. Mattison? I'm Martha Stark. Arthur and Matthew will be here any minute." Owen stepped forward to accept her outstretched hand. He saw a trim, composed woman of middle age, noting a few gray hairs among the auburn locks twisted into a bun at the back of her head. As their hands touched, she glanced over his shoulder. "Here they come now."

Along the gravel road through the cottonwoods came Arthur Stark and his son, Matthew. Their relationship was obvious. The man was tall, inches over six feet; the son was nearly as tall, and apparently still growing. Their stocky physiques were identical, their hair the same light brown.

An obvious difference was the father's uneven gait. As his left foot touched the ground, there was a slight hesitation as the right foot rose up, then a tiny lurch in the shoulder—a reminder of some old injury. But he walked with an easy rhythm and did not seem to be in pain. Owen walked a few steps toward the two. Matthew hung back, suddenly shy, but came forward when introduced. His handshake was nearly as vigorous as his father's.

"I'll leave you men to discuss your business," Mrs. Stark announced. "I'll have some refreshments ready when you come back." She entered the house.

"I thought we might look around the place," Stark said, "and see where Matt's project could fit in."

Owen said, "That's a basic decision Matt will have to make."

As the three walked back into the cottonwoods, Arthur Stark addressed Owen as if Matthew were forgotten. "As a school board member, I like the Smith-Hughes Act. It's good to have some federal money, and the support for teaching vocational agriculture shows somebody in Washington cares about farmers."

Was Owen being challenged? He cleared his throat. "Well, the program is based on showing the benefits of science, not just talking about them. Every student has to complete a major project, usually some kind of agricultural experiment."

Coming out of the cottonwoods, the group passed a half-acre vegetable garden. In late August, the garden was past its prime. But Owen could see the tomato vines were still producing, carrots and potatoes were still in the ground, and a few ripened ears of sweet corn were ready for picking. A few chickens scattered away from their path.

Matthew closed the distance between himself and the two men. "That's what I need to know about my project," the boy said. "It isn't really scientific. I mean, I won't develop a new breed of chicken or anything."

"Every experiment doesn't lead to something new," Owen said. "Some of them validate what we already think we know. I've seen the plans for your brooder house. People haven't used electric lights to keep chicks warm for very long, and you plan some arrangements that look brand-new."

Owen saw Mr. Stark nodding his head in agreement. "So you see," Owen continued, "your project will confirm the science and test new applications of it. Your teacher was right to approve it last year, and I hope you're ready to get started on it."

Matthew's smile was a silent sigh of relief, but his father wanted to continue the subject. Arthur asked, "Does your shop have the tools for a project like that?"

"We're close to it," Owen said. "We have a good table saw. We have basic things, hammers, T-squares. The electrical part we can figure out. But Matt will have to bring his own personal items, like a tool belt. Of course, he'll have to pay for the materials."

"It will be a substantial project," Arthur Stark said, "and takes a long time. Matt doesn't have much experience in carpentry, and he's never done anything that takes months and months. Will you be giving him close supervision?"

"I'll supervise when he needs it, but it will be Matt's project, not mine. Experienced or not, he looks like a strong, steady worker. Am I right, Matt?"

The younger Stark merely nodded.

As they walked on toward the barn, Owen asked how the idea of building a brooder house came about. Matthew confessed that the idea was his own. Like everyone, they kept a few chickens for the eggs and an occasional fryer. But if they were to raise chickens seriously, they needed a brooder house. His father had the dairy operation working well; if Matt raised chickens, he would have an income of his own, and he could save for college expenses.

Matt was now walking with the two men and talking freely. They examined three places in the farmyard that were possible sites for the new addition.

"Dad," said Matthew, "will I have to paint the brooder house that same tan color?"

Arthur Stark seemed amused. "I suppose not," he said. "White is probably the best color for a nursery."

When they returned to the house, Martha had set out lemonade and cookies in the parlor. Matthew took two cookies and went off to do chores.

"Mr. Mattison," Martha said as they settled into chairs, "I look forward to meeting your wife and helping her meet the local women. I hope you will both come to the reception and dinner for new faculty."

"I'm sure we'll be there. Ruby is eager to get acquainted."

"Do I understand correctly that you are newlyweds?"

"We've been married nearly two months." Was Mrs. Stark a small-town busybody? How much did he have to say to satisfy her?

But she did not press. She chatted about the attractions of Platteville and said she would introduce Mrs. Mattison to the Mizpah Society, the town's most active women's club.

"Don't keep the man in suspense," Arthur interrupted. "Tell him what 'mizpah' means."

"It's from the Bible, isn't it?" asked Owen. Was he too eager, like a trained animal?

"Yes, it's Hebrew for 'watchtower.' The club's project is restoring the cemetery on the hill east of town. We got help, including water from the tank up there, just two years ago."

Arthur Stark broke in. "They've done quite a job too. There was a bunch of old headstones and monuments up there, but it was all weeds, full of rats and rattlesnakes. They put in grass and trees and shrubs, really got the place organized."

Owen said, "I visited a student project out east on that road, just last week. The cemetery looks real nice, and it has a great view of the Rockies."

* * *

When Owen cranked the Model T and drove out between the gateposts, Arthur Stark turned to his wife. "You know, I think that Mattison boy is going to be all right."

"I liked him," Martha replied, "but he does seem awfully young."

"He's twenty-four, as I recall from when we hired him. Six or seven years older than the kids he'll be teaching and coaching. I'm not sure he really needs those horn-rimmed glasses he wears. Probably wears them to seem older."

"Well, they do make him seem more serious."

"He was good with Matt. Got him right into the grown-up conversation, assured him that his project is a good one."

* * *

After completing Monday morning chores, Arthur Stark fastened a collar to his shirt and selected a necktie. After he said his farewell to Martha, she watched through the window as he climbed into the Reo. She shook her head slightly, as if signaling her disapproval to the furniture.

The Reo started electrically without complaint. Arthur drove between the brick gateposts onto the county road. At the intersection, he turned south on the state highway and soon entered Platteville. He glanced toward the pickle-salting shed by the railroad station and remembered his own two acres of cucumbers. A block farther along Main Street came the large Platteville Mercantile store that stocked groceries, farm equipment, and kitchen utensils.

The barbershop was closed. Arthur couldn't make out the cardboard clock's hands that told the opening time, but Ollie Scott would surely open up soon. He stopped at the gas pump outside the garage and waited while the Reo's tank was filled. Then he turned back to the north, where Main Street led onto the state highway, which soon bent to the northeast, headed for Greeley.

Arthur settled into his seat, wondering if he could complete the sixteen miles in twenty minutes. It was noon when he got to Greeley and time for the lunch when he got to the hotel. Charley Vesser was waiting for him in the lobby outside the dining room.

Vesser rose from the chair with ease unusual for such a large man. Stark noted that Vesser's shoulders, developed by years of hoisting grain sacks, bulged beneath the coat of his business suit. "Hello, Arthur, you're right on time."

Stark grasped his friend's outstretched hand, responding in kind to the vigorous handshake. "Yes, the Reo cruises at forty or forty-five."

"Come on in, and I'll introduce you to some people." Before they could enter the dining room, a man dressed in a dark suit, wearing a plain necktie, hailed Charley Vesser and shook his hand. Vesser introduced Stark. "This is Reverend Davis, our 'kludd.'"

"That's 'kludd,' not 'clod,'" the minister said with a grin. "K-l-u-d-d. Means chaplain of the chapter. Welcome to our meeting." The minister inquired smoothly about Stark's occupation and family, asked after the health of a pastor in Platteville, and moved back into the lobby to meet some new arrivals.

Vesser led Stark into the dining room and up to the head table. Standing near a lectern was a mild-looking man of average build, wearing a pinstriped suit. "Arthur, this is the head of our chapter, the Exalted Cyclops, Dr. Gerald Ostrum. Gerry, this is Arthur Stark from Platteville."

The handshake seemed quite ordinary. "Charley tells me you're making a real difference in the Platteville School District. We need your kind of man in the Klan. We're dedicated to the same things, like raising a new generation of 100 percent Americans. We can help each other, so I sure hope you'll join with us."

"Charley's talked to me about it for quite a while."

"Well, Charley's one of my best 'kleagles'—recruiters, that is. If you're ready to join, we're having a shortened initiation ceremony at the end of the meeting. About half a dozen are coming in. Hope you'll be among 'em."

Other members came forward to speak with Ostrum, so Stark and Vesser took seats on opposite sides of the end of a long, narrow table.

Stark was surprised at how ordinary Ostrum seemed. Didn't at all match his title. What should an Exalted Cyclops look like anyway? He sought edification from Charley Vesser. "This Ostrum is a dentist here in Greeley, isn't he?"

"Yes, but his talent for organizing is wasted in dentistry. He's a real spark plug, and he is serious about the Klan's goals."

"I can't help saying, he seems too modest to be an exalted anything."

Vesser forced a chuckle. "When he has an order to give, he isn't modest about it. Best part is, he has ideas. Did you get a sense of that?"

"I sure didn't know the Klan is interested in the schools."

"You bet we are. Young people are the key. If you lose them to booze or to foreign influences, pretty soon you'll lose everybody."

The room was gradually filling with men in business suits. Arthur saw several complexions ruddy as his own, the mark of those who labor outdoors.

"Listen, Arthur, we can work together. Gerry is right. No matter what you do in the schools to train kids up, sometimes it just doesn't take. Kids get out of control before their parents realize it, so the Klan reminds them of what's right. We go to dance halls and throw out the booze. We put the fear of God into people who sneer at Prohibition." Vesser fell silent as a waitress delivered plates with roast beef, mashed potatoes, and vegetables. "The same thing goes," he continued, "for the kids parked in dark cars. A man in a hood shining a light in their faces gets their attention."

"My wife says that sort of thing is up to the sheriff."

"Hell, the sheriff of this county belongs to the Klan. He thanks us for our help."

"But Charley, can you always do what's needed here? The Klan's a national organization."

"Sure, part of the 'klecktoken'—the initiation fee—goes to the national

HQ. But each chapter deals with the problems in their own area. We don't take orders from anyone."

"Let me get this straight. The head of this Greeley group is called the Exalted Cyclops. Who is this Imperial Wizard I read about in the paper?"

"Oh, that's the big cheese down in Atlanta. He's got nothing to do with us."

As Charley Vesser attacked his roast beef, Dr. Ostrum appeared beside their table, knelt down, and placed his arm on Vesser's shoulder. "Charley, Harvey Burd has been sick a lot and wants to resign as 'nighthawk.' He couldn't even make it here today. Can I count on you to take over?"

Vesser laid his fork down on the table. "Well, sure, Gerry, unless someone who's been a member longer than me wants to take it on."

"Just wanting doesn't get the job done. You did most of the nighthawk's work last ceremony. Proved you can do it. I'll get you nominated." He clapped Vesser's broad shoulder and strode to another table.

Arthur Stark looked at his friend and raised an eyebrow. "What's a nighthawk? It doesn't even start with a k, does it?"

Charley Vesser chuckled. "The nighthawk is the keeper of the cross. He stores timber, burlap, and kerosene, then sets it all up for the next burning. Oh, and he presents candidates at the initiation ceremony."

Waitresses entered the room again, removing the luncheon plates and delivering a slice of apple pie to each place. Other women passed among the tables, refilling coffee cups. The hum of conversation died when Dr. Ostrum tapped against the lectern with a spoon.

"Excuse me for interrupting before you've finished your dessert. But there's a lot to do, and you all have other places to be. By rights we should have our initiation first, so our guests who wish to join could vote on the chapter business coming up. On the other hand, they should have a chance to observe the meeting, see what we're up to, and have a chance to back out if they get cold feet. Besides, it's better to finish a meeting on a high note, and that's the initiation. Does that suit everyone?

"Okay, the first item is an election to fill a vacancy among the officers. Harvey Burd is resigning as nighthawk because of ill health, and we need to elect a new one. Are there any nominations?"

A voice rose from the table visited by the Exalted Cyclops a moment earlier. "I nominate Charley Vesser." Another voice from the same table, "Move the nominations be closed." The motion was seconded from a table across the room, and a chorus of "ayes" was unleashed by "All in favor." The call for opposition yielded only silence, so the election of Charley Vesser by acclamation was announced, signaling a round of applause.

Dr. Ostrum read a notice from the Denver chapter that the annual boxing and wrestling tournament would be held in two weeks. A Greeley Klansman had volunteered to drive a carful to the tournament; those interested should contact him directly. A member reported his census of occupied cars parked in the dark along the Weld County roads. He concluded that Klan activity was responsible for a 60 percent decline in their numbers in just a month—and it had been a month of beautiful evening weather.

The Exalted Cyclops turned the lectern over to a committee chairman, who described planning for the second annual family picnic, to be held in the Rocky Mountain National Park the second Sunday afternoon in September. There would be a five-inning baseball game, and pony rides would be provided for the younger children. The women's auxiliary had agreed to supply the food. The meeting enthusiastically approved the plans.

Charley Vesser leaned toward his guest. "See what I mean? The Klan makes a difference. It even has activities for the family."

"Okay, I'm ready to join. Here's the ten bucks for your whatchamacallit, the klecktoken."

The Exalted Cyclops then asked members to introduce their guests who were considering membership. Host and guest stood, while each host extolled his guest as a fine potential Klansman. One guest was a familiar figure to Stark. It was Ollie Scott, the Platteville barber. No wonder his shop was closed.

No guest refused membership. The seven candidates were directed to line up, facing the head table.

"Arthur," Vesser said, "you're on your own. I've got to play nighthawk." He marched behind the head table, pulled a black extension cord from under the table, and unrolled it toward the wall.

"Our outdoor initiation with a cross burning is quite elaborate," Ostrum said from the lectern. "And it's very impressive. But rest assured, our indoor version still makes you a genuine Klansman, and the electric fiery cross has the same symbolic meaning."

Vesser returned to the table, reached beneath the cloth, and pulled out a wooden cross three feet tall and set it on the head table. It had a solid wooden base and Christmas tree–size lightbulbs running up the cross and along its arms. When connected to the extension cord, the cross spread a reddish glow. Vesser took a slip of paper from Ostrum and slowly called the name of each candidate, who then joined a line facing the cross.

"Candidates," the Exalted Cyclops declared, "know that the fiery cross symbolizes a Klansman's flaming zeal in the protection of the ideals that you will pledge yourself to cherish. To prepare for that oath, I will pose a series of questions to you. Your answers must be loud and clear. First, is the motive prompting your ambition to be a Klansman serious and unselfish?"

The assembled candidates mumbled their assent.

Ostrum cupped an ear with his hand. "I can't hear you!"

"Yes!" The seven candidates called out in unison.

"Are you absolutely opposed to and free of any allegiance of any nature to any cause, government, sect, or ruler that is foreign to the United States of America?"

"Yes!"

"Are you a native-born white, Gentile, American citizen?"

"Yes!"

"Do you believe in the tenets of the Christian religion?"

"Yes!"

"Do you esteem the United States of America and its institutions above any other government, civil, political, or ecclesiastical, in the whole world?"

"Yes!"

"Do you believe in and will you strive for the eternal maintenance of white supremacy?"

Arthur Stark heard his own voice join in the affirmative chorus. But there weren't a dozen black people in all of Weld County, and he was damned if he would go off to fight Denver's battles. Were they really listening to everything they claimed to agree with?

"Brothers," said the Exalted Cyclops, "I ask you to kneel before the cross and to join hands."

Stark stood still for an instant, wondering what was coming. The other candidates were hitching up their trousers to avoid stretching the cloth and lowering themselves to the floor. Ah, a lodge initiation. Not much difference. Ollie Scott had taken the position next to him. Arthur knelt and reached for the barber's hand.

"Repeat after me: I—state your full name . . ."

I, Arthur Preston Stark—

"In the presence of God and man, pledge, promise, and swear unconditionally . . ."

In the presence of God and man, pledge, promise, and swear unconditionally—

"That I will obey the constitution and laws and will conform to the usages and requirements of the Ku Klux Klan."

That I will obey the constitution and laws and will conform to the usages and requirements of the Ku Klux Klan.

"And will heartily heed all decrees, edicts, and instructions of the Imperial Wizard." As Ostrum spoke these words, Stark recalled Vesser saying the Imperial Wizard had nothing to do with them. It was a formality, like any lodge initiation; not the time to object.

I will heed all decrees, edicts, and instructions of the Imperial Wizard.

The Exalted Cyclops then declared, "By authority vested in me by the Grand Dragon of the Colorado Realm, I now declare and proclaim you citizens of the Invisible Empire, Knights of the Ku Klux Klan, and invest you with the title of Klansman, the most honorable title among men."

Chapter 2

MR. NEWTON MACLEAN, PRESIDENT of the board of the Platteville Consolidated Schools, wore a tight-fitting suit with a high-collared white shirt and striped tie. He looked as proper as he sounded, tapping his gavel lightly and declaring, "The meeting will come to order." He looked down at his two colleagues, who were not at all disorderly. The schools superintendent was equally silent. Four dozen chairs filled the large classroom, available for the public. All were empty.

"It looks like there are no burning issues to bring out parents or other taxpayers," Maclean said. "I wish that was because we've been good stewards of our trust, but I'm afraid it means this community is drifting along in blissful ignorance, with no sense of where we're going. I'll have a proposal to make about that when we get to new business. But the first item is the minutes of our final meeting of the school year, last June. Arthur?"

Arthur Stark, the secretary, reported. At their June meeting, the board gave formal approval to the district's contracts with two new teachers in the high school and three in the grade school. The superintendent reported on the purchase of new texts and other supplies. His plans for summer maintenance were approved. The board members signed seventeen diplomas for the graduating high school seniors. Arthur Stark closed his notebook with a tiny slap to indicate conclusion of the minutes.

Roy Thompson, the treasurer, seconded Maclean's motion approving the minutes, making a vote unnecessary. Maclean called on Superintendent Healy, who reported successful completion of the summer maintenance work and described preparations for the school year. Arthur Stark asked about equipment in the shop serving the vocational agriculture program. Healy mentioned some new tools and suggested a small fund to be committed after Owen Mattison, the new teacher, determined further needs. Stark supported the idea, which was agreed to unanimously. Finally, the superintendent reported that

63 students were expected to enroll in the high school, with 195 entering the eight lower grades. Treasurer Thompson expressed tentative optimism about district finances but called upon Superintendent Healy to caution the faculty against waste.

President Maclean asked if there was any new business. The other three men silently returned his gaze, and he said, "Hearing none, I will introduce an item of my own to which I have given a great deal of thought. I'm concerned by the wildness of our young people. The fact that liquor is now illegal just attracts them to it. The girls are wearing dresses that hardly reach their knees, and nobody has a sense of modesty any more. The music they want to hear is wild, and the dances they do are even wilder. When a boy comes to call on a girl, he won't sit with her on the porch swing. He wants to take her away in an automobile, and God knows where they'll go or when they'll come back."

Maclean removed the linen handkerchief from his coat pocket, shook it open, and mopped his brow. "I belong to the Methodist men's club, where we talk about the sorry state of our young people, but we don't do anything about it. We drift along with no sense of where we're going, despite two shotgun marriages in our church in the last eighteen months. Kids nowadays don't recognize the difference between right and wrong. If the churches aren't helping the kids figure that out, shouldn't the schools be doing it?"

"MacLean," Stark said, "I don't think you give enough credit to the churches, like our own Methodists. My children are in high school, and we get them to the Sunday school, where they get some of that teaching. But what about the ones who don't even go to church?"

"Exactly," Maclean said. He laid down his handkerchief and held up a book bound in black leather, which he grasped with both hands. "Where can anybody, whatever age they are, find guideposts to choose between right and wrong?" He began to punctuate his words by waving the book up and down in an arc of several inches. "It's here, in the Good Book. We can't control what the kids do when they're away from school, but we can help them see they have choices to make. I propose changing the classroom opening ceremony. In addition to leading the class in the Pledge of Allegiance, I want the teacher to read a passage from the Bible that guides students to choose right over wrong."

Superintendent Healy indicated his desire to speak by raising the forefinger of his left hand. "We do the pledge in every grade. Will this Bible-reading be in every grade? It will be over the little kids' heads."

Newton Maclean looked toward the superintendent. "Harold," he said, "I wanted to discuss this with you first. But when I called, you had finally gotten out of town for vacation. I didn't mean to blindside you."

Healy nodded to acknowledge the apology. Maclean plunged ahead. "The Bible should be read in every classroom. Little kids won't understand every word. But they'll hear those great words every morning, and they'll begin to remember them, like the multiplication tables. When the students begin to understand the words, they'll want to hear more."

Stark spoke again. "Maclean, if you are making a motion, I'd like to second it."

"Well, I am making a motion."

"Second the motion!" Arthur Stark beamed, delighted by Maclean's articulation of the problems that so disturbed him. At last, some sensible action. The board had a chance to make a real difference.

"A motion being made and duly seconded," Maclean said, "the motion is before us for discussion."

"Maclean," said Roy Thompson, "we need to know more details. Like, does each teacher choose the Bible passage for his or her own class?"

"No, the passages should be assigned by us, the school board. We have the responsibility, and we shouldn't delegate it. We will get advice from our local pastors. They could take turns recommending the passages, a month at a time. I'm sure Cobb will help us. With the Methodist preacher on board, it'll be easy to sign up the Presbyterians."

Treasurer Thompson spoke again. "Before we get too far along, I'd like to hear what Superintendent Healy thinks of the idea. Particularly, are there any hidden costs we should know about?"

Harold Healy tapped his pencil on the arm of his chair. "I don't see large cost problems. You would ask teachers to add about five minutes to their opening ceremonies. Unless you lengthen the school day by five minutes, that will cut into the time available for classes. In the high school, where we have six periods, that means shortening each class by fifty seconds. You could call those fifty seconds a cost, but I don't think teachers will complain unless you shorten their classes again for something else. The accrediting agency shouldn't complain. There could be some cost if the school is going to provide copies of the same Bible for every teacher."

President Maclean waved his hand casually. "There won't be any trouble getting uniform Bibles. Our church overordered them for Sunday school prizes. We can get a dozen or more just for the asking."

Healy laid down his pencil, hunched his shoulders, and bent forward. His voice suddenly sank to a near whisper. "The problem won't be cost. I see a different one. You mentioned two Platteville churches—our Protestant churches—and said their pastors would help pick Bible readings. What about St. Nicholas? Will you get their priest involved too? There are at least fifty Catholic kids in these schools. Will the priest choose some passages? Will Catholic parents want their kids to hear Bible verses picked by Protestant preachers? Will Protestant parents be happy when a priest does the picking?"

Newton Maclean pressed the palm of his hand to his forehead. "Harold, I appreciate you bringing up the politics of the situation, like you always do. And part of your job is to keep us from making political mistakes. But I don't think we have to consult any priests. Why does it have to be so complicated? We're all Christians. We're asking the teachers to read from a great work of literature that happens to include moral guidance. Who can object to that?"

The superintendent gazed for a moment at the ceiling. "You could tell parents their kids are studying the Bible as literature, but some of the faculty aren't qualified to teach literature. Will they be commenting on the passages they read?"

"No, no, that's not the idea at all. The teacher will only read the passage. In the high school, we can see if students will volunteer to read some. There won't be any comments or discussion, just those few great words. Food for thought, you might say. Then the school day will begin."

"And that's *all*?" Stark was disappointed.

"Oh," Maclean replied, "I have no illusions. One Bible passage won't make kids into adults. But they will hear a new passage every day."

Arthur nodded and spoke almost to himself. "Yes. There has to be two programs, one for now, aimed at kids who misbehave, and a long-term one for everybody. Parents—and the sheriff, if needed—handle kids who break the law. The school should take on the long-term need."

"Exactly," said Maclean. "Kids who have an immediate problem should take it to their parents or to their pastor. The Bible readings will help keep such problems from developing. Best of all, it's a chance for the three of us to do something for Platteville. Through us, the whole town can take a stand against the sinfulness of places like Denver and Chicago and Hollywood."

Arthur Stark nodded vigorously. "I don't think for a minute that a few words from the Bible will work miracles, but it's a beginning. It's a chance for this board to show where we stand, no matter what the town thinks. Are we ready to vote?"

Roy Thompson shook his head. "Like Harold, I'm wondering about the Catholic students or, really, their parents. Will they be happy about Protestants choosing Bible passages? Maybe we should announce that this Bible-reading program is under study and call a public meeting to discuss it."

"Thompson," Maclean said, "Every meeting we've had this year has been open to the public. If people missed our discussion tonight, it's their own fault for missing the meeting. If we called a special session, people would come and talk the idea to death, like tonight, only worse. The sooner this program gets started, the sooner it can do some good."

Arthur Stark agreed. "We have the authority to determine the curriculum. Let's go ahead and do it."

"I'm not against the idea," Thompson said. "I only wonder why we're in such a hurry. I won't oppose it. I'd be outvoted if I did."

President Maclean said, "I take that as a call for the previous question. All in favor of adding Bible reading to the classroom opening ceremony, please say 'aye.'"

Arthur Stark's "aye" rolled out firmly; Roy Thompson's was a weaker echo. Maclean indicated an affirmative for the record. "As there is no other new business," he said, "I'll entertain a motion to adjourn."

* * *

Owen Mattison hurried home from his orientation meeting with Superintendent Healy to find Ruby, dressed in clothes good enough for church attendance, attacking the living room furniture with a duster. "You don't have to shine things up," he told her, "just because my brothers are coming. They're family."

"Yes, they're family. But I've only met them once, and I want to show I can keep a decent house for you." Ruby moved on to the kitchen. "It's wonderful of your mother to lend us her piano."

Owen walked to Ruby's side. "She figured you wouldn't be happy without your music."

Owen's arm slipped around her shoulder, but Ruby returned to her dusting. "Why did the superintendent want to see you?"

"To make a long story short, he told me that I'll teach biology this fall and physics in the spring, on top of Vo Ag, shop, and PE, and coaching men's sports."

"So you'll be the science teacher."

"Only biology and physics. Healy will teach chemistry himself. He says I'm his only faculty member with a BS degree. And he can't have people with BAs teaching science. The accreditation people wouldn't like it. I told him I didn't even take physics in college. He laughed and said I'll get to learn it now."

"They didn't mention that when you were hired, did they?"

"What I would teach beyond the Smith-Hughes classes was left pretty vague. I was excited about coaching baseball and basketball, so maybe I didn't ask about it very carefully."

"But you don't really mind, do you?"

Before Owen could respond, they heard the sound of a Model T engine that stopped near their door. Owen marched across the room and yanked open the door before a knock could sound. Owen greeted his brother, "Hey, Lew, good job. You're here early."

Ruby patted her meticulously combed hair and followed Owen to the door. They welcomed Lewis Mattison and went with him into the yard.

The Model T truck was used for farm duties and hauling sugar beets. Now it carried a massive upright piano, wrapped with burlap and held by ropes. Peter Mattison, barely in his teens, was struggling to loosen the ropes, as Norman, second oldest after Owen, laid planks against the end of the truck bed to form a ramp. The three brothers were dressed in farm work clothes of varying age and condition. Owen recognized clothes he had worn before they were handed down the line of brothers. He climbed up into the truck bed to help Peter.

The piano rested on a dolly with hard rubber tires. When the ropes were cast aside, Owen and Peter pushed the piano to the back end of the truck bed. As Owen and Peter coaxed the front dolly wheels onto the plank, Norman and Lewis stood below on each side. When the second pair of wheels followed, the four brothers used all their strength to control the piano's plunge down the ramp.

"Made it!" Norman rejoiced.

"That's the hard part," Owen announced.

But the dolly did not roll easily. Coaxing the piano along threatened to topple it off the dolly. When the piano was finally eased to the floor and pushed into the position Ruby indicated, the brothers were winded. They stood back from the piano, staring at it as if they couldn't quite believe their accomplishment. The piano dominated the limited space of the combined living and dining room.

"Thank you, thank you," Ruby said. "It looks like it belongs there. Now after all that hard work, I have some sandwiches and iced tea ready."

"Not so fast!" Norman Mattison was wiping his brow with a white handkerchief. "I wouldn't mind a swallow of iced tea, Ruby, but you can thank us best by playing a couple of tunes on this beast. Pete, run and get the piano stool."

"It will be horribly out of tune," Ruby said. "The strings were stretched and loosened by the move—"

"Ruby," Norman said, "you credit us with better ears than we've got. We couldn't tell in tune from out of tune."

Ruby looked toward Owen for help, but he only smiled. Peter loped into the room and placed the stool before the piano keyboard with a flourish.

"Well, all right. You come get some iced tea, and I'll try to play something." Ruby moved to the dinner table and poured four glasses of iced tea. The brothers took them and found seats. When Ruby went to the piano stool, there were four chairs to hold the Mattison brothers. With the piano against one wall, and the four brothers seated, the living-dining room was stuffed.

Ruby picked her way through her in-laws to reach the piano stool. She placed her hands on the keyboard and began a lively tune. After a half-dozen notes, Owen recognized her favorite, *Kitten on the Keys*, while Ruby winced at the flat tone. Then in the midst of a run, she struck a key that sounded an octave too low; the sound was so blatantly misplaced that her audience joined in Ruby's laughter. She continued to play until another key produced similar results. She spun around to face her audience, shaking her head.

Norman Mattison grinned at her. "I reckon," he said, "now we understand your problem a little better."

"The piano tuner is coming tomorrow. No concerts until after that. And now it's time to eat." Ruby led the four brothers to the table with their chairs. Peter brought the piano stool to sit on, insisting that Ruby take a chair. She passed the plates of sandwiches and fruit she had prepared. Owen's brothers ate heartily and with appreciation. Owen caught her eye and smiled. Ruby grasped his hand under the table. *Owen is my best friend. My husband, my all.*

* * *

After Ruby's second successful driving lesson, Owen and Ruby strolled arm in arm to the Methodist Church for the new teachers' reception. Martha Stark greeted them warmly outside the church door and began describing Platteville's women's clubs as soon as Owen introduced Ruby.

Mrs. Stark recommended the Mizpah Club, which she had told Owen about in her own parlor, and expressed mock dismay that he had not informed Ruby of its delights. After summarizing the improvements already made in the cemetery, she invited Ruby to attend the next meeting. The invitation had official standing, since Martha headed the membership committee, and she promised a reminder telephone call with the details.

Mrs. Stark spied another guest walking from the street toward the church. She lowered her voice. "That's Isabel Nelson. She's alone because her husband was killed in the war, just a week before the armistice. So sad."

The newcomer was dressed in a chemise that barely covered her knees, and her honey-colored hair was bobbed. Owen need not have worried that Ruby would be the only one to experiment with flapper fashion. Mrs. Nelson seemed older than both Ruby and Owen. Ruby thought she could be an older sister.

"Isabel, this is Owen and Ruby Mattison. Owen is our new Vo Ag teacher and coach. This is Isabel Nelson, she's been teaching literature in the high school for—my goodness, is it two years already?"

"Actually, it's three." Ruby felt Mrs. Nelson's handshake was as firm as a man's. Ruby was delighted. "Welcome to Platteville," Isabel said. "It is a friendly town, provided you don't bring too many new ideas."

"I know," Owen said. "Mrs. Stark's husband tells me the same thing about the farmers. He says they have trouble accepting new agricultural practices."

"I believe it," said Isabel Nelson. "Or take music, for example. Platteville isn't even ready for ragtime, not to mention jazz."

Ruby wanted to ask for musical details, but Martha Stark took control. "Irene, I've been telling Ruby about the Mizpah Club."

"Oh yes." Mrs. Nelson turned toward Ruby. "It's not just a social organization. We actually do things and get to see the results. You'll love it if you have any interest at all in gardening."

With more guests arriving, Martha Stark directed them inside to a large basement meeting room, where partitions separating Sunday school classes were shoved against the wall, child-size chairs stored, and adult tables set up. Planks laid on sawhorses made a food table. Scattered clusters of people talked quietly. The men wore celluloid collars with Sunday suits, and the women exhibited varying compromises between flapper fashion and Edwardian primness.

As Owen and Ruby entered, School Superintendent Healy left one of the groups and came to meet them. "Hello, Mattison. Good to see you again. This must be your bride."

Owen presented Ruby.

Healy said, "It's great to have some fresh young faces around, do a world of good for Platteville. We've got to get you connected with the right folks. You met Martha Stark at the door, now come over here and meet the preacher."

Healy guided the Mattisons toward a group of five people. He stopped beside a man wearing a dark coat with a sober tie. "This is Reverend Dan Cobb, pastor of First Methodist. Reverend, let me introduce Owen and Ruby Mattison. Owen is our new coach and vocational agriculture teacher."

The clergyman shook hands enthusiastically and introduced the two couples beside him, members of the church who were also parents of schoolchildren. Arthur Stark, who was acquainted with all but Ruby, who Owen introduced quickly, suddenly joined the circle.

Stark looked around him. "Has Harold told you about the new policy we adopted at the last board meeting?" Receiving only negative signs, Stark forged ahead. "We've been wondering what the school can do about the wildness of young people today. We've agreed that from now on, opening ceremonies in each classroom will include a Bible reading."

"A fine idea," Cobb said. "Who will do the reading?"

Stark glared at Superintendent Healy as if daring him to make a negative comment.

"Normally," Healy said, "the teacher will do the reading. In the upper grades, a student volunteer may be appointed occasionally. He will have plenty of time to practice at home before his turn comes."

Ruby noticed Healy's presumption that student readers would be male. She felt the time was not ripe for complaining about such oversights.

"You see," Stark said, "we'll choose the readings and publish the list in advance. We'll choose readings for their moral content, but not by ourselves." He turned to Cobb. "We'll ask our ministers to suggest passages. We hope you'll be willing to help, Dan."

"Of course, Arthur. I see lots of possibilities. We might have the same theme for readings in school on the weekdays, and for Sunday services, plan sermons around them. I assume you'll be asking Jed Rollins." He named the Presbyterian pastor.

"Oh yes," Stark said. "We thought if you'd take turns, it won't become a burden. Maybe each of you could advise us a month at a time."

"There would have to be a little coordination, but I'm sure that Jed and I can handle it."

Martha Stark walked up, announcing that dinner was ready. Six newcomers to be welcomed—five new teachers and Ruby—and there would be six tables. Would Ruby mind being separated from her husband, so there could be a newcomer at each table?

Ruby shrugged her shoulders slightly for Owen, smiled at her hostess, and followed Mrs. Stark to the food table.

Owen was not pleased by the separation from Ruby, but he saw familiar faces when George and Susan Lydell sat down at his table. He thanked them for the picnic on their land and told how Ruby enjoyed it, even finding columbines and claiming them for a centerpiece. The Lydells urged Owen to bring Ruby whenever it was convenient.

Then George Lydell asked a question Owen did not anticipate. "Mr. Mattison, did you follow the news in July about this fellow Scopes, down in Tennessee? The schoolteacher?"

"I remember the name, but I didn't follow the trial." Owen did not add that he had been on his honeymoon in July.

"Well, this Scopes was teaching biology, in high school, I believe. And he was teaching this evolution theory that's contrary to the Bible."

"Yes, I remember that, but I never heard how the trial came out."

"He was convicted. Tennessee has a law against teaching the idea, but I don't think we have that law in Colorado."

"Not that I know of."

"Well, it looks like our boy Ronald will be taking your biology class, along with Vo Ag. We wonder if you'll be teaching this evolution thing."

Owen was glad he had just taken a mouthful of pork chop. He could think while he chewed. And chewed. And then took a drink of water before replying. "Well, I won't teach that men came from monkeys. We'll cover Mendel's laws of heredity, about dominant and recessive traits, because it's important to know how a breeder can improve his herd and to understand hybrid corn. It's a very basic class, so we won't be reading any Darwin."

Mrs. Lydell entered the conversation. "Mr. Mattison, it's comforting to hear that. I'm sure it's just a stage, but Ronald tries so hard to pick fights with his father. This evolution idea is the kind of thing he wants to argue about."

Owen noticed that all other conversation at the table had ceased, and the two other couples joined the Lydells in looking at him. "Well, I'm surprised to hear that. Ronald seemed real shy when I was out at your place."

"I suppose that's so," Mrs. Lydell said, "you being his new teacher and all. But he won't stay shy very long. He'll try to argue with you. I just hope he stays respectful."

A mother at the end of the table spoke up. "Our Bobby talks like he knows more than his father and I can ever learn—and he's only eleven!"

Appreciative laughter went around the table, inspiring other parents to describe the dubious joys of parenthood. Owen let Charles Darwin slip from his mind.

* * *

Owen and Ruby walked two blocks home through the lingering twilight of an early September evening. Many front porches were occupied, some by a couple in the porch swing, others by children, a few by entire families. Owen described the intrusion of the Scopes evolution trial on his dinner.

"Oh," responded Ruby, "I had an experience kind of like that." She wanted to tell Owen about the incident but wondered how to introduce the topic. *That problem is solved, but I can't tell the story practically in public like this.* Ruby nodded toward the porch they were passing. "I'll tell you about it when we get home."

They were soon in the privacy of their little house, where Ruby told her story in a quiet voice.

"Everyone was very courteous to me and to each other in public, but their private talk was different. I overheard some snide comments about Methodists, right there in the Methodist Church. I was combing my hair in the little powder room under the stairs. Two women were waiting to use it, and the second one said some nasty things about Catholics. They didn't know I could hear them through the door."

"What kind of nasty things? Or snide things, for that matter."

"It was about liquor. The first woman said that some of the Methodist men go to temperance meetings on Sunday after visiting speakeasies in Denver on Saturday night. Then the second woman claimed the Catholics have liquor delivered to their doorsteps. She said all the bootleggers are Catholic and that the Platteville priest gets so drunk nobody can understand him. Lots of the prayers are in Latin, she said, which nobody understands even when he is sober."

Owen was silent, digesting Ruby's news. "Maybe," he said, "the Lydells aren't unusual. I got the idea that if I was going to teach evolution, they wouldn't want Ronald in the class. Some other parents probably feel the same way."

"What did you tell the Lydells?"

"I said we wouldn't have time for Darwin, we'd be so busy with other topics."

Ruby nodded, smiling. "So you ducked the question of agreeing with the evolution theory."

"They didn't ask that straight out, so I didn't answer it. I'll bet that's how old Professor Johansen would handle it."

"Probably. But how would he deal with this one: a couple of the ladies at my table ganged up on me after dinner and very sweetly asked if we've found a 'church home' in Platteville."

"How did you answer?"

"I explained we were both raised as Baptists and said we were disappointed there's no Baptist church here. I said most Sundays, we will either visit my aunt in Longmont or your folks near Windsor, and go to church with them."

Owen drummed his fingernails against the table for a moment. "You know," he said, "Professor Johansen told us that we'd carry the message of scientific farming into communities where it's controversial, and we shouldn't get involved in other fights. His example was politics—he said we shouldn't register as either Republicans or Democrats. Maybe that applies to religion too."

"How would you apply it?"

"Let's not join a church in Platteville. If people ask, we'll tell them what you told those busybodies about trips to Longmont or Windsor."

"Well, I still belong to my home church in Illinois. I never transferred when I went to college."

"I think that's just fine. Let's leave it that way."

Ruby smiled. "Somehow it feels good to have that decided. I feel like some celebrating."

"So make a joyful noise."

Ruby walked to the newly tuned piano. The syncopated sounds of *Kitten on the Keys* challenged the darkening night.

* * *

When setting the date for the faculty reception, Martha Stark did not consult widely with Platteville organizations. She was unaware of conflict with a meeting of the St. Nicholas Altar and Rosary Society until she received declinations from potential Catholic guests. She had never intended a strictly Protestant party.

Mary Gorman, secretary of the Altar and Rosary Society, learned about the school board's Bible-reading plan from her husband, who had overheard customers talk in his store. The customers had attended the dinner for new faculty and talked to Arthur Stark. Since Catherine Koblenz was the president of the Altar and Rosary Society, Mrs. Gorman assumed she would devise some response. But Catherine deferred to her husband on religious matters, so Frederick Koblenz waited in Father O'Donnell's study while the priest finished his time in the confessional.

Koblenz looked through the rectory window toward the walls of the church. He remembered his grandfather's description of the congregation's early years, when itinerant Irish priests held Mass for German immigrants in the Koblenz living room. When his father led the congregation in building the first small church, it functioned as a mission outpost served by visiting clergy. O'Donnell was their first permanent priest; Fred had led the drive to build the rectory, which was barely six years old.

"Frederick, my son!" Father O'Donnell bustled into the room. "It's a pleasure to see you."

As usual, Koblenz felt soothed by the priest's Irish joviality. After a brief exchange of pleasantries, he was ready to broach his subject. "Father, have you heard about this new school board policy?"

"Aye. And I'm very disturbed by it."

"They want to begin the school day with a reading from the Protestant Bible, but that's proscribed. What should we tell our children?"

"I'm afraid the teaching of the church is very clear. It is an occasion of sin. Each person must choose whether or not to remain in the situation."

"That's asking a lot of a first or second grader."

"And we will not leave the decision up to the little ones. But those who have been confirmed are expected to understand their faith and even to defend it."

"So we may expect something from the seventh and eighth graders, and certainly from the high school students. They should be ready to quietly walk out."

"Exactly. Now when does the new board policy go into effect?"

"They haven't bothered to notify parents, so I don't know for sure. I believe that it's on Monday, the first day of school."

"That leaves the weekend for us to get ready. Or—for you." The priest shook his head sadly. "I can't help much in my homily. The bishop doesn't want us to get involved in local political questions, although he may see this as one we can't avoid being public about. The young people's groups can take it up, and there'll be time for parents to give guidance to their children. Catholic students should not feel they are facing this alone."

"Father, I'm glad you feel that way. My wife and I will get started, organizing this thing. Would you be able to meet with any parents who have questions?"

"Of course."

"I only wish we had a Catholic school in Weld County. Then we could have some confidence in our children's education."

"Ah, but this is not a Catholic community. The children may be better off facing Protestant attitudes while they are young."

* * *

Half a dozen Klansmen rode horses. They gathered west of the town named Loveland and entered the Big Thompson Canyon at dusk. Five cars of Klansmen followed an hour later. Arthur Stark drove his Reo touring car, giving a ride to Ollie Scott and picking up Charley Vesser and another klavern member in Greeley. The trip from Platteville and back again would be more than a hundred miles.

The autos were on time for the rendezvous in a pasture a hundred yards below the roadhouse. When the cars entered the pasture and turned off their headlamps, the sudden darkness seemed complete, but the light of the nearly full moon soon proved adequate. Men got out of the cars, pulled on their white robes, and then held the horses while riders dismounted to don their own costumes.

When all were robed and masked, nearly thirty men formed a quiet circle around their leader. Exalted Cyclops Ostrum quietly reviewed the plan. The horsemen would surround the building. When patrons fled, the riders would first herd them toward the cross that would burn on the mountain above, but eventually let them back into the parking lot. No firearms were to be exhibited except for rifles carried by the Exalted Cyclops's four guards. Klansmen from Loveland were tending the cross, so Charley Vesser was not needed as nighthawk. Stark and Vesser would enter with Ostrum, to lead the inspection party.

The riders mounted up, leading the way onto the road, with the others following on foot. A light was flashed toward the mountainside, and a cross burst into flame. Two automobiles came along the highway; one headed up the canyon, and a moment later, another headed down toward Loveland. Rather than pause to view the parade, both cars accelerated past the hooded figures.

When the Klan reached the open ground around the roadhouse, the horsemen surrounded the building, speaking softly to calm their mounts.

Above the front door, several naked lightbulbs illuminated a sign: THE HALFWAY HOUSE.

Sounds of jazz music seeped out of the building. Arthur Stark estimated that four dozen autos were parked near the front door. Embarrassed when his words issued in a hoarse whisper, Stark spoke to Charley Vesser. "Why are we so damn quiet? People can't hear anything in there with the racket that jazz makes."

"We have to take them by surprise, Arthur. Otherwise it won't work."

When Ostrum's party reached the front door, a guard tested the doorknob, which turned easily. He glanced at Ostrum, who nodded. The guard yanked the door open, held his rifle in the position of port arms, and marched into the building beside his leader. Another guard marched on Ostrum's other side, followed in turn by Stark and Vesser.

The Klansmen entered a single large room designed for dancing. There were small tables with chairs in one end, and in the middle was a raised platform where half a dozen musicians were playing. Couples dipped and swirled on the dance floor, unaware of their visitors. The Klansmen paused on the edge of the dance floor. A girl shrieked when she saw the hooded figures. Some dancers paused, looking around in confusion; others headed for the back door, and the band stopped playing.

The Exalted Cyclops's declaration filled the sudden silence. "Stay where you are, we wish you no harm. Do not try to leave the building. It is surrounded by mounted guards. If you have been obeying the law, we will only beg your pardon for intruding. You must remain in your places while we make that determination."

Flanked by the two rifle-carrying guards, Stark and Vesser strode briskly across the dance floor toward a swinging door behind the group of tables. Arthur could keep up, but the rapid motion accentuated the jerk in his stride. The hood covering his face could not hide his gait. But why should anyone there know him? It was a different part of the county and a different crowd. Surely there were no Methodists in the dance hall.

They reached the group of small tables and began to walk through them. Several tables held teacups, most of them resting on saucers. Stark noted that some of the cups contained a clear liquid, but he saw nothing that looked like tea or coffee. *Bathtub gin.* The first time he actually saw it.

A few couples who had been sitting out the dance sat frozen at their tables, stunned by the visitation. As Vesser and Stark neared the swinging door that had to lead to a kitchen, one of the couples clasped hands and edged toward the wall. The boy was tall and awkward, on the edge of manhood, and the girl wore a knee-length chemise. Arthur Stark barely glanced at the couple as he hurried past, yet the youth's figure was familiar. *By God, that was the oldest Koblenz boy.* Stark saw him graduate from high school—even signed his diploma—the year before.

Led by one of the riflemen, the inspection party burst into the kitchen. They found a table, cupboards, a range holding nothing but a teakettle, and a sink. A man standing at the sink set a gallon jug on the drainboard beside two similar containers.

"Hold it right there!" Charley Vesser shouted. "You've been pouring the stuff down the drain! Let me see that."

He shouldered the man aside, then picked up and shook each of the jugs. "All empty. But you couldn't pour out the smell. Here, take a sniff." He thrust a jug toward Stark. No need to get closer—the odor of raw alcohol was unmistakable.

Vesser grabbed the arm of the man by the sink. "What have you got to say about this?"

The man shrunk away from his hooded questioner. "Them jugs was here when I came in tonight," he said. "You will have to find out who rented the hall last." When none of his captors challenged this assertion, the man took courage, pretending to ignore the riflemen. He pulled his arm out of Vesser's grasp. "Listen, this here's a respectable operation. We put on a dance, keep the young people off the roads. Sell 'em some tea or coffee and cookies."

Arthur Stark spoke through clenched teeth. "You can't make tea or coffee when there's no fire in your stove! And there's no tea or coffee in those teacups out there. It's booze!"

The man's voice took on a wheedling tone. "We ain't responsible for what people bring in with them. Most of the guys carry flasks. You should check them."

Charley Vesser turned away, walking toward the kitchen door, and spoke to his fellow Klansmen. "This fellow is hopeless. He's lying through his teeth, but we can't prove it. We've got to tell Gerry."

Vesser led the group back through the swinging door to the dance floor. Their leader had moved to the bandstand, now deserted by the musicians, and the patrons were drifting toward the two doors. Vesser whispered his urgent sentence into Ostrum's ear.

The Exalted Cyclops, who had taken off his mask, mounted the bandstand and called out to the retreating patrons, "It won't do you any good to run. Running away won't change the law. We know what you've been doing here, making a mockery of the U.S. Constitution, but we haven't found evidence we can take to the sheriff. So we're going to let you go. But be warned! We'll be back. You know who I am, because I've filled some of your teeth. We're all your neighbors, and we want to be your friends, but only if you obey the law. The Klan will follow you wherever you go, if you break the law.

"Those of you still living with your folks, I say to you, go home to your parents and confess where you have been, and tell them who you saw here. Tell them, whether or not they care how you behave, the Klan cares. Now go!"

The building emptied quickly. The mounted Klansmen chased several couples toward the burning cross but then turned them, like stampeding cattle, back toward the parking space in front of the building and allowed them to drive away. As the last of the dance hall patrons departed, Klansmen began to walk back down the highway.

Arthur Stark and Charley Vesser walked together.

"There were a lot of familiar faces," Vesser said. "Kids who've come into the store for years with their dads, others who've shopped for themselves. I'm glad Gerry took off his mask and said that we're all neighbors, but I'll keep mine on. There are other feed stores in Greeley that people can go to."

"I didn't expect to find Platteville people there," Stark said, "but I recognized one kid, Fred Koblenz's oldest boy. Koblenz has a big place on the other side of town from me."

"Koblenz . . . isn't that a German name?"

"Yeah, they're one of the original families in town. Fred's grandfather was one of those German Catholics the railroad brought in fifty years ago."

"So the kid you saw tonight is Catholic."

"Well, yeah, he must be."

"It figures. You know Catholics are wets, they opposed Prohibition. All the bootleggers are Catholic. They want the Pope to take over in America."

Stark nodded, not really listening. His first Klan raid got their attention and gave the young people something to think about, but there was no violence. It was good to stand with the Klan, showing young people the path of righteousness. As he climbed into the Reo, Arthur glanced up at the cross, still blazing on the mountainside. *Something to be proud of.*

Chapter 3

IT WAS THE FIRST day for classes at Platteville High. Owen was the designated faculty sponsor of the junior class, so all fourteen juniors reported to the science classroom for roll taking, announcements, and the opening ceremony. Owen read over the roster of student names three times in advance and practiced the Bible reading twice. He wore a brand-new shirt and tie for the first day and recognized nervousness that he would never admit to Ruby. He was comforted by thinking the students could be nervous too.

Four of six junior girls took seats in the room. Did only girls dare show enough interest in learning to arrive well before the tardy bell? Owens's question seemed answered as the first boy marched through the door, carrying a cap in his hand.

The muscular youth did not seek a seat but resolutely approached Owen's stool behind the counter that held a sink and equipment for chemistry experiments. "Mr. Mattison? I'm Frank Koblenz."

Owen glanced at his roll, confirming the boy's name was listed as Francis. Owen shook the offered hand. "Hello, Koblenz, glad to meet you. Can I help you with something?"

His resolution faded from the boy's eyes. "Well . . . uh huh . . . it's about that." Frank pointed a finger toward the Bible on the counter and quickly withdrew his hand. "I guess you'll be reading something out of that."

"Yes, I will, after the Pledge of Allegiance."

"Well, we—everyone who goes to St. Nicholas Church—aren't allowed to read or hear your Bible." Koblenz twisted the cap in his hands until it was a wrinkled ball. Owen nodded encouragement. The boy hated this responsibility but carried it out. Owen saw he had spunk. "So," Koblenz said, "when you read from the Bible, uh, we have to leave the room until you're done."

"You keep saying 'we.' So others are involved, and you're their leader?"

A look of misery flooded Koblenz's face. He nodded.

"Well, I won't force you to listen to something you aren't supposed to hear. I'll have to talk to the principal, but there isn't time now. When you go, just be sure you're back in five minutes." Koblenz nodded again, as relief conquered misery in his face. "Now please find a seat."

Owen counted the fourteenth arrival as the tardy bell rang. He introduced himself, writing his name on the blackboard to end speculation that he might be descended from the fourth president, and called roll. All were present, so he seated them in alphabetical order, to facilitate future roll taking. "Now all stand and face the flag."

The American flag was in a front corner of the room, its staff standing in a metal holder. Owen faced that corner to lead the pledge. Fifteen right hands were placed over fifteen chests, and fourteen quiet voices followed Owen's lead.

> *I pledge allegiance*
> *to the flag*
> *of the United States of America,*
> *and to the Republic*
> *for which it stands,*
> *one Nation indivisible,*
> *with liberty and justice for all.*

"Please take your seats." Owen reached for the Bible and pulled it across the countertop. The swish of leather over stone was the only sound in the room. "I shall now read from the First Epistle of Saint Paul to the Corinthians."

The room stirred as Frank Koblenz rose from his seat. Three students looked from side to side at their neighbors. A tall, slender youth with blond hair raised half out of his chair. Owen glanced at his roster; the boy was Bruno Gorman. Frank Koblenz had reached the end of his row of desks.

"Mr. Koblenz," Owen said, "I understand you believe you are not allowed to listen to this. You and others who attend St. Nicholas may leave the room for five minutes, at least for today."

Frank Koblenz turned toward the door, his footsteps more purposeful. Bruno Gorman stood up, glaring at the girl sitting beside him. Hesitantly the girl stood up, and Owen checked his roster. Oh. Margaret Fitzgerald.

Fitzgerald, Koblenz, and Gorman reached the door together.

As the three students passed into the hallway, Owen began to read, "Though I speak with the tongues of men and of angels, and have not charity, I am become as sounding brass, or a tinkling cymbal."

Owen read on, glancing at the class after each few verses. They were quiet but not particularly attentive. Were they so familiar with the passage that they were bored? Was his reading the problem? He recited the final sentence with a measured cadence but almost in a whisper, "Now abideth faith, hope, charity, these three. But the greatest of these is charity."

Time for the threesome to come back. Time for a bell dispatching them to first period classes. There was a hand up in the back row. "Mr. Lydell."

"Mr. Mattison, do you teachers expect us to learn from everything you tell us?"

The class suddenly seemed more attentive. The Catholic students came in. Owen waited for them to take their seats, grateful for the extra time in which to formulate his response.

"I can only speak for myself," Owen responded, "but that's sure the way it ought to work."

"And you teach biology and scientific farming?"

"Yes." Owen did not like the questions' trend.

"So," the Lydell boy continued, "you won't read something to us unless it's established fact."

The class had to know Lydell was setting a trap. Fourteen pairs of eyes looked at Owen, awaiting an answer. "Well, your English teacher will have you read Shakespeare, but not because she thinks the play is literally true."

"But a play is something made up, it's not science. Can we believe what's in the Bible? Was the world created in just six days? Did a snake really give an apple to Eve?"

"Mr. Lydell, the passage I read had nothing to do with the creation of the world. You should be thinking about the meaning of faith and charity, not worrying about Adam and Eve."

As the Catholic students were settling in their seats, the bell sounded shrilly in the hallway. Owen dismissed the class. He hoped the relief he felt did not show in his face.

* * *

Doubling as chair of both the membership and program committees, Martha Stark made her promised telephone call to remind Ruby of the September Mizpah Club meeting, planned for the Methodist Church basement on Thursday. Ruby accepted the invitation with gratitude.

Martha's voice sounded metallic as it continued over the wire. "Ruby, I've heard wonderful things about your piano playing. Your neighbor, Anne Morgan, is a friend of mine. She tells me that she and her husband sit on their front porch nearly every evening to hear you play."

Ruby paused. *It really is a small town. The main source of entertainment is gossip about the neighbors.* She said, "Mrs. Morgan came over to welcome us the first week we were here, but I haven't seen her since."

After casual questions about Ruby's musical interests, Martha confessed that the pianist intended as the mainstay of the club's program had been called out of town by a family funeral. Martha invited Ruby to play two or three numbers of her own choice.

"That's very kind, Mrs. Stark, but you must have other members who play."

"Please, you must call me Martha," the older woman said. "Yes, we have a number of members who play at home, but nobody is confident enough to play in public. It's terribly short notice, but if you can't play, we won't have a program at all."

"Well, there are only one or two numbers I could play from memory. Would you mind if I brought sheet music?"

"God bless you, Ruby. If you will play, bring as much sheet music as you like. If you wish, I'll help carry it to the church."

Ruby laughed, declaring her ability to carry enough music for a fifteen- or twenty-minute program.

* * *

On Thursday afternoon, Martha welcomed Ruby at the church door. They went down to the basement together, where Martha led Ruby to a group of women and introduced her to Ruth Herman, the club president. Mrs. Herman shook hands warmly and introduced the other three women. Ruby already knew Mrs. Lydell.

The group returned to the topic of the day. "We've been discussing the Catholic walkout at the school," Mrs. Herman reported. "Our club has several Catholic members, but none of them came today."

"I should think not!" declared Susan Lydell. "You know the students didn't dream this up on their own. The idea came from their parents, who probably got it from that priest."

Ruth Herman turned to Ruby. "Mrs. Mattison, did any of your husband's students walk out?"

"Well, yes, he said that three of them walked out. But one of them explained beforehand why they had to do it."

"Isn't Mr. Mattison the junior class advisor? So all the juniors are in his homeroom?"

"Yes, I believe so."

Susan Lydell broke in, her voice tense. "Ruth! Isn't Mary Gorman's son Bruno a junior?"

Mrs. Herman nodded. "Yes, Bruno is a junior."

"I bet he's one who walked out, right?"

36

Ruby frowned. The time to change the subject was past. "I did not," she said, "ask Owen for their names."

Susan Lydell ignored the reproach. "Frank Koblenz is a junior too. This whole thing was planned by the Gormans and the Koblenzes."

When Martha Stark spoke, her voice was cold. "I believe that the Catholic Church itself objects to the King James Bible. It isn't only Catholics in Platteville."

"I don't understand why," Susan Lydell said with an air of finality. "We're all Christians, and the Bible is the Bible."

Ruth Herman declared it was time for the meeting to begin. She walked to a rostrum and asked the members to take their seats.

By invitation, Ruby sat next to Martha Stark. Glancing around, she estimated the attendance at more than two dozen.

The secretary's minutes of the previous meeting were accepted. The treasurer reported solvency but said they must raise funds to finance future projects. The program chair recommended reactivation of the planning committee to establish a priority list of projects for the Mizpah Cemetery. She proposed a cake sale to begin gathering funds. The two proposals passed easily.

Finally Martha Stark introduced Ruby as a prospective member who had graciously, and at the last minute, agreed to provide the afternoon's entertainment.

Ruby sat down at the piano and adjusted the position of the stool. Without announcing its title, she played *Kitten on the Keys*. A flashy number, Ruby played it to emphasize the flash. When the tune finished, the applause seemed more than polite.

Ruby turned toward the audience. "For a change of pace, I'll play something that really belongs in a church. It was written by Sir Arthur Sullivan, better known as the partner of Mr. Gilbert. It's called 'The Lost Chord.'"

Ruby arranged the sheet music and launched the majestic beat and harmonious chords of the hymn. She finished with a flourish, and the applause was even more enthusiastic. Was there anything they didn't like?

When the applause died, Ruby announced, "Scott Joplin's *Maple Leaf Rag*," and she swung into the number. When she finished, the applause was sustained, but she rose from the piano stool and began walking to her seat. The women nearer her own age seemed more enthusiastic than the older ones. There were many calls for an encore. Before she could sit down, Ruth Herman asked her to honor them with another number. Ruby suppressed a grin. If the older ones were offended by ragtime, they were in the minority.

She returned to the piano and drew sheet music from her modest stack. "The first number I played for you, *Kitten on the Keys*, was written by Zez

Confrey, my favorite contemporary composer. For a final number, I'll play another of his tunes. Here is *The Greenwich Witch*."

As Ruby played the lively number, she felt a kind of rhythmic unity with her audience. They all liked Confrey. His music made them want to tap their toes, but it didn't scare anybody. The explosion of applause when she finished confirmed her judgment.

As the ladies gathered at the refreshment table, Ruby saw Isabel Nelson moving through the crowd. She was wearing a chemise of the same design as her dress at the faculty reception, but a different fabric. When Isabel greeted her, Ruby had the comfortable feeling of recognizing a compatriot.

"Ruby, that was marvelous. I told you Platteville wasn't ready for ragtime, and you made a liar out of me. They loved it. Thank you."

"It was my pleasure," Ruby said.

"Better still," Isabel continued, "it took people's minds off the walkout. You must be as tired as I am of talking about it."

Pleading another commitment, Isabel departed when Martha Stark brought Ruby a cup of tea with a sugar cookie. "Ruby, you've earned this ten times over. Your playing was wonderful."

"Thank you, Martha. I'm glad you enjoyed it."

"Have you ever given piano lessons? Our daughter, Irene, seems to have some talent. But she simply outgrew her teacher. She'd like to resume lessons if we can find a suitable teacher."

"I've never taught piano, but I taught home economics for a year before we were married and loved it. It would be a luxury to have just one student at a time. Let me discuss it with my husband."

Women eager to compliment Ruby on her playing surrounded the pair. Ruby concentrated on keeping track of the new names. When the circle finally grew thin, Susan Lydell and Ruth Herman came up. After praising Ruby's performance, the two older women turned to Mrs. Stark.

"Martha," Susan Lydell began, "I didn't get to ask you what Arthur wants the school board to do about the walkout."

"I'm not sure they have to do anything. The students aren't running off to a pool hall or something. They come back in after the Bible reading."

"But that isn't maintaining discipline," Mrs. Herman objected. "You can't let students pick some requirements to meet and others to ignore."

"You know," Susan said, "it's like that Klan raid on the roadhouse in Big Thompson Canyon. I don't approve of the Klan, but I agree with their argument: you can't decide to obey some laws and not others."

Martha Stark's voice was icy. "Susan, you cannot compare unlike things. Whatever the Ku Klux Klan chooses to do has absolutely no connection with rules laid down by our school board."

* * *

The Platte Valley high schools did not have the enrollment or funds to support football teams, so they played speedball in the fall. Speedball, developed by the Platte Valley coaches, was based on soccer's continual movement and minimal physical contact. Owen had played varsity football at Ft. Collins, and he hoped to coach football someday. He had never seen a speedball game, but he had a rulebook, and he knew something of soccer.

He held tryouts for the speedball team the second week of school. The number of boys who appeared for the tryouts—mostly residents of the town who did not take the school bus onto the county roads—was enough to form a team with a few substitutes. Owen had to choose the starters, assign their positions, and remind them all of the importance of practice games to sharpen skills and assure school victories.

The tryouts were after school on Wednesday. Owen made careful notes, studied them at home, and announced his choices Thursday, with the hopeful players gathered around in a semicircle. Those named as starters walked over to form a separate group.

Owen read a quarter of his alphabetical list before he came to the name of Bruno Gorman, another junior. He called out "Bruno Gorman" and watched as the lanky, blond youth walked toward the first team. Since some seniors did not make it, would their teammates resent the juniors?

As Owen continued reading names, he overheard the stage whisper come from another junior. "Hey, Bruno," the boy hissed, "is the Pope gonna let you play speedball? Did you get a telegram from Rome?"

The Gorman boy did not answer. Owen finished the list and urged those not named as starters to attend after-school practices, giving his speech about their importance. Then he announced position assignments and reviewed the rules. Only the goalkeeper was allowed to touch the ball with his hands. Owen was impressed by the height, large hands, and quick reaction time shown in the tryouts by Bruno Gorman and named him as starting goalkeeper. Those present were divided into two teams for a practice game.

As Bruno Gorman walked past the line of forwards toward the goal, Owen heard an exchange between two of the forwards.

Providing his version of a priestly chant, the first boy sang in a deep baritone, "Where in the hell is the incense pot?"

The response imitated an altar boy with a sharp falsetto, "Down in the cellar 'cause it's too damn hot."

"Knock it off!" Owen nearly shouted. "You're here to play speedball, not make fun of your teammates."

Bruno Gorman's face was blank and pale.

* * *

At dinner that evening, Ruby told Owen about meeting the Mizpah ladies.

"They liked my playing, but they couldn't talk about anything but the walkout at school. Before the meeting even began, Susan Lydell wanted to know who walked out of your classroom. I told her that I didn't ask you for their names."

Owen grinned. "Good for you. We don't need the whole town telling us what to do. You don't need to worry about this kind of stuff."

"Well, the whole town is curious, and I'm curious too. So tell me," Ruby smiled at Owen, "how did it go today?"

Ruby's smile melted Owen's hesitation. "The three students walked out again, like they have every day this week. The others razz them until I have to quiet them down. Worse yet, the bad feelings are spilling over into other activities. This afternoon was our first speedball practice. I put a Catholic boy, Bruno Gorman, on the first team and made him the goalie. He's a junior, and I thought the seniors might resent him. But he was razzed by another junior on his own team."

"At the Mizpah meeting, Susan Lydell asked Martha Stark what her husband wants to do about the walkout. Martha said they don't have to do anything, since the students come back in after the Bible reading."

"Did she give any hint that her husband feels the same way?"

"No. Maybe she was just trying to quiet Susan down. I know I wanted to."

"What you said doesn't sound like Arthur Stark. Mrs. Stark is wrong, because school is really being disrupted. Protestant students resent Catholics getting out of listening to the Bible, so they pick fights. And parents are going to take their kids' side."

"You don't have fistfights at school, do you?"

"There have been a few scuffles down in the grade school, but our students know enough to take their fights elsewhere. I really don't understand how there can be so much bad blood. Ollie Scott, the barber, says the Catholics are the oldest congregation in town. You would think they would understand each other better by now."

"Platteville has a lot of social organizations, including half a dozen women's clubs. Except for Mizpah, the biggest and strongest clubs are organized in the churches, so it's possible to have an active life without friends in any other church."

Owen was happy to satisfy Ruby's curiosity. With the gossip flying around town, she should know the facts. And she sure seemed to understand what was happening. "Owen, I need to ask you about something else. Martha Stark asked if I could give piano lessons to their daughter, Irene."

"You don't need to do that. We don't need extra money. We may not live in a palace, but I can support you. People don't need to think that you have to work."

Ruby was dismayed by Owen's pride in being the breadwinner. She chose her words carefully. "Owen, if I earn a dollar or two a week teaching piano lessons, nobody will think I am taking your place. We could use a dollar or two to get those new curtains. Taking care of this little house is not a full-time job. I've been playing the piano a lot and reading a lot, but what I need is a good reason to get out of the house."

"Well, let's talk about details. Where would you give these lessons? Sounds like you won't ask Irene Stark to come here."

"That would not work for two reasons. She'd be forced to miss her bus, and our house is just too little. A student learning the piano is not giving a concert. You couldn't get away from the noise."

"So," Owen said, "you would go to the Stark place."

"Yes. I'd have to take the Ford, and you know I can handle it. We would schedule things so my piano lessons won't conflict with your inspection of student projects."

"You've thought about this a lot, haven't you?"

"Yes, I have. I think it's a real opportunity."

Owen looked across the dinner table. Ruby's plate was nearly emptied, and she had not touched the silverware lying across it for several minutes. His own meal was long completed. But how could they complete the conversation?

"How does this sound?" he asked. "Tell Martha Stark you can visit them to meet Irene, see if the two of you get along, and be sure she really wants to take lessons. If she does, you make the commitment. The Starks are solid people, and you'll be doing them a favor. But you aren't hanging out a shingle, or whatever it is that music teachers do to advertise. If anyone else wants you to give lessons, we'll talk it over again."

"Well," replied Ruby with a toss of her head, "I don't plan to advertise in the Greeley *Tribune*. Of course we'll talk it over if anyone else wants me."

Owen said, "Now let's look into that apple pie I saw out in the kitchen."

* * *

Frederick Koblenz gave the telephone number to the operator and waited for the ring, which was answered promptly by a female voice.

"Hello, Mrs. Stark? This is Fred Koblenz calling. May I please speak to Arthur?"

41

"I'm sorry, Mr. Koblenz, but he's at a school board meeting. May I take a message?"

"Oh, I didn't realize that a meeting was scheduled."

"It's an emergency session. To discuss the walkouts, I believe."

"That's the very thing I want to discuss with Arthur. I think there's a great danger of misunderstanding. Misunderstanding the Catholic point of view, I mean."

"Arthur will be sorry he missed you. Can he reach you in the morning?"

"It would be best if I call him. But please pass along my greetings to him. And thank you, Mrs. Stark, thank you very much."

Koblenz placed the receiver back on its hook very carefully, because he had wanted to bang it down. He walked into the living room, where his wife was reading a magazine.

"I was too late. Arthur is already at an emergency school board meeting."

"Maybe you should attend the meeting."

"I couldn't get in. Since they haven't announced this meeting, it will be closed. Anyway, I want to talk to Arthur privately, where I can get him to listen. If the board is determined to act, they may do something they will live to regret."

* * *

The board was indeed determined to act. As soon as the letter they drafted could be printed, every student was given a copy to take to their parents.

PLATTEVILLE CONSOLIDATED SCHOOL DISTRICT
Platteville, Colorado
October 9, 1925

Dear Parents:

Recently the school board decided to include the reading of the Bible, without comment, as a part of the opening exercises each morning in each room of the school. There was no intention of causing any hard feelings on the part of anyone. The passages selected to be read were the same in all rooms, and were selected with the express aim in view of containing nothing sectarian or denominational, but rather, to contain thoughts dealing with right living and being good, as opposed to being bad.

However, certain pupils have been violating the rules of the school by walking out of the rooms during the opening exercises. This practice is purely uncalled for; it is tending to break down the morale and discipline of the school, and it is causing hard feelings to exist between the pupils. All of this, of course, is not for the best interests of the school.

Therefore, the board has decided that they will enforce the rule that there shall be no leaving of the rooms during the opening exercises. The enforcement of this rule will become effective Monday, October 12.

Trusting that we may have your cooperation, we are

  Yours very truly,
  The Board of Education,
  Platteville Consolidated Schools, District No. 118.
  Newton D. Maclean, President
  Roy C. Thompson, Treasurer
  Arthur P. Stark, Secretary

Chapter 4

LATE FRIDAY AFTERNOON, FATHER O'Donnell telephoned the bishop, who accepted the need for legal action and recommended a Denver lawyer named Milton Thayer. The bishop promised to brief Thayer on happenings in Platteville. When Fred Koblenz called, Thayer readily agreed to the meeting.

Koblenz left Platteville at nine o'clock on Monday, drove directly to the Daniels and Fisher department store in Denver, located the lawyer's office across the street, and found a parking place. He was early for the ten-thirty appointment.

Koblenz had barely settled into a chair indicated by the receptionist when a ruddy-faced man, whose bulk strained his vest buttons, emerged from one of a row of glassed-in offices. Curly gray hairs on the back of his neck were beginning to hang over the collar, which had been loosened. "Mr. Koblenz, I'm Milt Thayer. Please come into my office."

As Koblenz followed Thayer, he thanked the attorney for seeing him on short notice.

"Lawyers sometimes deal with emergencies," Thayer said, "just like physicians." He waved his guest to a chair and sat down heavily at his desk. "And the Platteville situation sounds like an emergency."

"Well, yes. The school board has issued an order to our students they can't follow and still obey the teachings of the church."

Thayer smiled the ingratiating smile that won over juries. "You'll want to adjust your thinking a little on that one. This society does not recognize a single Church, with a capital C, but many churches. And the legal tradition is, or we like to think it is, the state treats all religions equally."

Fred didn't need a civics lecture. But maybe the lawyer was making his point. Fred asked, "Aren't school boards part of the government?"

"They are. And you feel your school board isn't treating your faith equally."

"They don't seem to care how they treat us. I don't know if they even understand why we object to the King James Bible."

Thayer pulled a long pad of yellow paper to the edge of his desk and took a pencil from a leather cup. "Let's go back to the beginning. You keep referring to 'we.' You are a Catholic parent, and you are speaking for other Catholics with children in the Platteville schools."

"Well, I wasn't elected by anybody. A group of us got together with the priest at our St. Nicholas Church. He called the bishop for us, and I agreed to make the trip to Denver. The rest you know."

"Fine. In the eyes of the law, you are speaking on your own behalf and that of all persons similarly situated. It will be a class action suit."

"A lawsuit? Wouldn't that take a lot of time? We told our kids to stay for the Bible reading today, but that can't go on much longer. Can't something be done sooner?"

"Yes. Because the situation is urgent, I'll first attempt to proceed ex parte. That means I'll ask the judge for a preliminary ruling without even listening to the school board's arguments. Then when the time comes for a permanent ruling, the school board will object. And then there will be the equivalent of a trial. The business of the law is to settle disputes, and yours is with the Platteville school board. So you'll be suing them."

"I have to sue to get action by the court?"

"Exactly. Now let's review the facts," the lawyer said. "There is no parochial school in Weld County, and your children are required by law to attend the Platteville public schools."

"That's right."

"And the school board decided to supply moral instruction by having the teacher read Bible verses every morning. They are reading from the King James Bible. Why do you object?"

"For two reasons. First, we believe children should not confront words from a holy book without guidance. Any reading should be with the help of adults who have religious training. Second, the King James Bible was translated by Protestants who imposed their ideas on it. It is proscribed. For a Catholic to read the King James Bible is a sin."

"So you encouraged your children to walk out of the Bible readings."

"Yes."

"And when the school board requires them to stay, they are requiring those children to sin."

"The board doesn't see it that way. You should have a look at this." Fred pulled from his inside coat pocket the school board letter of October 9 and unfolded it as he handed it to the attorney. "They sent this letter home on Friday."

46

Thayer read the page quickly, underlining a passage with his pencil, and then peered at his prospective client. "They say here, the passages were chosen 'with the express aim of containing nothing sectarian' in order to 'contain thoughts dealing with right living and being good.' Do you believe that?"

"Oh, I don't think they set out to attack our religion. They believe their own motives are pure, and they don't see how their entire Bible can be considered sectarian."

"Would you be happy if they took the readings from a Bible approved by your church?"

"No, the students would still lack adult guidance. Anyway, the school board would never approve selections from a Catholic Bible, for fear of upsetting the Protestant parents."

"Protestants are the majority, and they elected the school board. So it naturally represents Protestant attitudes. You are saying, in effect, the school board has shown itself to be incapable of treating Protestants and Catholics equally."

Despite the lawyer's impersonal manner, Koblenz felt his cause had passed some kind of test, and his confidence in Thayer was growing. He offered a smile of his own as he answered, "That's a good way to put it."

"It's the kind of situation that sends you to the Constitution, which guarantees individual rights regardless of majority opinion. You feel the school board is denying your freedom of religious belief."

Fred Koblenz vigorously nodded his head. "That's right."

"I personally believe," Thayer continued, "the actions of your school board are prohibited by the federal constitution's First Amendment, applied to the States by the Fourteenth Amendment. But the U.S. Supreme Court hasn't made much headway in defining which freedoms the States must protect. Earlier this year, in the Pierce case, they wrote that parents do have the right to have their children educated where and by whom they think best. That's a beginning, but the precedent doesn't reach to your case. However, the Colorado Constitution picks up the idea of religious freedom in article 2, when it guarantees freedom of conscience. Later on, it prohibits any support for a religious sect by the State. So you will appeal to the district court to enforce the Colorado Constitution."

Fred hoped he saw a chance for action, not just words. "What do I have to do?"

"I will call the district court in Greeley this afternoon, warning you will seek an emergency writ of mandamus on Wednesday, represented by me. That particular writ should be a little stronger, and maybe it will last a little longer than an injunction that is labeled as preliminary from the beginning. When they give me a time, either on Wednesday or later, I'll telephone you, and you can meet me at the courthouse. I'll prepare the case and present it. All you have to do is show up as the plaintiff."

"And do you think we have a good chance of getting this thing, this writ?"

"I never guarantee what any court will do. But there's a good chance, or I wouldn't take the case."

Another detail had to be nailed down. Fred said, "We haven't discussed your fee."

"My partners and I don't try to get rich on civil liberties cases. Nobody could put a value on winning this case—you parents are not seeking a monetary settlement. So I'll work for expenses. Five cents a mile for any traveling, plus twenty dollars an hour for time spent in court. Does that sound fair?"

"More than fair."

Fred felt their parting handshake as the kind friends use to say good-bye. He recognized the untidy attorney as a friend, as well as a professional skilled at persuasion. It all combined to give Fred new confidence in the future of his cause. Since a mild celebration was in order, he treated himself to a meal in the Daniels and Fisher tower lunchroom.

* * *

Classes finished at three o'clock, so Owen scheduled the speedball practice for three fifteen. To build fundamental competencies, he invented drills and man-to-man contests. To drill the goalies, he lined up five players twenty feet from the goal, gave them two balls, and asked them to take turns kicking goals. In a game, the goalie would never face more than one ball, so he admonished the players to allow the goalie a chance to get set before kicking either ball toward the goal.

The goalkeepers took a stance in front of the goal, ready to leap in the direction the ball was kicked. The best goalies could sense the kicker's direction and throw themselves in that direction in the split second before the kicker's foot hit the ball. Owen told them to watch the kicker's eyes for a hint of the kick's direction.

Goalies practiced at each end of the field while other players practiced skills in the midfield area. Owen tried to observe all this simultaneous activity, but his attention kept returning to the goal defended by Bruno Gorman. Gorman's large hands captured the ball readily, and he often sensed what direction the kick would take. He made three saves in the first quarter hour of practice, while the other goalie watched every kick sail into the goal. Owen heard no repetition of his teammates' digs at Bruno's religion. Owen felt he had found an answer to the school's problem. Give the Catholics a chance to prove themselves, to show they belong.

Owen felt he should get five new players to attempt goals. He walked along the sideline nearly to the goal, seeing Gorman return two balls to the kickers. Owen wanted to halt play before any more kicks were attempted. He tooted his whistle and saw he had Gorman's attention. As he was calling "time out," a ball sailed through the air. Gorman's rush to that side came as the ball sailed past. A second ball rocketed from the other side of the field, striking Bruno's face with a loud slap.

"Hey! I called time out!" Owen moved toward Gorman, who sank to the ground holding his face in his hands.

"Not my fault, I didn't hear that," the kicker mumbled. Owen knelt by the injured player. Bruno's face was contorted by pain and shock. His nose bled furiously, bloodying the palm of one hand and the fingers of the other. He pulled a handkerchief out of his pocket and inhaled with loud, shuddering sniffs, nearly sobbing aloud.

Owen peered into the youth's eyes, and then held three fingers before his face. "How many fingers?"

"Th-th-th-three."

Owen helped Bruno stand up. "Looks like you'll live. Go wash your face, get some cold water on that nose. Come back when you feel ready." He patted the boy's back.

Students gathered from all over the field to watch. As Bruno pushed his way through the circle, a falsetto voice came from the crowd. "Whatsa matter, choirboy? Did him hurt his wittle nose?"

Gorman held out his hands and blindly pushed his way through the crowd, which seemed to part reluctantly.

Owen turned toward the five who had been kicking goals. He felt his face flush. "There was no reason on earth for that to happen, whether you heard the whistle or not. You were told to hold off kicking the ball until the goalie had a chance to watch out for it. If you can't obey a simple instruction, you don't belong here."

Owen heard a voice from the midst of the players, just loud enough for him to hear. "Sure, Coach. Whatever you say, Coach." He could not identify the speaker, but the sarcasm was unmistakable. He felt the warm flush of anger in his face and turned aside from the aspiring athletes.

* * *

Ruby stopped the Ford near the Stark farmhouse. As she set the brake, Martha Stark came out of the door, wiping her hands on her apron, and greeted the guest. "Irene is up in her room, supposedly doing her homework. In case she didn't hear your arrival, I'm to give her a call."

Ruby smiled. "It's hard to surprise anyone when you're driving a Model T."

The women walked through the kitchen and living-dining room to the parlor. The room was also a library, as two of its walls were given over to bookshelves. In the center of a third wall stood the upright piano. It had an adjustable stool by the keyboard, and a dining room chair was drawn up next to the stool. How nice, a place for the teacher. These Starks were serious about piano lessons. Did Martha provide the chair, or was it Irene's idea?

Irene joined them before Ruby could decide how to pose the question. Irene had some of her father's height and unfortunately, much of her father's square jaw. When introduced, her shy smile was what mattered.

"You two need to get acquainted," the girl's mother stated, "and I have work to finish in the kitchen. I'll leave you to it."

Martha was barely out of the room before Irene turned to Ruby. "Mrs. Mattison, I'm really glad to meet you. Thank you for coming."

"Please, Irene, call me Ruby."

The shy smile returned. "I heard you played ragtime at the Mizpah meeting."

"Yes, and they liked it. Although some of the older members weren't so sure."

"If I could play ragtime, I wouldn't have the nerve to play it for Mizpah."

"Well, I took the curse off by also playing a hymn." As Irene laughed, Ruby sat on the dining room chair and waved the girl toward the piano stool. "It's time to see how much piano you've already learned. Is there a number you could play for me, from memory?"

"Golly, the only thing I might remember is the piece I played in a recital two years ago. It's real simple and real dull, and I don't really like it."

"What's the number?"

"Well, it's 'Old Black Joe.'"

"Yes," Ruby said, "that is pretty dull. If you're going to play something by Stephen Foster, it should be 'Camptown Races.'"

Ruby looked over the music lesson books Irene used with her former teacher. Irene lost her shyness and began talking about that aging spinster. Pointing to a simplified march in the *Tom Johnson Third Year Music Book*, Irene announced, "She only let me play this one with the metronome running."

"Irene, I guess it's time for a decision. Would you like me to give you music lessons?"

"Oh yes, would you, please?"

Together they examined more of the collected music, both in lesson books and sheets. The piano and most of the music came into the household when Irene's aunt developed such crippling arthritis she could no longer play. The sheet music included classical numbers, ragtime, and some jazz; but Irene wasn't ready to attempt advanced pieces. Finally, toward the back of the Tom Johnson book, they found a version of "Camptown Races." Irene would spend the week mastering the notes. At the next lesson, they would concentrate on the rhythm.

Although Ruby said this was merely a get-acquainted session, Martha Stark insisted on paying her the dollar for a regular lesson. Irene walked with Ruby out to the Ford. Ruby adjusted the spark, decided the engine was warm enough not to need the choke, and spun the crank. The engine caught at once, and Ruby climbed into the seat. With a word of admonition about piano practice, she waved and drove out through the gate.

The return trip seemed brief on the now-familiar road. Platteville's streets carried little traffic at this hour. Men weren't home from work yet, but kitchens were beginning dinner preparations, and boys raked leaves in several front yards. Ruby was delighted to reach the little brown house before Owen came home. She could teach a music lesson and be home in time to fix dinner. Ruby shook down the ashes in the stove and added paper and kindling to the embers. Soon she could add coal to the flame.

Nearly an hour later, Owen came into the house. He went immediately into the kitchen. Barely greeting Ruby, he began audibly to sniff the cooking odors. As he reached out to lift the lid from the iron skillet, Ruby lightly slapped his hand.

"You know better than that. You'll get all you can eat when it's ready."

"It smells like chicken."

"So there, you didn't have to peek to find out what's for dinner." Ruby turned back to the crookneck squash she was peeling. She laughed when Owen bent down to nuzzle behind her ear and pretended to threaten him with the paring knife.

"Feisty," Owen labeled her attitude. "You must have had a good day. How did your meeting go with the Stark girl?"

"Irene has musical talent. Better yet, she has lots of interest and is willing to work. I've agreed to weekly lessons."

"You didn't waste any time getting that set up."

"We even went through the music they have there, and I've got her working on 'Camptown Races' for next week."

"That's a good old tune."

Ruby began slicing the squash she had peeled. "And Martha insisted on paying me a dollar, calling it the first lesson. Now it's your turn. Tell me about your day. Did you have walkouts again?"

"No, they are obeying the school board. The three Catholic kids just sit there, looking miserable."

"If they are unhappy, they won't get much out of the readings."

"Of course not. It divides the school. There wasn't any razzing of the Catholic kids in class today, but there was some trouble during speedball practice this afternoon."

Ruby slipped the squash slices into a pot of steaming water on the stove. "What happened?"

"I picked Bruno Gorman, one of the Catholic boys, for starting goalie. He was doing fine. Then when I was starting to call a time-out, Gorman was paying attention to me, not to the kickers. He got hit in the face by a ball. Gave him a bloody nose."

"Was it an accident, or was he hit deliberately?"

"Hitting him in the face was an accident because none of them can kick that accurately. Aiming at him was deliberate. The kickers were using two balls, and I told them not to kick a ball until the goalie had a chance to see it coming. That was a second ball, and it came about two seconds after the first one. If they were following directions, it wouldn't have happened."

"It sounds like the goalie wasn't badly hurt."

"No, he wasn't. I checked him over and sent him in to wash his face. The worst part was, the Gorman kid acted like it was the end of the world. He did everything but bawl like a baby."

"Wasn't he reacting to more than the bloody nose? You said the Catholic kids were miserable."

"Well, the only way they can be accepted is to participate in everything they can, but they've got to be grown-up about it."

Ruby lifted the cover off the iron skillet and began turning the chicken pieces over with a fork. "All right, big brave husband, how about putting some bread on the table?"

* * *

On Thursday, Fred Koblenz hurried both the milking and breakfast. He drove to Greeley without speeding and got to the district courthouse with minutes to spare.

Earlier on Wednesday, he had listened to Milton Thayer request a writ of mandamus directed to the school board. The judge promised, because of the urgency of the situation, to render judgment the next day.

Koblenz now entered the courtroom, which was filling with spectators, and marched forward to take a seat next to Thayer.

Koblenz saw all three members of the school board sitting in the front row of spectators. People were still filing into the room. He addressed Thayer in a near whisper, "Looks like a real crowd."

"The word gets around quickly about a case like this."

The bailiff appeared at the door and commanded, "All rise." The judge marched in with a swirl of black robes and took his seat on the bench, laying a slender manuscript before him. When the people facing him regained their seats and the courtroom was quiet, the judge cleared his throat.

"I have prepared a formal order, which I will eventually read, but I want to explain the thinking behind it. First, let me outline the situation. At the beginning of the school year, the Platteville school board decided opening ceremonies in each classroom would include, for moral instruction, a reading from the Bible. Each teacher was given a copy of the King James Bible, and the board decided which verses would be read. The readings are the same in every class, and the teacher offers no comments. But the Catholic Church finds the King James translation objectionable, and Catholic students walked out of the classroom in protest.

"This protest was peaceful, and the students returned to their seats quietly when the reading was over, but they never knew exactly how long an individual reading might take. The walkout by Catholic students, which the faculty tolerated, led to resentment by the students required to remain. Last Friday the school board sent a letter home with the students, claiming the walkouts were detrimental to the school and would no longer be permitted.

"This letter led Mr. Koblenz, on behalf of all Catholic parents, to petition this court for a writ of mandamus, which is a court order to a public official—in this case, an independent agency of local government—to perform a duty. The petitioner argued Bible reading is a religious exercise, and the King James Version is a sectarian document. And therefore, the Bible-reading exercise is contrary to law, as expressed in article 2, section 4 and article 9, sections 7 and 8, of the Colorado Constitution. The petition would have this court ban the Bible reading as part of the opening exercises. Failing that, the petitioners ask that the school board be required to rescind their rule of compulsory attendance at the Bible readings."

Fred Koblenz felt his mind wandering. *Get to it, Judge!*

"Now, we may ask, what right does this court have, to make decisions on the behalf of the school board? The board's authority comes from the people through the constitution. So does the authority of the courts. Thus the courts cannot presume to run the business of the schools. However, it is the job of the courts to propound the constitution, to say what it means. I cannot find in the constitution's phrases any indication that the reading of moral precepts from the Bible, without comment, can be described as a religious service. Clearly the constitution does prohibit religious services in the public schools. But simple Bible reading, without ritual or even comment, is not a religious service. Therefore it cannot be prohibited.

"However, the guarantee of freedom of conscience in article 2 is very clear. Since Catholic parents are convinced readings from the King James Bible are dangerous to their children's faith, the school board's requirement of compulsory attendance at the Bible readings is contrary to the Constitution of Colorado. That is the reasoning behind the writ of mandamus, which I will now read."

Frederick Koblenz paid no further attention to the judge's words. Half a loaf is better than none. He glanced at Arthur Stark, who was frowning and shaking his head.

When the judge finished reading his brief order, there was a smattering of applause in the courtroom, which called forth a longer and louder chorus of boos. The judge pounded his gavel and declared the court adjourned.

Koblenz grabbed Thayer's hand and pumped it, thanking him profusely. A crowd gathered around the table, clamoring for conversation. Suddenly, on the fringe of the crowd, Koblenz saw the tall figure of Arthur Stark. Koblenz dealt as quickly as he could with his co-religionists, then walked toward his adversary, offering to shake hands. But Stark kept his arms folded, and Koblenz had no interest in a confrontation.

"Fred," said Stark, "I can hardly believe you made all those charges before that judge and prevented him from hearing the board's side."

Koblenz labored to keep his own voice quiet. "I can't believe that your board made its decision without consulting us."

"You haven't heard the end of this, Fred. It is only the beginning."

* * *

The only customer in Oliver Scott's barbershop reclined as hot towels softened his beard. The door opened, admitting an elderly man wearing farmer's coveralls. The newcomer turned to the coat rack, hung his sweat-stained hat on a hook, and turned toward the barber.

"Hello, Ray," Scott said, "I haven't seen you since last week. How's the missus?"

"Same as always. Gossiping with the neighbors over the fence or somebody over the phone. I couldn't stand it. I had to get out of the house." Raymond Dodsworth, a retired farmer, sat down heavily in a chair beneath the wide mirror and began searching in a stack of magazines in the next chair. "Hell, Ollie, where's the *Police Gazette*?"

The barber reached to the counter behind him and picked up a tabloid paper. "Here's the one for this week. I saved it for you."

Dodsworth pushed himself out of the chair, took the journal, and settled down with it. "That's damn good of you, Ollie, but I still don't need a haircut. Anyone else comes in, you can tell them that they're next."

Scott stropped the razor vigorously on the leather band hanging from the chair and applied himself to shaving the customer. Dodsworth was absorbed in his reading. When the shave was completed, Scott applied rose water to the gleaming face and a light dusting of powder to control the gleam.

The barber asked, "Are you a stranger to these parts?"

"No, I'm out of Denver. It has been in my territory for three years, so I've gone through Platteville many times, but this is the first call I've made here."

"What's your line?"

"I represent the National Cash Register Company. We've got a new electric number that store owners really like."

Ray Dodsworth put down his reading. "Not many stores in Platteville," he announced, "that would have a use for your gadget. Must take a huge sales volume to make it worthwhile."

"It doesn't cost as much as you might think. It should be perfect for a place like the Platteville Mercantile next door. Pretty busy place, isn't it?"

"I've traded there for thirty years," Dodsworth said, "and I seldom have to go anyplace else. Most everybody feels the same way, so they do an impressive business."

"Say," the salesman said, "tell me what I should know about the owner. Name of Gorman, isn't it?"

"His old man started the place. It's been in the family a long time."

The customer was reaching into his pocket for coins, a process normally not interrupted, but Ollie Scott felt called to enter the conversation. "The first thing you might want to know about Johnny Gorman is his religion. He's a big cheese in the Catholic Church."

The salesman began to count coins from one hand into the other. "I'm not sure what your point is. Are you telling me that he won't want a new cash register because the old one was blessed by a priest?"

"No," replied the barber. "I was just warning you not to insult the Pope or tell dirty stories about nuns."

"Oh, so you've heard some of those stories too."

Scott chuckled, and Dodsworth guffawed in his chair. Scott accepted the coins as the salesman said, "There's a little extra there. Thanks for the advice."

The salesman retrieved his hat, opened the shop door for a man coming in, and marched back onto Main Street. The new entrant was a young man who dressed to make himself seem older, with a three-piece suit, a four-in-hand necktie, and a watch chain across his vest. He greeted Ollie and Ray.

"Hello, Harry," the two men chorused. Dodsworth added, "If you want a haircut, get in the chair. I'm just here to get out of the house."

"OK," said Harry Singleton, cashier of the Farmers' State Bank. To Scott he said, "The usual, Ollie. Can you finish in time for me to get to the bank when it opens?"

"Ten o'clock? Easy." Scott applied his comb and scissors.

Singleton spoke up from the barber's chair. "Did you fellas hear about the big court decision yesterday?"

Dodsworth answered, "So the school board can't make Catholic kids listen to the Bible? It's crazy."

"Art Stark is really sore about it," Scott added.

"If I understand it," Singleton said, "the Catholics object to the Protestant translation they're using."

"Well," Dodsworth replied, "I can't see that there would be much difference. The Bible is the Bible, even if it was written in Greek or something."

"I'm surprised by Fred Koblenz," Scott said. "His family has lived here as long as there's been a Platteville. They've always gotten along fine with the rest of us. Why raise a fuss now?"

"Maybe," Dodsworth said, "he thinks that it's high time for his people to be running things."

Ollie Scott was so taken by this idea that he let his scissors fall silent. "I know Art Stark. He's upset by the way young people behave nowadays, and so is Newton Maclean. They're trying to do something to teach the kids how to live right. Why should Fred be opposed to that? Is he all for jazz and short skirts and bathtub gin?"

"I don't think so," Harry Singleton said. "I'll bet he thinks it's up to the parents and the church to straighten out the young people, not the schools." Scott plied his scissors again.

"Harry," Dodsworth said, "you don't have any kids, do you?"

"Yes, we do. Our daughter, Lucy, will be four in a couple of months."

"As someone who has raised seven kids," the older man continued, "I can tell you that parents are usually grateful for any help they can get. When kids won't listen to anybody at home or in church, maybe they'll listen to somebody at school."

The scissors slowed as Ollie Scott emphasized each word with a loud snip. "Sometimes kids are like mules. You hit them between the eyes to get their attention."

Harry Singleton laughed. "I don't think we want the schools doing that. At least, not literally."

Scott closed the scissors. Now he emphasized his words by waving their point in the air. "The Klan, over to Greeley, has been doing something like that, raiding roadhouses and breaking up petting parties in parked cars."

"The Ku Klux Klan? My God," Singleton said, "we better not depend on *them* to straighten out the kids!"

Ollie Scott decided not to mention his Klan membership.

Chapter 5

THE SCHOOL BOARD MET in their usual classroom. President Maclean proposed the private meeting for Saturday afternoon, after his colleagues agreed there was no need further to consult public opinion, since all three were wearied by constituent reactions. The problem for discussion: could any action by the school board avoid offending Protestants, appease Catholics, obey the court, and unify the school?

Arthur Stark declared his position upon taking his seat. "We had good reasons to require Bible readings, and those reasons are still valid. I'm damned if I'll give up the readings because the Catholics don't like our Bible."

Maclean nodded. "I share your sentiment. After all, I proposed the idea. But we need formal discussion. And therefore, I call the meeting to order."

Harold Healy strode into the room and slipped into the seat at the end of the table. Maclean turned to Stark. "Let the minutes record," he said, "the presence of Superintendent Healy."

"Newton," Stark said, "can't we just thrash this thing out? Does everything have to be so all-fired formal? Do I even have to keep minutes?"

"Arthur, you don't need to record everybody's arguments, but you'll need to report any formal action we take. This is an official meeting. The law allows us to hold private meetings at our discretion."

Because the school superintendent shared his impatience with Maclean's formality, Stark addressed the latecomer. "Harold, just before you came in, I said I'm damned if I'll give up the Bible reading. Our reasons for requiring it are still good."

"That's true," Healy responded, "but we can't defy the court. I have a proposal to offer, if the president is ready to entertain proposals."

"Well, I suppose I am," Maclean said. "If you've got some way of dealing with that writ of whatever-it-is, let's hear it."

"We have to build on the fact that Catholic parents don't object to moral instruction, they object to the way we do it and to the text we're using. So we should set up moral instruction they can support. When we send Catholic students to their own class comparable to the Bible readings, Protestant students won't have reason to be jealous anymore, because the Catholics won't be escaping something."

Roy Thompson, the board's treasurer, spoke up. "Sounds good, but it can't be that simple. Who is going to teach this class? It won't take more than five minutes, so it won't amount to much."

"That's the beauty of it," Healy said. "We'll ask the Catholic parents, and maybe the priest himself, to recommend some layperson we can hire. They can't object if they choose the teacher."

"Why do you say 'layperson'?"

"Just think of the ruckus there would be if we got a priest or a nun in here to teach!"

Thompson slumped in his chair. "For a minute there," the treasurer said, "I thought we could get a priest or nun and not have to pay them."

"If we tried that," Healy said, "we'd be crucified. Lawyers would come, waving the constitution, yelling about separation of church and state."

Arthur Stark voiced a rising sense of outrage. "You mean, in order to read a little bit of the Bible, we have to pay for a separate Catholic class?"

"Here's how it would work," Healy said. "It's now the last week of October. There are seven weeks of school before Christmas vacation, counting Thanksgiving week. That's ample time to consult the Catholics, make all the arrangements, and begin the special instruction when school starts again."

Thompson intervened. "You didn't say how we're going to pay this new teacher."

"The new teacher will be strictly part-time," Healy responded. "We'll only pay a few dollars a month, and the teacher will probably be more interested in supporting the Catholic faith than in making money. When the fiscal year began, you established a contingency fund. You've set aside part of it to pay that lawyer we had to take on. You would commit the balance to cover the new salary."

"Yes," Thompson said, "that would work. Then we'd make it part of the regular budget next fiscal year."

"Wait a minute," Stark nearly shouted. "I'm dead set against this new teacher as a permanent arrangement."

"Don't forget," President Maclean said, "we don't have the final word of the courts. Our lawyer has objected to the writ issued by the district court—he says he filed a demurrer. That requires a reconsideration of the issue, and we'll get to present our side. Then whoever is unhappy with the result will appeal to the Colorado Supreme Court."

Roy Thompson agreed. "Our lawyer says it will take two or three years to get a decision from the Supreme Court. That will take us beyond the current fiscal year, but it won't make the special Catholic instruction permanent."

Stark was not mollified. "The whole thing sounds too one-sided. We cave in on requiring attendance at the readings, and then we finance special treatment for Catholics. If it's a compromise, they should give up something."

"They don't think they have to give up anything," Maclean said. "They've got the court on their side, at least for now."

"But they should make some concession to us in return for the favor we're doing them. How about the seven weeks of classes before it goes into effect? Are they going to keep on disrupting things? What do they do when they walk out, just wander the halls?"

Superintendent Healy spoke up. "We've got the high school kids studying in their library. We haven't had walkouts in the grade school, but those parents complained about the readings. If their parents request it in writing, we send the grade school kids to wait in chairs we set up in the hallway. They take a drawing or something with them."

"Well," said Stark, "why can't the Catholics have their kids stay in the Bible readings for seven weeks, in return for having their own instruction after Christmas?"

"Arthur," Maclean said, "if you can get the Catholics to promise that, more power to you. But they should be approached informally. Haven't you known Fred Koblenz for a long time?"

"Yes, I have, and I'd like to try talking to him."

"All right, it's time for the board to take formal action, so you'll have something to talk to him about. Are you prepared to make a motion?"

Stark consulted his notes. With coaching from the others, he constructed a two-part motion. The board would recruit a new part-time teacher, with the help of local Catholics, and commit the balance of the contingency fund to finance the new hire. The motion carried unanimously.

* * *

Ruby sat next to the piano stool while Irene Stark played "Camptown Races." A week earlier, Ruby suggested the tempo should be like galloping horses; now the bobtail nag dashed around the track. Irene also mastered the repetitive exercises, and her fingers were becoming very nimble.

Irene finished the number and turned to Ruby for a reaction. Ruby murmured her appreciation and approval. She was ready to discuss a new assignment, but Irene's face clouded over.

"Irene, are you all right?"

"Well, y-yes . . . Ruby, do you mind if I ask you a personal question?"

"Not at all."

"Well . . . how long have you worn your hair bobbed?"

"Let's see . . . nearly five years. I got a short haircut for the first time, my freshman year at Ft. Collins."

"So you didn't have to get permission from your parents?"

"No, because I was in Colorado, and they were in Illinois." So Irene wanted to cut her hair, despite parental objections. The girl's shyness returned full force. Ruby wanted to encourage her without causing trouble. "Of course, bobbed hair is even more fashionable now. I hardly ever saw it before I went to college."

Irene was silent for an instant. Then she blurted, "My father says it's the flapper hairstyle."

"Well, yes, it is. But flappers don't have a monopoly."

"Ruby, could you . . . I mean, have you ever . . ." Irene was nearly overcome with hesitancy but seemed determined to finish her question. "Ruby, do you ever think of yourself as a flapper?"

Ruby turned halfway from Irene, looking back over her shoulder with a raised eyebrow, mocking the pose of a movie star. "My dear, a true flapper is never married. If she is, she'll never admit it. But I am a happily married woman."

Irene laughed. "You look just like the posters outside the Rex Theater."

Ruby was pleased by Irene's changed mood. Best keep up the act. She held two fingers to her lips and then drew them away, blowing out imaginary smoke. "A real flapper drinks gin and smokes cigarettes and flirts with other women's husbands. We never do that in Hollywood."

Irene laughed hilariously. Ruby ground out her imaginary cigarette in an imaginary ashtray. "Now young lady, we must get back to your music. Your mother will wonder what's gotten into us."

Irene's laughter faded into giggles, and she became silent. Ruby assigned new scales and exercises for the following week. They searched the sheet music together until they came upon a George M. Cohan tune, "Forty-five Minutes from Broadway." Ruby's first requirement was that Irene have fun at the piano, and the lively waltz from an old Broadway show was exactly right. As the lesson drew to a close, Ruby offered praise. "Irene, at the rate you're going, in two or three weeks, you'll be starting on ragtime and jazz."

"Oh, Ruby, do you really think I'll be ready?"

"Yes, as long as you keep on practicing."

Ruby and Irene walked together toward the back door. They paused in the kitchen, where Martha Stark was beginning dinner preparations. Martha asked if Owen was enjoying his teaching. Ruby answered affirmatively. When

Irene was distracted, Martha slipped the dollar payment into Ruby's hand. Irene regarded Ruby as a friend more than a teacher, and Martha did not want to remind her daughter of the paid relationship.

Irene followed Ruby to the Model T. As Ruby took her stance by the radiator, Irene asked, "Could you teach me how to crank your car someday? And how to drive it?"

Ruby paused. "I don't think so. Sometimes it has an awful kick, and you can't play the piano very well with a broken arm." She smiled at Irene to take the sting out of the rejection. "Better ask your father if you can learn to drive. Maybe ask him sweetly to teach you."

Ruby pulled the choke with her left hand and spun the crank. She released the choke, spun the crank again, and the engine lurched into life. Sliding onto the seat, she adjusted the spark and throttle. She bade Irene farewell and drove out through the gateposts.

Arthur Stark walked in from the barn just after Ruby's departure, joining Irene on the doorstep.

"Oh, Daddy, she's so nice. I love playing the piano again."

"I saw the two of you from down by the barn. I'm not tickled by her hairstyle, but I'm impressed by the way she handles that Ford."

"Well, I asked her about cranking it, and she said it could break my arm. But your car has an electric starter . . . Lots of women are driving cars now . . . Please, would you teach me to drive the car?"

"I think knowing Mrs. Mattison is giving you notions. First you want to cut your hair, now you want to drive the car. You forget you're barely seventeen years old. Stick to learning the piano, that's what we're paying her to teach."

* * *

Owen walked through the front part of the house into the kitchen, where Ruby stood at the kitchen table. She concentrated on molding a reddish lump to fit in an enameled baking pan. Owen tiptoed behind her and encircled her waist with his arms, pleased by her yelp of surprise. "Meat loaf! That's great. You make the best meat loaf ever."

Ruby turned around in his arms, returning the embrace. "Owen, you're easy to please. You eat whatever I put in front of you and want more."

"Well, you spent all that money to major in Home Ec, and it paid off. You learned to cook."

Ruby turned out of his arms. "Give me a chance to practice what I've learned." She picked up the pan, carried it to the stove, and slid it into the oven. She asked, "How did the speedball practice go today?"

Owen sat on the only kitchen chair as Ruby took dishes out of the cupboard to set the dining room table. "The practice was all right. Bruno Gorman is doing real well as goalie, and there wasn't any razzing about religion. But the big news is, I got called away from practice to take a long-distance telephone call."

"That's something new. Who was it?"

"It was the sports editor of the Greeley *Tribune*. He asked me to send him a report on the speedball game with Ft. Lupton. He said they get coaches to report the games because we're sure to be there. And I should send items about the school or athletics, without being asked. They'll pay me twenty-five cents a column inch for anything they publish."

Ruby silently carried plates and silverware to the dining room table. She returned to stir a pot on the stove. "That should be interesting," she said. "But isn't there a problem? Reporting on your own team, won't you play favorites?"

"It won't be a problem. You've seen the paper. They don't give their correspondents' names."

Ruby grinned at him. "So with no byline, nobody can hold you responsible?"

Owen acted as if a tiny cloud crossed his personal sun. "I don't see how I can play favorites if I just tell the score and describe the best plays."

"I'm sure you'll be a model of objectivity. And you can make sure the reader appreciates your team's coach." Ruby cringed, surprised by her own sudden sarcasm. *Will Owen be offended?*

Owen gave no sign of offense. "Writing for the paper will be fun," he said. "I've never had any problem with writing things, and it will bring in some extra money."

"You weren't the only one to get a phone call today. Mine wasn't long distance, just from the other side of town. It concerned one of your students, Margaret Fitzgerald. Nearly everybody seems to call her Maggie."

"She's one of my walkouts, but she's doing all right in biology class. Who called you?"

"Her mother. Apparently Maggie is a friend of Irene's, and Irene tells her all about each lesson. Maggie took lessons from Irene's former teacher until she lost interest. Maggie claims I would get her interested again."

Owen fought to keep his voice low. "You promised we would discuss this whole thing before you take on any more students."

"That's what we're doing." Ruby walked the few feet of the dining room table and pulled out a chair. "Come and sit down."

Owen went to the table and sat opposite Ruby. "So what did you tell Mrs. Fitzgerald?"

"I told her that I'd have to discuss it with you, find out if I can use the Ford.

Then if you approve, I can go for a get-acquainted visit with Maggie, to see if she really wants lessons from me."

Owen pursed his lips. Ruby wondered what would happen if he said no. She had to help him understand her feelings.

"You know," Owen said, "since I'm going to get paid by the *Tribune*, we won't need money from more music lessons." He folded his hands and rested them on the table.

Ruby reached across and covered his hands with her own. "Owen, you know I'm not primarily interested in the money. I'd want to do something like teaching piano even without being paid. It gets me out of the house and lets me feel useful."

Ruby stared into Owen's eyes. She pulled her hands away from his for an instant and then grasped them firmly. "I won't teach piano very long after I get pregnant, and I won't even think of teaching after there's a baby to take care of. I want your child, more than anything in the world. They say that when you really want to get pregnant, it won't happen, so I really need the music lessons. If I just sit in this little house waiting to get pregnant, I'll go crazy."

Owen clasped Ruby's hands tightly as tears welled in her eyes.

Suddenly her nose twitched. "The peas are boiling dry!" Ruby bounded out of her chair and in three strides was tending the stove.

* * *

Arthur Stark wanted to confront Fred Koblenz on his own home ground, where Stark could control the environment. But he had spoken harsh words to Koblenz in the courtroom, and Fred would not be in a receptive frame of mind. In the end, Stark telephoned his boyhood friend, told him that the school board wanted them to speak, and asked Koblenz to suggest a meeting place. Koblenz invited Stark to come out to the Koblenz farm after dinner.

Daylight was fading as Stark guided his Reo into the Koblenz yard to park beneath a tree. Some of the farmhouse windows were already warmed by the glow of oil lamps. As Stark approached the front porch, the screen door opened, and a young man stepped out. Stark recognized the oldest son, the one he had seen at the Halfway House, but he did not remember the name. What could he say?

Before that decision was needed, Frederick Koblenz followed his son outside. "Hello, Arthur. Have you met my oldest boy? This is Emil. Emil, this is Mr. Stark."

Stark said, "Hello, Fred," to his host. To the son, he said, "I saw you graduate a couple of years ago, Emil. I remember you had a fine record in high school."

"Thank you, Mr. Stark."

Stark smiled. No sign of recognition by the boy. Because of the darkness, maybe he wasn't recognized at the roadhouse. Just as well. It was not the right time to tell Fred Koblenz about the Klan.

Emil walked toward Stark's Reo, volubly admiring it. Stark offered Frederick Koblenz a handshake, which he accepted.

"Arthur, I'm glad you're willing to shake my hand. Last time we met, that wasn't the case."

"In the courtroom." How long did Koblenz bear a grudge? It couldn't hurt to eat some humble pie. "Fred, that was rude, and I apologize. I couldn't believe we didn't have a chance to tell our side. I was surprised to see you, and I forgot my manners."

Emil made appreciative sounds while walking around the Reo. His father explained that Emil was an auto mechanic, and delaying his sweetheart's courtship to examine an interesting automobile was normal behavior. The older men bade Emil farewell and entered the farmhouse.

In the living room, Fred's wife, Catherine, greeted Arthur, who briefly grasped her extended hand and declined her offer of a cup of tea. They passed on into the dining room, where Emil's younger brother rose from his place at the table strewn with books. He was introduced to Arthur, who responded, "I'm glad to meet you, Walter. As a member of the school board, I'm glad to see you doing your homework. Seeing you buckle down makes all those dull meetings worthwhile."

They left the youth rigid with silent anger at his father. He wanted to be called Walt.

Stark followed Koblenz into the parlor, a comfortable but little-used room. Two oil lamps gave soft light and made dark shadows on the walls. The host returned to the door and began to close it. "I assume you'd like some privacy."

"That's a good idea."

The men sat in armchairs facing one another. Koblenz was willing to follow his guest's conversational lead, so they chatted about their respective sons. Stark realized that Koblenz was proud of Emil's mastery of gasoline engines.

Stark described Matthew's brooder house project, but he feared that no amount of small talk would soften his host's attitude, so he moved toward his purpose. "Fred, I'm glad you could see me on such short notice."

"Least I could do. I don't know if Martha told you, but I did try to telephone you about the Bible reading. You were already at a school board meeting."

"She did tell me. I didn't return your phone call right away, and then I didn't want to bother you on the weekend. When I called on Monday,

Catherine said that you were in Denver. But none of that really matters, now we've gotten together."

"After the lawsuit and all," Koblenz replied, "I think I'd better listen to whatever you want to say."

"I think you realize," Stark began, "why we decided to add Bible reading to the opening ceremonies. The kids are so wild nowadays, with their jazz music and crazy dances. The girls all want short hair and shorter dresses—"

Stark was about to mention gin and Prohibition, but he remembered Emil Koblenz at the roadhouse and began again. "We just felt that we need to do something to give students moral guidance, help them see the difference between right and wrong."

Fred Koblenz nodded his head slightly but remained silent. Hoping this was a good sign, Stark plunged ahead. "We think you agree about the need for moral guidance, but we appreciate that you don't like the way we're going about it. We propose to establish something you can really get behind, because you—the Catholic parents, with the help of your priest—will select both the text and the teacher. If their parents request it, we will excuse Catholic students from Bible readings to attend this special instruction."

"So," Koblenz said, "the board is willing to recognize the difficulties they've made for Catholics. That is promising."

"During the seven weeks between now and Christmas vacation, we'll consult with you folks and hire the person you recommend. He—or she—will begin when school opens again in the New Year."

"I suppose this person will be part-time."

"Yes. Of course, the pay will be negotiated, but the board has committed our entire contingency fund to finance it."

"Let me ask a question. I'm not being ungrateful, I just want to know. Do you think we could have gotten this by talking with the school board, without a court order?"

Stark inhaled a deep breath, feeling a sudden thirst for the tea he had declined. "I don't believe," he said, exhaling, "it would do any good for me to speculate on that. The fact is, our schools have been disrupted, and the board is making a generous offer to solve the problem."

"I grant you that. It is generous."

"Fred, I've come here tonight to see if you folks could respond to that, give a little because you're getting so much."

Koblenz stiffened. "What do you have in mind?"

"For four days last week, your students stayed in the Bible readings, and it didn't seem to harm them at all."

"They were there because your board ordered them to be there. We made it clear to Superintendent Healy that they were there under protest."

"But you don't claim any of them were hurt by it. If they can stand four days, they can stand forty days, and there are less than thirty school days until Christmas vacation. So those few weeks can run without disruption, could you keep your kids in the Bible readings until Christmas?"

Stark saw Koblenz's jaw clench. His host spoke slowly and forcefully. "Arthur, you still don't understand. You want our children to listen for six weeks to a book that is proscribed. If they pay attention to the words they hear, they will sin. To do that for thirty days would eat away at their souls. Now I don't think you want them to sit there with their hands over their ears. They are better off walking out, and the school is better off without students defying school authority inside the classroom."

"Fred, maybe you're the one who doesn't understand. Can't you realize we never choose passages for some Protestant meaning? We only pick them to give moral guidance."

"Most passages don't guide very well without interpretation, and you aren't providing anyone in those seven weeks to supply that guidance. The walkouts will have to continue, but I will make you a promise. If any Catholic student disrupts any school activity or vandalizes any school property, we will double whatever punishment the school decides on."

Arthur Stark stood up. He had known Fred for over thirty years. They had played baseball together in the summer and went out on Halloween to tip over outhouses. What could they agree on now? "Fred, that promise is worth a lot, and I'll take it back to the board. But I'm disappointed that you won't give a little. Remember, we haven't heard the last word from the judges."

"All right, Arthur. But let's not wait to see each other in court. If we keep on talking, maybe we can keep things from getting bitter."

* * *

"Good afternoon, Mr. Mattison." Owen paused at the gymnasium door to exchange greetings with Isabel Nelson, who led a women's exercise class in the absence of a coach.

"Hello, Mrs. Nelson. Could I get you to call me Owen?"

"Owen, that wouldn't do if students were present, so I won't get into the habit. I'm glad you were able to come teach the women about basketball."

Owen saw the girls coming down the hall. They were wearing long bloomers and middy blouses, ready for gym, and the front ones were nearly within earshot. "To tell the truth, Mrs. Nelson, I've never seen a girls' game, but I've read the women's rules."

Isabel Nelson lowered her voice as the girls began filing through the door. "Well, I've seen one women's game. Do you doubt female ability to play basketball?"

"Well, it isn't a contact sport, so nobody should get hurt."

"You still sound skeptical."

"I just wonder if they have the agility to change direction quickly while they handle the ball."

"Agility? You forget that some of these women have danced the Charleston. Anyone who does that can surely play basketball."

Owen grinned. "You have a point. And the women's rules do limit the amount of running around they have to do."

A bell signaled the end of the passing period as the teachers entered the gym. One section of the bleachers had been folded down from the wall, providing the girls with seats. Isabel Nelson took roll; only one of the high school's thirty-three girls was absent. Next, she explained that basketball season was about to begin, and the Platte Valley League would sponsor women's games. They would play basketball in gym class to acquaint women with the game, then see if enough wanted to try out for a school team. She introduced Owen, saying that he would explain the game, and if Platteville fielded a team, he would share coaching duties. Finally, she asked for questions.

A hand went up at the rear of the group. "Mrs. Nelson, does this mean the school will take the women's team to play at other schools, like the boys' teams do?"

"Exactly like the men's teams. Most games will be scheduled the same day we play that school's varsity. The women's game will begin about an hour before, and both teams will travel in the same bus."

Mrs. Nelson's final sentence triggered a buzz of conversation. Untroubled by this impact, she turned the meeting over to Owen and took a seat on the folded-out bench. Owen stepped out before a suddenly interested group of girls to explain the game. He picked a basketball out of a box on the floor that contained half a dozen balls.

"How many of you have ever played in a basketball game?" No hands were raised. "How many have ever seen a basketball game?" Owen counted four hands. "OK, I better start at the beginning. Basketball games are played by two teams of five men—I mean, players—each."

Owen pointed out the baskets at each end of the gym and explained the markings on the floor. "Each team attacks the goal ahead of them and defends the goal behind them. Each team has two forwards, two guards, and a center. The big difference between the boys' and girls' games is this: when the girls' team attacks, their guards cannot cross over the centerline to support the attack. When they defend, their center and forwards cannot cross the centerline to support the defense. This protects you from overexertion."

There were no questions at that point, so Owen discussed scoring. "You win the game by scoring more points than your opponents. Points are scored in two different ways. The first is when you make the ball drop through the hoop during regular play. That's called a basket and scores two points. Then the referee can award you one or two free throws if somebody interferes with you. That's called a foul. The referee stops play by blowing his whistle, and then you stand behind this free throw line."

Bouncing the ball, Owen walked into the free throw circle. He required three attempts until, blushing furiously, he sank a successful free throw. Owen turned toward the girls. "Each time you sink a free throw—it's harder than it looks—you score one point." He held the ball against his hip and walked toward the girls' benches.

"Because this is an indoor game, played on a hard floor, there are important rules that limit what you can do. First, you can't intentionally make physical contact with your opponent. If you do, the referee will call a foul. Second, you can't carry the ball when you move from one place to another. If you have the ball and want to move, you have to bounce it on the floor. That's called dribbling."

Owen dribbled to the center of the gym and back. "But you only get to dribble once. When you stop, you must keep one foot planted on the floor until you can pass the ball to a teammate or shoot a basket." Holding the ball in front of his chest, Owen pivoted on his right foot and thrust the ball in different directions to tease imaginary opponents.

"There's one other basic thing you should know. If one team causes the ball to go out of bounds, the referee will stop play—like this." Owen raised the whistle dangling from a string around his neck to blow a short blast. "The referee will then give the ball to a member of the opposing team, who will throw it in to a teammate from the sidelines."

Owen dragged the box to the center of the court and pulled three more basketballs from it. "The first thing you need to do is get used to handling the ball. Please form up in four lines here, facing me."

Owen realized that none of the girls wanted to seem eager. He recognized Margaret Fitzgerald in the first row of benches. "Ms. Fitzgerald, I'd like you to be the first person in the line over here." As the girls filed onto the court, Owen gave a basketball to the first person in each line.

"Here's the drill. The person at the head of each line will take the ball and dribble it toward the basket, as fast and as far as she is comfortable with. She can try to sink a basket, if she thinks she's close enough. Then she will pass the ball back to the next person in line, who will do the same. After you've passed the ball back, you go back to the end of your line to take another turn. Is that clear to everybody? OK, begin."

The girls began slowly but picked up speed, as the motions became familiar. Some could dribble only at a slow walk and also control the ball. A few threw the ball so clumsily that it would not reach the girl at the head of the line, forcing her to chase the ball. Soon the gym was full of sound—balls bouncing, girlish laughter, and derisive comments.

Owen walked to the sideline and sat down next to Isabel Nelson. "I think we'll get enough volunteers to make up a squad. Some of them will like playing basketball, but so far they're mostly interested in traveling with the boys. We should be on the lookout for talent, for girls we can encourage to join."

"I think," Mrs. Nelson said, "Maggie Fitzgerald is one who should be encouraged."

* * *

As the congregation sat down after the second hymn, seven Klansmen marched in step down the center aisle of the Presbyterian Church. Two ranks of three men followed a solitary leader. All wore white robes with cone-shaped hats. They were neither masked nor armed.

Harry Singleton sat with his wife and his daughter, Lucy, on the aisle six rows from the front. Pastor Rollins stood quietly behind the pulpit as heads turned in the congregation to watch the silent marchers. The only sound was the heavy tread of the intruders' shoes on the carpet. Lucy turned to look past her father as the sound approached their pew. She gazed up at the stern-faced men in white and blanched.

"Mommy! Daddy! I don't like those funny men." Lucy's face collapsed and sobs began. Her mother took Lucy into her arms and whispered words of comfort.

As the Klansmen approached the pulpit, Gerald Ostrum spoke out loudly. "Pastor Rollins, we come in peace and ask to join your worship."

The preacher did not seem surprised. He said, "If you are peaceful and abide by our customs, you are welcome."

Ostrum reached through a slit in his robe near his pants pocket to withdraw an envelope. "Let us begin by making this presentation." He opened the envelope and took out an oblong piece of blue paper, which he held toward the preacher.

Rollins came down two steps to accept, examining the shape handed to him. "Why, it's a check for one hundred and fifty dollars! Thank you!"

Ostrum, the Exalted Cyclops, turned to face the congregation. His guards took positions on either side of him, also facing the congregation, and folded their arms.

"We are pleased to make this donation," Ostrum announced, "because we respect the work that you are doing in the community. I happen to live in Greeley, but our membership reaches throughout the Platte Valley, and I hear nothing but good reports about what your congregation is doing. What you are accomplishing conforms to the purposes of our organization, so we are happy to support it.

"I wish we could stay for the remainder of your service, but we have other calls to make. With your permission, though, I'd like to offer a prayer before we go."

Rollins invited Ostrum to the pulpit. Standing behind it, the Klansman stretched his arms wide and called upon God to wipe the illusion from the eyes of those who believed it fashionable to consume liquor and in other ways defy the law and God's commandments. He solicited God's blessing for the Platte Valley, its people, and its products. Finally, he called for God's help in leading young people onto the path of righteousness.

Then the seven robed figures marched back through the sanctuary and were gone. Rollins made no direct reference to the visitors, continuing the service as set forth in the church bulletin. His sermon was based on the story of the Good Samaritan, with the moral that persons should not be judged by their backgrounds but only by their actions. Harry Singleton wondered if this was a plea to tolerate the Klan.

The recessional hymn was sung as the choir went out of the sanctuary, followed by the congregation. Harry carried Lucy, whose cheerful disposition was again on display. He freed a hand to return the pastor's greeting at the door. The Singletons emerged into the crisp November air. They were not inspired to seek out gatherings of friends, as they would on a July Sunday, but they did stop to greet the Thompsons. Both as treasurer of the school board and as a manager at the pickle factory, Roy Thompson had many dealings with Singleton's bank.

Thompson patted Lucy's head. "I don't blame you for crying, Lucy. Those men were really scary." He turned his attention to her father. "What did you make of that visit, Harry?"

"I didn't like it. It seems like the Klan is trying to buy respectability. And from the way Pastor Rollins acted, he must have known they were coming."

Chapter 6

RONALD LYDELL DROPPED OFF his schoolbooks on the back porch, turned up his coat collar against the chill November evening, and hurried to the barn, where he found his father and brother in a stall with a mare and her foal. The foal had been given to four-year-old Robbie, just as Ronald had gotten a colt to care for, train, and eventually ride. Robbie named the foal Star because of white hair splashed against his dark forehead.

Star was eight days old. He had barely worked the wobbles out of his long legs when sickness made him unsteady again. The foal was lying on his side, with Robbie sitting beside him.

"Hi, Robbie, how is Star?"

Robbie turned a tear-stained face toward his older brother. "We can't get him to eat!"

George Lydell finished lighting a lantern and hung it from a nail above the manger. "Hello, son, I'm glad you're home. I need you to stay here and help Robbie while I get some things done. I want to try this one more time before I go."

Lydell reached under the foal with both arms and gently lifted it to its feet. The foal's long forelegs trembled, and his front hooves touched the floor listlessly. His head was guided toward his mother's teat. The foal began to suck, but his actions were tentative, unlike a foal's normal lusty appetite.

"I told Mr. Mattison about Star," Ron Lydell reported. "He just shook his head and said we should call the vet."

George Lydell removed his hands and knees from the foal's sides. It trembled but remained upright. Ron saw Robbie kneeling in the shadows at the back of the stall, his lips moving silently. George Lydell lowered his voice almost to a whisper. "The vet was here an hour ago. He says it's the shaker foal syndrome, results from a bad infection. All we can do is try to get some food

73

into him. If that doesn't work, the final stage comes when his breathing gets interrupted. Then we'll have to put him down."

The foal's forelegs continued to shake. When the mare shifted her weight, the foal's hindquarters wavered, and then he tumbled to the floor. Ron stepped forward to help drag the foal away from his mother's back hooves.

"I'll go get the milking started. You stay with Robbie, try to get the foal to eat. Try every five minutes. Come tell me if his condition changes." George Lydell walked to the end of the stall and squatted beside Robbie. Unable to offer honest words of encouragement, he patted the boy on the back, rose, and strode away.

Ronald could do nothing to make the foal more comfortable, so he sat down cross-legged beside Robbie. The small boy's lips moved again.

"Hey, Robbie, who are you talking to?"

"God."

"You mean . . . you're praying?"

Robbie nodded.

"Do you think that's going to help?"

"Mama says God can decide to take Star away from us. I'm asking him not to."

Ronald's pulse pounded with anger. How stupid, telling a kid that God decides when little horses die. Better to find out where the infection came from. The words "God has nothing to do with it" formed in his mind.

Before he could say them, a sudden memory paralyzed his throat. Ronald felt seven years old again and saw his baby sister, Erin, lying in a box lined with white satin. He heard his mother's voice. "God has decided," she said, "to take Erin to be with him in heaven."

Ronald sat silently as the memories faded, and his pulse subsided. Then he got up, went to the foal, and picked it up as his father had done. He half carried Star to the mare and, with the foal leaning against his leg, guided it to nourishment. But the connection was soon broken. Star was unable to swallow. Milk dripped from the foal's mouth to splash in the musty hay beneath their feet.

Ronald lowered Star to the floor near Robbie. "Robbie, you look after Star for a minute. I've got to go get Dad."

* * *

The gymnasium was filling with noisy echoes when Owen walked toward Isabel Nelson sitting with the Platteville women's basketball squad. It was their fourth league game, their second at home, and Owen felt the English teacher no longer needed his assistance. She had asked his help for one more game, and he agreed, since he had to be there in an hour for the men's game.

Mrs. Nelson rose from her seat to greet Owen. "Thank you for coming," she said. "Unfortunately, there's a change in plans. The referee who was scheduled for this afternoon called in sick, and they are asking you to take his place."

Owen shook his head at the same old problem. The school tried to do everything a bigger school did; but there were barely enough students, and definitely not enough staff members, to keep it all running.

He reported to the small table where Harold Healy, the school superintendent, was set up to function as both scorekeeper and timekeeper. "Mr. Healy, I can referee the girls' game, but I'll be coaching the boys. It wouldn't look right to referee at the same time."

"That's taken care of, Mattison. We telephoned the bank, and Harry Singleton can be here in time for the boys' game. He was a star player a few years ago, you know. If he gets here early, I'll ask him to referee for you, so you can help Mrs. Nelson."

"That won't be necessary. All Mrs. Nelson needs is some self-confidence, and that will come with experience."

The opponents were from Ft. Lupton High School, Platteville's archrivals. Ft. Lupton was a larger town, a dozen miles away on the road to Denver, and its high school enrollment was nearly triple that of Platteville. The size disparity was a fine excuse for losing and a source of redoubled pride if the Platteville Bears should win.

Owen took off his necktie and hung the cord attached to a whistle around his neck. As the players lined up for the tip-off, Owen saw that Maggie Fitzgerald was starting at right forward. He wanted to cheer on the Catholic kids' achievements, yet Maggie was the only girl player whose religion he knew.

Owen lofted the ball up between the opposing centers. Although the Ft. Lupton girl was a few inches taller, the Platteville center timed her jump perfectly and tipped the ball to Maggie, who dribbled toward the goal, passed the ball to the other forward, received a return pass, and shot for the basket. The ball rolled around the rim and fell outside it; but Maggie dashed underneath, grabbed the ball, and made the game's first score.

Owen settled into the rhythm of the game, rushing from end to end of the court. He used the whistle to signal when the ball went out of bounds, but he seldom needed to call a foul. The rules curtailing the girls' movements slowed the game's pace. Furthermore, their style of play was not confrontational; physical contact between players was genuinely accidental. There were fewer time-outs for free throws, reducing the total time used for the game.

The two sides were evenly matched (or were equally incompetent, as Harold Healy later said), and they alternated baskets. Platteville maintained the lead throughout the first quarter but were overtaken in the second, and finished the first half four points behind. However, the Bears were revitalized in the second half, regained the lead in the fourth quarter, and won the game by three points.

The Platteville girls were jubilant. Owen did not walk among them as he did not want to jeopardize the appearance of objectivity essential to officiating. He signaled to Isabel Nelson, and she left the circle of girls to talk with him.

"Congratulations!" Owen said. "You have soloed."

"What do you mean, soloed?"

"You coached a full game all by yourself. And you won!"

"All I did was send in a substitute when somebody got tired. You taught them their skills."

"Well, you must have given them a fine pep talk at half time. They really perked up in the second half."

Isabel Nelson looked at the floor, and Owen thought he saw a faint blush cross her features. "Well, I did say a few words, rather to my surprise. Something about upholding the honor of womanhood. You know, I hadn't appreciated how feminism and athletics go together."

Owen grinned. "I learned that when Ruby—this was before we were married—beat me at tennis."

Isabel said, "I gather your male ego recovered from the blow, since you did marry."

Owen searched his mind for a rejoinder, trying to remember something of Dr. Freud's terminology, as Isabel returned to the bench for her coat. The Platteville girls were leaving the gym as the boys filed in to take over the benches. Mrs. Nelson wished Owen and his team good luck; other obligations prevented her from staying to watch.

Owen replied, "With Ft. Lupton leading the league, staying for our game would be cruel and unusual punishment. Coaching is enough. You don't have to be a fan too."

Isabel Nelson laughed appreciatively and took her leave. Owen was pleased that Isabel and Ruby were becoming friends. Isabel appreciated Ruby's sense of humor, and they served on the same committee in the Mizpah Club. The two of them would make a good pair, like sisters bringing new fashions and music and even ideas to Platteville.

All the folding bleachers had been let down from the walls, and the gym was filling. Students who did not need to catch busses drifted in. Townspeople came in, looking for entertainment. Owen recognized old Ray Dodsworth, who made the barbershop his second home. Harry Singleton came in, stripped off his coat, loosened his tie, and asked to borrow Owen's whistle. As he handed it over, Owen caught himself grinning. So far the day was going well.

As the game progressed, Owen's good feeling evaporated. The Ft. Lupton boys were larger and a little faster. They penetrated Platteville's man-to-man defense because the defenders had trouble keeping up with their attackers. In frustration, Platteville players fouled their opponents. Harry Singleton called foul after foul, but Owen felt all the calls were justified. The Ft. Lupton players made nearly half their free throws. When the first half ended, Platteville was six points behind.

The school provided no locker rooms, so the teams gathered at opposite ends of the gym for the half-time break. The eight students who made up Platteville's entire male basketball prowess sat in a semicircle on the floor.

Owen paced back and forth between the ends of the semicircle while he spoke. "These guys are big, and they are fast. But you can beat them. The problem is when they are about to break through the defense, you foul them. When you foul them, they make hay with free throws. Then you get worried about fouling out, so you freeze up and let them through to score."

Owen lowered his voice, hoping to emphasize his conclusion. "This. Has. Got. To. Stop. The man-to-man defense isn't working, so we are going to change to a zone defense, although we haven't practiced it much. If an attacker is moving out of your zone and you don't see a defender in the next one, of course you stay on him. But you shouldn't have to. Whenever a sub comes in for you, be sure he knows what zone you were defending. When you don't have to follow attackers all over, you should have energy left to go on the attack yourselves.

"When you're throwing in from out of bounds, try to get the ball to someone closer to the basket. Get it to a forward if you can. The guards don't have to take the ball down every time. Now are there any questions? All right, go get a drink of water—but not too much. And let's see if we can win this game."

The second half started auspiciously. Overconfidence led some Ft. Lupton players into carelessness, and they missed more shots. At the same time, Platteville's shooters found a new accuracy. Platteville's score crept upward until, early in the fourth quarter, the score was tied. This shocked Ft. Lupton out of its lethargy, energizing their attack just as the Platteville Bears were tiring.

When Harold Healy signaled the game's end, the score was Ft. Lupton thirty, Platteville twenty-seven. Owen gathered his eight stalwarts to congratulate them for coming so close to victory.

* * *

"It was pretty bad. First he couldn't swallow. And then he couldn't breathe." Ron Lydell waited until the other students filed out of the classroom to tell

Owen of the foal's death. "We got Robbie back in the house. Dad carried the colt out into the pasture while I carried the lantern and the rifle."

"Did you bury the foal then, in the dark?"

"No, I think Dad is burying him this morning before Robbie comes out."

As the Vo Ag teacher, Owen expected questions about farm problems. He remembered the worries George Lydell and his wife expressed about Ronald studying evolution. Agricultural science dealt with the here and now, not the origin of things. And the biology class had the same approach as Vo Ag.

"You will want to know," Owen said, "exactly what caused that infection, to keep it from spreading. It could be a mistake to bury the carcass in the pasture, where other animals come to feed. You should ship it to the animal husbandry lab in Ft. Collins. They can do what's called a necropsy to determine the cause of death. And I think it's free."

"Golly, would that work even if we have to dig up the carcass?"

"I'm sure it would, but your dad probably knows about the lab and may already be shipping it."

"How long will it take to get the results?"

"It will take a few days. Do you have a telephone at your place?"

"No, the line hasn't come out our way."

"I know the people at that lab. I can get them to phone here with the results, so I can pass them on to you. That would save a day or two, if your dad ships the carcass."

"Gee, that would be great. I'll tell him."

* * *

Arthur Stark stared at the document before him on the table. Its title took up four inches in a column half as wide as the paper, running down the left margin:

THE PEOPLE OF THE STATE OF)
COLORADO, on the Relation of)
FREDERICK I. KOBLENZ,)
Petitioner
• vs-   RULING.
NEWTON D. MACLEAN, ROY C. THOMPSON,
and ARTHUR P. STARK, as
Members and President, Treasurer, and)
Secretary of the Board of Education of the)
Platteville Consolidated Schools, District No.)
118, of the State of Colorado, Respondents)

It was the decision of the district court. As he waited for his colleagues to arrive at the school board meeting, Arthur Stark began reading the opinion for the third time. He intended to summarize it in his minutes of the meeting.

> The respondents, sole directors of the Platteville Consolidated Schools, District No. 118, by demurrer question the sufficiency of the Alternative Writ of Mandamus issued from this Court on October 14th last, on the verified petition of Frederick I. Koblenz, a taxpayer and the father of pupils of school age entitled to the benefits of and there being no parochial school, required to attend schools maintained within said District at public expense, who sues on behalf of himself and all others similarly situated.

Arthur saw Newton Maclean come in the schoolroom door, so he turned to the decision's eleventh and last long page, skipping past the legal arguments and citations from the record of the Colorado Constitutional Convention of 1875, to assure himself that the conclusion remained unchanged:

> The Convention had the opportunity to exclude the Bible from the schools of the State, as the petitioner contends was done, but the proceedings show that it specifically refused so to do. The demurrer therefore must be and accordingly is sustained.

Maclean sat down as usual at the head of the table, exchanging greetings with Stark as Roy Thompson came in. "I saw Harold parking his car," Thompson said. "He'll be here in a minute."

"Roy," Arthur said, "it looks like we've won, for a change."

"So I understand," the accountant replied. "Now we have to decide what to do about it."

"Isn't that obvious? We enforce the rule that nobody leaves the Bible readings. We rescind the motion we passed last time. I'm sure that you won't mind getting your contingency fund back."

"I'm calling this meeting to order," Maclean said, "so this discussion will be on the record."

Stark opened his notebook to acknowledge the chairman's authority.

"Arthur," Thompson continued, "we can't go back to how things were when we passed that motion. We've acted on it. You told Fred Koblenz about our plans, for Pete's sake. Harold has gotten recommendations for teachers to give Catholic instruction. I've been assuring Catholics that their kids won't have to worry about the King James Bible."

As if on cue, Superintendent Healy rushed into the room and took the remaining seat at the table. Arthur recorded the time of Healy's arrival.

"Harold," Newton Maclean said, "Roy has just pointed out that implementation of the plan for separate Catholic instruction is well advanced. He says it's so far along, it would be hard to back down. Fill us in on your activities."

The superintendent had consulted Fred Koblenz, Mary Gorman, and Father O'Donnell himself. All three were pleased with the plan. All three named the same candidates for the position, and the consensus first choice was a Mrs. Helena Parker. Mrs. Parker was the most popular Sunday school teacher at St. Nicholas Church. She had trained to be a nun but left the convent before taking final vows to marry her childhood sweetheart, who a few years later was killed in a railroad accident, leaving her comfortably well-off. She would be available for interview by the board.

"Hold on a minute," Arthur Stark said. "This is all based on the assumption that we are going ahead to hire someone. But now the district court has knocked down its own order, and we don't have to let the Catholic kids out of Bible reading."

"I don't think," Maclean said, "we want to start a civil war in Platteville. We've given a lot to the Catholics, and we can't take it back without causing an explosion."

"Besides," Thompson joined in, "the final word will come from the State Supreme Court. If we call off the special Catholic instruction before it begins, then we have to reinstate it, we'll really have egg on our faces."

"Well." Arthur Stark looked from one colleague to another. "I got into this issue believing we have the authority, as well as the responsibility, to determine the curriculum and establish all formal exercises for our two schools. We should have the courage of our convictions. We know the Catholic walkout all but destroys the Bible readings' effectiveness. Therefore I move that the motion passed last meeting, which committed the contingency fund to paying for a new part-time hire, be rescinded. May I speak in support of my motion?"

"You've already done that," snapped Newton Maclean. He added quietly, "I'm sorry, Arthur, but your motion fails because it has not been seconded."

* * *

The morning after telling Owen of the foal's death, Ronald Lydell reported that his father had dispatched the carcass to Ft. Collins. Three days later, Owen was called to the principal's office to take the call from the lab.

When the biology class ended, he asked young Lydell to stay a few minutes. "Ron, I got the report from Ft. Collins. They're mailing a full report to your father. He should get it in a couple of days. They say your foal was killed by botulism."

"Botulism? I've heard of that, but isn't it a human sickness?"

"It's the same microbe. It's even more toxic to horses than to humans, but it's usually fatal to either one."

"I remember, you get botulism by eating beans that aren't canned right."

"Exactly. That's where the pressure cooker comes in."

"But that foal didn't eat any beans," Ronald said. "He didn't eat anything at all, because he wasn't weaned. And the mare isn't sick."

"That bothered me too, so I looked it up. The spores of this microbe can exist for years in the soil, particularly when it's damp. When livestock eat infected material, like forage, the microbes multiply in their intestines. But that doesn't explain your case, because the foal never ate solids. The second way the disease spreads is when the toxins are absorbed through a wound."

"But the foal didn't have a wound, either."

"Oh, but he did. Every foal has a kind of wound. Apparently he absorbed the toxins through the stump of the umbilical cord."

"So he was lying down in some place that was infected, and the microbes only had to touch him to make him sick."

"That's my understanding."

"So we should find the infected place and keep other livestock away from it."

"Particularly your horses. Cattle get the disease, but they aren't as susceptible as horses."

"I'll tell my dad. I knew there was a scientific reason for that colt to die, and now we know the truth. My mother tells my little brother, Robbie, that God decided his colt should die." Ronald Lydell shook his head sadly. "Isn't that silly?"

Owen chose his words carefully. "Ronald, you can't ask me to take sides in a conversation you ought to have with your parents."

* * *

Their families showered Ruby and Owen with holiday invitations. Ruby said either they felt no bride should have to prepare a holiday feast, or they realized the little house in Platteville could not contain a real party. Only after they had a child or two, Ruby said—not to mention a bigger house—would she bundle everybody onto the train to show their grandchildren to her parents and relatives in Illinois. Since Owen's parents were only a few miles away, Ruby and Owen decided that they would take Thanksgiving dinner with Ruby's

Aunt Margaret in Longmont and spend three days at Christmas with Owen's family near Windsor.

Ruby insisted on contributing to the Thanksgiving feast. She volunteered a sweet potato and pecan casserole made from a North Carolina recipe supplied by her mother's relatives. The dish would cool on the road, but it could be warmed in a corner of the oven.

Owen had not taken the Model T's top down since fastening it in early September. He repeatedly offered to put up the side curtains for Ruby before she left to teach music lessons, but she always declined, pointing out that no student lived more than four miles away. Thanksgiving Day was cold and overcast, threatening snow, so Owen put the side curtains in place. Their function was more symbolic than actual, and Owen admonished Ruby to dress warmly. The Ford's engine started with little complaint, which Owen took as a positive sign.

Owen drove to Main Street, turned south, and soon reached the familiar state highway. As they approached the bridge over the South Platte that would take them west toward Longmont, Owen and Ruby glimpsed the Lydell property with its stand of cottonwoods, their favorite local picnic place.

"I don't expect more picnics until May," Owen spoke loudly over the Model T's clatter. "We can't get into the high mountain valleys until late June."

Ruby reached up a gloved hand to adjust the scarf around her neck. "It's been two months since we ate outdoors, and I'm ready to eat indoors until spring."

Their car bounced along the unpaved road, climbing gentle rolling hills, to descend on the far side. The frontal range of the Rockies filled the horizon ahead of them, the snow on the mountainsides showing pure whiteness despite the cloudy day. Rain two days before left puddles stretched into deep ruts by auto wheels. Owen steered carefully when traversing muddy segments of the road. One time, after wrenching the front wheels out of steep ruts, he shouted to Ruby, "When it gets a little colder, the ground will freeze up. Then we won't have to worry about mud."

Despite these difficulties, and thanks to the absence of flat tires, they traveled the twenty miles to Longmont in less than forty minutes.

Owen and Ruby were happy to enter the warm house. Aunt Margaret introduced Owen to the other guests, all of them Ruby's distant relatives. Ruby joined the women bustling about the kitchen on missions of varying importance, leaving Owen in the parlor to talk politics with the men. A general opinion soon developed. Spending his days with bankers, industrialists, and politicians, President Coolidge had forgotten his rural roots in New England. Thus Coolidge failed to realize that farmers, particularly in the West, did not share the prosperity so obvious on Wall Street. Regardless of which party won the legislative contests, Republicans were more to be trusted than Democrats.

Soon all were called to the meal that, in its abundance and variety, signified the prosperity of those who prepared it. A second cousin who taught in an Episcopalian Sunday school offered lengthy thanks for the bounty spread before them. Then the serving dishes were passed around the table. Much later, as Owen cleaned his plate, they came around again. He wanted more of the sweet potato casserole, so he took turkey and cranberry relish to go with it. When the meal drew to a close, Owen felt stuffed. Offered his choice of pumpkin, mincemeat, and apple pies, he accepted servings of pumpkin and apple.

When the table was cleared, children were excused to play games, the women returned to the kitchen to wash the dishes, and the men returned to the parlor, where their talk drifted into sports, beginning with the prowess of Babe Ruth. When Owen admitted that he was the coach at Platteville, the others insisted on hearing analyses of games with various opponents and, finally, a critique of girls' basketball. None of his listeners had seen a girls' basketball game, but all regarded them as displays of unladylike behavior. At that point, the women returned to find places in the parlor, leading Owen to hope for a change of subject.

Aunt Margaret realized his hope with a vengeance. "Owen," she said, "we asked Ruby a question in the kitchen that she said you could answer better."

"Ask away," Owen said. "I'll do my best," sounding more confident than he felt. If Ruby had to duck a question, it wouldn't be any fun for him.

"We've been hearing rumors," their hostess said, "of trouble in the Platteville schools. Something about Catholic students walking out in protest? And something about a judge taking sides."

"Well, the judge getting involved didn't have anything to do with a crime." The expectant looks of his suddenly attentive audience made Owen feel trapped. There was no way to turn their thoughts back to Coolidge.

"Maybe," he said, "I should begin at the beginning. Before school began this fall, the school board decided that in every classroom, after everybody recites the Pledge of Allegiance, the teacher will read a passage from the Bible that emphasizes good behavior."

Owen saw some heads nod, and Ruby's Uncle Will murmured, "Good idea." Aunt Margaret demanded, "What could the Catholics object to in that?"

"Well, the selections are from the King James Bible. As I understand it, the Catholic Church forbids reading that translation. In fact, they don't much encourage people to read any version of the Bible all by themselves, without someone who is trained to explain it."

The Episcopalian cousin spoke up. "Do students—either Catholic or Protestant—ask you to explain the passages you read?"

"We're not supposed to. We were told to read the passages without comment. None of my students have ever asked a question. Of course, that's only the Protestants. The three Catholics in my classroom walked out the first day and have only been there for the readings about three times. But one of them explained to me in advance why they felt they had to do it, and they try to go out without raising a fuss."

Aunt Margaret asked, "Why did they stay those three times?"

"The school board decided to enforce the rule that every student must be present for the full opening ceremony. Our principal felt that we couldn't let the walkout go on after that, and the students didn't try to keep it up. Then the Catholic parents went to court and got a kind of emergency order saying that Bible reading is fine, but the board can't require everybody to stay and listen. So we're still reading the Bible. And Catholic students, at least the high school students, are still walking out."

"I think," Uncle Will said, "that is exactly the difference between us and the Catholics and has been since Martin Luther. We believe the individual should consider the Word of God in the Bible, by himself. The Catholics think there should be a bunch of intermediaries to help."

"Well," Aunt Margaret said, "we don't have a very good record of agreeing on what the Word means. Some believe in infant baptism, others don't. Some baptize only by immersion, others only by sprinkling. We only agree on having water. When they hear about dippers arguing with sprinklers, you can't blame the Catholics for not reading our Bible."

The parlor was silent for several long seconds. While Owen wondered if he should try to break the silence, Ruby spoke up. "I was baptized in a river in Illinois," she said, "and it was a wonderful experience, but it doesn't seem right for a church to put a water tank next to the pulpit."

Ignoring Ruby, the Episcopalian cousin spoke up. "Aunt Margaret, it sounds like you think it's all right for Catholic kids to walk out of the Bible readings."

The hostess's voice was suddenly sharp. "I'm sure of one thing. God is not a God of revenge. He will not turn aside an innocent child from the gates of heaven for being baptized in the wrong way, or for not being baptized at all."

* * *

The four Lydells—George and Susan, the parents; Ronald and Robbie, the sons—shared their Thanksgiving table with Susan's sister and her family. When all eight were seated, George Lydell offered thanks. "Heavenly Father, we thank thee for this company and that we may be together on this special day. We thank thee for this bounty, that we may enjoy the harvest thou hast guided us in bringing forth from the earth."

Ron Lydell saw his father glance at his younger brother. Robbie was sitting quietly, head bowed as he had been taught. Although his face was abnormally pale, Robbie showed no signs of the sobs that had shaken his small frame.

George Lydell continued, "O Lord, help us, we beseech thee, to accept thy will. Teach us that life itself is thy great gift, and that what thou givest can be taken away. We know that we can never fully understand thy purpose, but we beg thee, use us to achieve it."

Ron wanted to scream. It wasn't God who killed Star, it was a microbe! But he dared not speak out.

His father concluded, "So we pray again, as you taught us, 'thy kingdom come, thy will be done, on earth as it is in heaven.' Bless this food to our use, and us to thy service. We ask it in the name of Jesus Christ, our strength and our Redeemer. Amen."

A quiet chorus of amens echoed around the table. The food was passed. Ron was biding his time, and eating was a great comfort as he waited. The meal progressed like any other Thanksgiving feast. When the table was finally cleared, Susan and her niece brought in the pies. When dessert was finished, Robbie began to nod off at his seat and was taken to bed for a nap. After helping clean up, the guests departed, wanting to drive home before dark.

Ron Lydell confronted his parents at last. They were sitting at the dining room table, resting from the rigors of the day, when Ron sat down with them. "Dad, Mom, there's something I need to talk to you about."

"Go ahead, Ronald," his mother said.

"Dad, I could tell when you asked the blessing that you were talking to Robbie. Especially the parts about accepting God's will and that life is the gift of God."

"I don't know, son. Do you really think he could understand, in the middle of all those thee's and thy's?"

"He's heard words like those once a week or more for five years. I'll bet he understands more than you realize. But I'm talking about a lot more than your blessing, Dad." Ron looked at his mother, who seemed distressed, then back to his father. "Both of you have been telling Robbie that his foal's death was God's will. You've been encouraging him to believe in a myth, instead of facing the truth."

"Truth," Susan asked. "What is truth?"

"The truth is that Star was killed by botulism!" Ron nearly shouted at his mother. He leaned over the table, putting his face close to hers. "And botulism is caused by a microbe. It is called *Clostridium botulinum*."

George Lydell's voice was stern. "What your mother is trying to say, if you'll give her a chance, is that two things can be true at the same time. The foal was killed by the microbe. And that was God's will."

Ron shook his head. "If I said something like that in biology class, Mr. Mattison would fail me, and he should. The scientific method finds truth by conducting experiments that can be repeated by other scientists."

"Fine," George Lydell said, "but there are other ways to know things besides scientific experiments."

"But we're talking about Robbie. When you're four years old, you either figure things out for yourself, or you learn them from someone you trust, like your parents. What you're telling Robbie keeps him away from the truth, and he can't be kept away forever. Don't you understand? Robbie probably killed his own foal. God had nothing to do with it. When Robbie carried buckets of water to the mare, they were heavy for him, and he splashed water on the floor of the stall, which is covered by old hay and straw. That made a perfect place for the microbe. When Star was born, it was like a trap was set for him."

George and Susan Lydell were silent for several seconds. When Susan spoke, it was in cold, measured tones. "I forbid you to tell that to Robbie. Right now, it would practically kill him. And you aren't even sure it's true."

Chapter 7

RUBY ACCEPTED MEMBERSHIP IN the Mizpah Club. Expecting to pay her way, she was embarrassed when Martha Stark asked the club to waive membership dues, after Ruby agreed to be their regular pianist. In addition to solos, this meant playing the piano for group singing, which Ruby enjoyed. She was delighted by the club's activities, helping with the fall cleanup of the Mizpah Cemetery and contributing a cake and two dozen cookies to the October bake sale. Ruby was elected secretary of a committee chaired by Isabel Nelson, to plan further cemetery improvements for the spring. In November, driving home from a music lesson, Ruby detoured up the cemetery road, simply to admire the view of the snowcapped Rockies.

The Christmas meeting was Ruby's third as the official club musician, and she shared its planning with Martha Stark, the program committee chair. Martha agreed that music was essential to Christmas, more than any other holiday. Ruby wanted the club members to sing their hearts out.

When members gathered to talk before the meeting began, the turnout was the largest Ruby had seen. Ruth Herman, the club president, introduced Mary Gorman to her. "You know," Ruth said, "the Gormans have Platteville Mercantile."

Ruby realized that the Catholics were back. Everyone could agree on Christmas.

The business meeting was mercifully short. Mrs. Herman declared that every member had to sing heartily to earn her share of the refreshments. Ruby took her seat at the piano, where she had a book of accompaniments for the familiar Christmas carols, and some not so familiar. Isabel Nelson distributed printed booklets of Christmas song lyrics, so the members would not be lost if called on to sing beyond the familiar first verse.

Ruby called for additional verses only if the first verse was particularly successful, or more than one verse was familiar, as with "Silent Night" and

"We Three Kings of Orient Are." The group entered wholeheartedly into "O Christmas Tree," so Ruby called for the German lyrics, "O Tannenbaum." The voices began uncertainly but grew stronger as singers found the right place in their booklets. Ruby suddenly remembered that no public singing in German was done during the war, and she wondered if Isabel would be offended. She looked away from her music long enough to find Mrs. Nelson in the crowd. The war widow was singing valiantly.

Ruby smiled at her music. The club was really warmed up; not a Scrooge, or Mrs. Scrooge, in the bunch. When she called for "O Come, All Ye Faithful," the women seemed to achieve better harmony than ever. When the first verse ended, Ruby called out, "Now let's sing the Latin version, 'Adeste Fidelis.' The words are on the next page."

Ruby first played the closing bars of the song to establish the tune. The singing was ragged at first, as women struggled with unfamiliar words, but there was one loud soprano, fuzzy but on key. Ruby stole a quick look at the group. If she was not mistaken, the leading voice belonged to Mary Gorman. Too bad there was no more Latin in the songbook.

When Ruby tried to end the singing, there were calls for favorites that had been missed, followed by a request for a reprise of "Away in a Manager." Then the ladies surrounded the refreshment table, thirsty for tea and ready for Christmas cookies or a slice of fruitcake. The babble of conversation seemed like water breaking over a dam.

Ruby moved toward the table and found herself in line next to Susan Lydell and the elderly Mrs. Dodsworth. Both women thanked her for her playing.

Then Mrs. Dodsworth lowered her voice. "I suppose," she said, "it's a good thing to have Mary Gorman and her friends back. They must not be mad at us any more. But I didn't see that any of them brought any food to share."

"I don't see how they could be mad," Susan said. "They're getting the school board to hire a special teacher for their kids, at our expense."

Ruby hardly knew Mrs. Dodsworth, and she feared Susan would give her the wrong impression about the school's troubles. "It's my understanding," Ruby said, "that the new teacher will be strictly part-time. She'll only teach the Catholic kids for five minutes each morning while the others are at the Bible reading. She won't get much pay."

"Well," Susan said, "I thought it would be more extensive than that."

They reached the refreshment table. Ruby accepted a cup of tea and took two small cookies. She bit into a cookie shaped like a Christmas tree, covered with bright green sugar. Suddenly she felt at peace with the world.

* * *

Owen awakened to see the early light of dawn seeping into the guest bedroom of his parents' home. For a second, he could not place himself. Aware of Ruby's familiar warmth, he worked back from that. The blankets were heavier than in their Platteville house. Of course. There was no heat in the second floor of his parents' home except for minor warmth radiating from the chimney bricks. You could leave the hall door open for warm air drifting up the stairs from the coal stove in the living room, but they had closed the door for privacy.

Memories of the day before arranged themselves. The flat tire on the road west from Greeley. The bitter cold in the Model T, snow spitting from the sky despite the sunshine, and their arrival in time for him to help with the milking while Ruby settled down in the kitchen with his mother. Now it was the morning of Christmas Eve.

The mattress shifted as Owen sat on the edge of the bed to reach his socks. Ruby stirred but did not seem to waken. However, as he was pulling on his shirt, Ruby's eyelids fluttered open. "Do you have to go so early?" Her voice was heavy with sleep.

"Yes, I'm going to help Pa and the boys with the milking." Owen pulled on his trousers.

"Don't you ever take a vacation? Don't the *cows* ever take a vacation?"

"Ruby, you're still dreaming. You know a dairy farmer's life starts with milking the herd morning and evening. That's partly why I became a schoolteacher."

"Do you have to help? They get along without you when you aren't here."

"Sure. But if I don't show up in the barn this morning, I'll never hear the end of it from Norm and Lewis. They'll say I use my wife as an excuse to duck chores. You go back to sleep. Breakfast will be after milking, about an hour and a half. If you aren't downstairs on time, I'll fetch you."

"I should be downstairs, helping your mother."

"I think the family rule is, the bride gets her beauty rest while the groom goes to work." Owen walked to Ruby's side, bent down, and kissed her cheek. "Now you catch up on your rest." He closed the guest room door behind him and skipped down the stairs to find Kate Mattison emerging from the downstairs bedroom. "Good morning, Ma. Has Pa already gone out?"

"Yes, a few minutes ago. And the boys left before that. Owen, could you take out the ashes?"

"Sure, Ma, just like old times."

Owen went to the kitchen stove and eased the rectangular bucket from beneath the firebox. Raising the handle, he carried it to the back porch and set it on the floor to pull the door closed. He took his coat and cap from their peg, picked up the ash box, and carried it along the road through the cottonwoods.

There, on the side of an abandoned irrigation ditch, was the pile where ashes were dumped. He carried the box back to the kitchen and slipped it back into the stove. A fire was laid in the firebox, so Owen held a lighted match to the paper beneath the kindling.

Hearing her son's activity, Kate Mattison abandoned the dining room table she was setting and returned to the kitchen. "Thank you for doing that, Owen. Is Ruby on her way down, do you think?"

"I hope not. I told her to get some rest."

"I see you've got your coat on, for going to the barn. But could you sit for a minute?" She took a step to the counter and returned with a full glass, which she set on the kitchen table. "I poured some milk for you."

"You know I'd never turn down a glass of Jersey milk." Owen pulled a chair away from the table and sat down. He swallowed half the milk as his mother was seating herself.

"I won't keep you, but I want to say something privately. Ruby is a fine young woman, and I'm grateful to you for bringing her into the family."

"I'm glad you like her, Ma."

"We talked about a lot of things last night, and she happened to mention the music lessons she's giving. I asked her what you think of them, and she said you don't seem very happy about it."

"Ma, she can only do one lesson a day, after her students are home from school. She's got four students, so she's off in the Model T four afternoons a week. It's cold now, and she barely gets home before dark."

"Owen, I don't think you're unhappy because of the weather. Maybe you don't understand the real reason yourself. I thought about the two of you for a long time last night, and I just want to say this: young women are doing things nowadays that we wouldn't have dreamed of in my day. And they're doing them very well."

Owen suddenly thought of girls filing into the gym wearing bloomers and middy blouses. Isabel Nelson had pointed out they could dance the Charleston, demonstrating athletic aptitude.

"Ruby has a lot of talent," Kate Mattison said, "and sharing it is as good for her as it is for those she shares it with. The world is changing, and you must not feel that your wife working outside your home makes you less of a man. You should be proud of her."

Owen drained the last of the milk from his glass and carefully put it down on the table. "Of course I'm proud of her, Ma, and I love her music."

"All right, Owen. I just wanted to give you an idea to think about. Now I'll let you get on out to the barn."

Chapter 8

OWEN WAS AT HOME in the science classroom. He taught biology the first semester; now he would teach physics. He perched on his stool at the front of the empty room, ready for the first school day of 1926. So far the new year felt a lot like 1925. He remembered the opening day of school in the fall, when most of the girls came in before any boys. Had he been that reluctant—not so many years ago—to seem interested in learning?

Maggie Fitzgerald breezed in, walking to her accustomed seat. Her smile was a ray of sunshine on a gloomy day. "Good morning, Mr. Mattison."

"Good morning, Ms. Fitzgerald. Congratulations on your game against La Salle, back before Christmas." Owen remembered the sparse audience chanting, 'Go, Maggie, go!' "I saw you make the winning basket."

"Thank you, it was fun. And happy New Year."

As Maggie settled in her seat, Ronald Lydell entered. Remembering the barrage of questions he raised in biology class, Owen wondered if Christmas had done anything to calm Ron's rush to become the town atheist. Was Ron's younger brother reconciled to the foal's loss? A teacher should not invade the privacy of a student's family. Owen exchanged nods with Ron.

The students crowded in during the final seconds before the tardy bell. When it rang, all fourteen juniors were on hand, although three boys were just sitting down. Owen rose from his stool and stood before the blackboard.

"Welcome back. I hope you all had a grand Christmas. By now you have digested the turkey and will be wide awake and ready to learn." Owen combined a slight grin with peering over the top of his eyeglasses. "Today's main announcement concerns the new special instruction for Catholic students. You have all heard about it—this is how it will work.

"Everybody will report to this room for roll taking and announcements, for anything that affects the entire junior class. We will recite the Pledge of Allegiance. Catholic students whose parents have requested it in writing will then report to Mrs. Parker in the auditorium. Instead of coming back to this room, you will remain there until the bell, then go directly to your first period class. Are there any questions?"

Owen saw the three Catholic students stare straight ahead. Surely they hated being singled out for special treatment. He made eye contact with each one in turn. "Very well. There is no need to sit down again when the Pledge of Allegiance is finished. You may leave the classroom. Don't expect a signal from me. Mrs. Parker is waiting for you, and you are free to go."

When the pledge was completed, the three students gathered their books, and Frank Koblenz led them out of the room. The boy sitting nearest the door hissed a malediction at his three classmates, but Owen could not hear the exact words. He decided to hold his admonition for the next occasion.

When the door closed, Owen said, "We begin our readings for the new year with a familiar passage. It is the Ten Commandments, found in the book of Exodus, chapter twenty."

* * *

Owen sat at the dining room table, using two forefingers to tap out a report of the Platteville boys' basketball victory over Hudson High School. The Remington portable typewriter was brand-new, purchased with his earnings as a correspondent for the Greeley *Tribune*. After Ruby put away the last of the dinner dishes, she sat down at the end of the table with that day's copy of the newspaper.

Suddenly Ruby interrupted the tapping. "Owen, what do you know about this?" She brought the paper, laid it beside the typewriter, pointed to the item, and returned to her seat.

> Platteville, Jan. 8. The membership of the Mizpah Women's Club is clearly divided between the regulars and the flappers. The flapper's badge is her bobbed hair. Whether her haircut, like Samson's, will take away her strength, remains to be seen.

Owen read the paragraph and chuckled. "Well, it's true, isn't it?"

"I don't care about that. I want to know where it came from."

"Gee, I don't know. The paper has correspondents in Platteville I don't even know about. We never meet or anything."

"So you had nothing to do with it." Ruby's voice was stern.

"Not a thing. Cross my heart."

Ruby relented. "I've had short hair as long as I've known you. If you don't like it, please tell me to my face. I don't need to find hints in the newspaper."

"Ruby, I love your hair, long, short, or in-between. Haven't I told you that?"

"Maybe you have." Ruby brushed back a chestnut lock that wanted to tumble over her forehead. "But not since long before we were married. Of course, I know you Mattisons never talk about your feelings."

"That's right. You're better off to judge us by our actions, not our words." Owen took a short step to the end of the table and gathered Ruby into his arms.

* * *

Frederick Koblenz hastily backed his Studebaker into the street in front of the Ft. Lupton farm machinery store. He jerked the transmission into first gear. The car lurched forward, the engine roared, and Fred shifted into second, following a horse-drawn farm wagon. Fred swung into the middle of the street, despite traffic headed his way, and passed close to the wagon. The team reared, and their driver cursed, but Fred sped on to the edge of town. The street became a narrow highway headed north to Platteville as concrete pavement gave way to frozen mud mixed with gravel. When the Studebaker skidded on the road around the sharp corner of a cornfield, Fred battled to regain control. Time to calm down.

Damn the Klan. They would love to know they got him upset. If he wrecked the car on the way home, they would count one fewer target. He hated to worry Catherine, but she needed to know about this. He began planning what to say.

Fred parked the Studebaker in its shed and hurried into the farmhouse. His wife was working near the living room stove, with her mending spread out over half the sofa. He greeted her and stood by the stove to warm his hands.

Catherine asked, "Were you able to get the parts you wanted in Ft. Lupton?"

"Yes, no trouble about that."

"When you didn't get home, I thought you went on to Brighton, looking for them."

"No, the reason I'm late is different, and I need to tell you about it." Fred moved a basket of stockings out of the way and sat on the sofa. "When I finished at the store, I saw some men in white robes going into the Congregation of God Church there on Main Street."

"I've never heard of that church."

"It used to be the Baptist Church. When they built a new building, this crowd took over the old one. Anyway, then I saw some signs for a public meeting of the Ku Klux Klan, and I recognized those cone-shaped hats they wear. So I asked one of them if he was going to the Klan meeting. He said he was, and I was welcome to come along."

"You went to a Klan meeting? That's crazy. What if someone we know saw you going in?"

"Someone we know would realize I was going in only to find out what was going on."

"Into a Protestant church? You aren't supposed to be curious about them."

"It was a Klan rally, not a service. It says something about that church when the Klan could meet there. Most of the pews were occupied, so I stood in the back of the church as long as I could stand it. Then I came home."

"What made you leave?"

"Cathy, it was appalling. I was so upset, even after I got back in the car, that I nearly ran down a team pulling a wagon. The speaker was introduced as a local preacher, and he talked really smooth, like a salesman. At first his tone was so reasonable, you almost forgot he was selling hate. When he got warmed up though, he started to rant. Hate the Jewish bankers, they caused the war. And now they're bottling up all the money on Wall Street, causing unemployment. Hate the Negroes, they threaten the purity of the white race. Most of all, hate the Catholics. It seems that we're the bootleggers, our women are the whores, and we're preparing the way for the Pope to march into Washington."

"It sounds like what we've heard from the Klan before."

"Putting it all together was new, at least to me. He claimed there is a conspiracy between the Jews, what he called the 'nigrahs,' and the papists—us—to take the country away from the '100 percent Americans.' The politicians are joining the conspiracy, and only the Klan is left to defend the country. It sounds silly, but the crowd was buying it."

"I thought the Klan was fading away. That leader in Indiana—what's he called?—you saw the item in the *Tribune*."

"The Grand Dragon, something-or-other Stephenson."

"Right, he was charged with rape and murder. And Mayor Stapleton, down in Denver, repudiated the Klan and got the American Legion to take them on."

Fred Koblenz shook his head, saddened by the need to explain. "Everything you say is true. The Klan is mixed up in scandals in other places, but none of that involves the Klan here in the Platte Valley."

"Wasn't that a recruitment meeting in Ft. Lupton? Maybe they've had resignations because of all the scandals, and they're desperate to fill up again."

"Maybe. But when they get desperate is when we have the most to fear."

"Fred, you keep saying 'we.' Do you mean members of our church, our family, or what?"

"I mean anyone the Klan has picked to hate. And I feel vulnerable myself. I did sue the school board, and they are all Protestants."

"Do you think the Klan has something to do with the school board making our kids listen to their Bible?"

"I don't think there was a connection in the beginning, because different people are involved. But both the school board and the Klan finish by attacking our church. The worst thing is that the school board's decisions are the same as law."

* * *

After basketball practice, Owen walked through the late January twilight to the Vo Ag shop, a separate small building in a corner of the school grounds. After gathering his notes for the next morning's classes, he took a moment to inspect Matt Stark's brooder house.

At Owen's suggestion, Matt had modified the structure to make it more rigid. The redesigned frame was complete, and Matt was beginning to attach the siding. He learned through hard experience the old adage, "Measure twice, saw once." Now the angles were true, and the miniature house had a look of strength. Matt truly earned the good progress grade Owen gave him.

Owen turned out the lights and was locking the door when he heard a woman's voice. "Oh, Mr. Mattison! Owen!"

With a moment's thought, Owen placed the voice: Isabel Nelson. She had used his first name, so all the students must have gone. "Hello, Isabel, what can I do for you?"

"I wanted to ask about one of your students. That is, I think he's one of your students."

Owen swung the door open. "Come in, I'll tell you whatever I know." He held the door open for her, and then switched on the electric light.

His guest looked around the room. "This is really interesting. I've never seen your shop before."

"I'm afraid it's pretty crowded. In Vo Ag, we do both carpentry and automotive work. There's a group working on that old tractor in the corner, and the biggest carpentry project is this brooder house that Matt Stark is building."

"I have Matt in composition class. He's very talented. It's a great relief when the son of a school board member is not a dunce."

Grinning, Owen pulled another chair to his desk and waved Mrs. Nelson toward it. He sat, folded his hands on the desk, and looked at her.

"The student I wanted to ask about is Bruno Gorman."

"Well, Bruno is in my homeroom, but he isn't in the Vo Ag class because he lives in town. He took biology as a sophomore, before I came, and I guess he's saving physics for his senior year. I know him best through athletics. He did a good job as goalie on the speedball team. At first, he was razzed a lot about his religion. But that's died out, since he proved himself as a goalie."

"I think it's the razzing about religion that bothers his mother. She came to see me, complaining about a short story I assigned from the American Lit anthology. Do you know the Edgar Allan Poe story called 'The Pit and the Pendulum'?"

"No, I've heard of Poe, but I don't recognize that title."

"It's one of Poe's tales of horror. The narrator is a prisoner of the Spanish Inquisition in a medieval dungeon. He first escapes death by avoiding a deep pit in the center of his cell. Then he is bound to a wooden cot while a sharp blade on a swinging pendulum is lowered toward him, aimed at his heart. He escapes that by getting rats to eat his bonds. Then the iron walls of the dungeon heat up and begin to close in on him, squeezing him back toward the pit. Finally he hears trumpets sound and is saved because the city of Toledo has been captured. And Poe writes, 'the Inquisition was in the hands of its enemies.'"

"So it's a story about the Inquisition? Wasn't that centuries ago?"

"I wondered the same thing, so I looked it up. The Spanish Inquisition was officially ended in 1820, so it's been just a century. But the kings of Spain, not the church, operated that. My point is that Poe's story isn't about religion. It's about how it feels to be in a dungeon, trying to avoid death. There are a few mentions of tortures devised by monks, but the Inquisition is only mentioned in the opening and closing paragraphs."

"Exactly why did Mrs. Gorman object to the story?"

"I'm not sure that she actually read the story, but she really read me the riot act. She said the story gives a biased picture of the Catholic Church, that it confirms student prejudices, that Poe was an ignoramus who wrote obscene poems, and that I should have better sense than to use that book."

"That's pretty strong. How did you answer her?"

"I told her there's a statewide committee that screens textbooks, and we can purchase books not on their recommended list only by action of our local school board. The book she complained about was recommended."

"Did that satisfy her?"

"No. She just shook her head, as if she couldn't believe me. Then I suggested she take her complaint to the school board. That made her mad, and she stormed out of the room."

"I reckon she doesn't expect sympathy from the school board."

"No. When it got a bigger result than I expected, I was ashamed of making the suggestion. What I wanted to ask you is, how is all of this affecting Bruno?"

"Well, Bruno doesn't take after his mother's bad temper. He stays calm, and he's able to concentrate. Goalies have to be able to focus. Although early in the season, he got hit in the face by a ball and raised a fuss that was way out of proportion." In fact, Owen had nearly catalogued Bruno as a sissy. Judging him by that one emotional outbreak would have been unfair.

Mrs. Nelson stood up. "From what you say, Bruno is not suffering, at least not now. I wonder if other kids were giving him a bad time, which would explain his mother's interest."

"It's hard on the Catholic kids to be singled out to be sent out of the room every morning, away from their classmates. But I think Bruno has adjusted to that as well as any student I know."

"I'm glad to hear it." Mrs. Nelson fastened the belt around her coat. "I so enjoy Ruby's piano playing at Mizpah meetings. She plays modern music so well, the ladies discovered they like it. And I don't hear any more complaints that our skirts are too short. Please say hello to her for me."

"I certainly will."

Chapter 9

THE SECOND DAY OF March, Owen found his way through blustery winds and snow flurries to Ollie Scott's barbershop. Ray Dodsworth sat in his usual chair with his usual magazine and waved Owen into the barber's chair.

As Scott began to snip Owen's hair, Dodsworth asked about the baseball schedule. League games would begin the last week of March, and Owen named their opponents. The retired farmer approved of the lineup and pronounced the games Platteville's best spring entertainment. "I like to watch the game in the afternoon, hurry home for a quick supper, and take the missus to the evening show at the Rex Theater."

As Dodsworth launched a description of the current feature film, Owen wondered what his life would be like with Ruby when their planned children—Ruby insisted on at least three—would be grown up and moved away. If he were retired, what would fill his days?

After leaving the barbershop, Owen began planning for baseball tryouts, fearing the time available to shape up a team might prove too short. He had statistics and lineups saved by the previous coach indicating that five of the 1925 varsity players graduated that June. Matt Stark, then a sophomore, was the first baseman. Surprising, since Matt had not turned out for other sports.

The second week of March began clear and calm. In Tuesday's announcements, Owen proclaimed baseball tryouts to begin on Wednesday. When the Vo Ag class was busy on their projects, he strolled over to where Matt was nailing siding to his brooder house. Matt put the hammer down.

"Matt, I see you were first baseman on the varsity last year. Will you come out for baseball this year?"

"Yes, Coach, I will."

"How come you didn't turn out for basketball or speedball?"

"My dad needed me, he was shorthanded. But he's got a new hired man to help with spring planting, so I can play. Dad wants me to go out for it."

"That's good news. I'll see you there tomorrow afternoon."

On Wednesday, most of the male high school students appeared for tryouts, confirming the importance of baseball to Platteville that Dodsworth had proclaimed. But no magic eliminated the demands of spring planting. Did other farmers take on hired hands to let their sons play ball? It seemed more likely to Owen that boys shortchanged their schoolwork to handle both sport and farm work. How athletes found enough time to play was usually not a coach's concern, unless he was also teaching something like physics.

Owen wanted a team with strong basic skills. For batting trials, he told the line of waiting batters to hit as hard as they could, but make the pitchers throw strikes. Volunteers took up positions in the field. Owen noticed that Matt Stark's claim on first base was unchallenged.

Owen told the hopeful pitchers that for batting practice, they should not try to strike anybody out but only get the ball over the plate in the strike zone, so the batter could show his stuff. Owen served as umpire to call the strikes and balls. Each of the aspiring pitchers faced three batters, and then joined the line of batters.

A dozen batters made solid hits. Right-handed batters who swung late drove the ball toward first base, where Matt Stark caught three foul fly balls, two fair ones, and many grounders. Owen concluded that Stark played first base like he owned the position. That could be confirmed in due course. When the batters completed their turns, Owen called in the fielders to try batting or pitching, and asked for more volunteers to take the field positions.

Owen agreed when Frank Koblenz asked to play third base. Koblenz had scored two solid hits in batting practice, and unlike several others, he did not grow frustrated and swing at wild pitches. If he could field as well as he batted, he deserved a spot on the first team. With Matt Stark at first base, how well would they work together?

Koblenz handled hits very well, but he did not invade the shortstop's territory. When both of them got under a pop fly, Koblenz yielded. Owen wondered if the boy was aggressive enough for the first team.

The question was answered by the fielders' trials. Owen stepped up to the plate with a slender bat for fungo hitting. He tossed up a ball, grasped the bat with both hands, and hit the ball as it descended, sending it in a precise direction.

At third base, Koblenz displayed his aggressive nature. Instead of waiting for a ground ball to reach him, Frank ran forward to meet it, shortening a runner's time to reach first base. His throws to the first baseman were hard and accurate. When Owen lined a hard drive that skimmed along the third base line, barely in fair territory, Frank leaped to his right to stop the ball. Both of his feet flew into the air, the ball slammed into his glove, and he managed to hold on to it when he crashed to the ground. Then he got to his knees and fired the ball across his chest toward first base.

Matt Stark was guarding first base. Frank's throw bounced once on the way, but Matt caught the ball easily. "Great throw, Koblenz!" Matt shouted.

Owen had found his third baseman. Stark and Koblenz would work together just fine.

After a second day of tryouts to give everybody a chance, Owen posted the varsity and second team rosters on Friday. Every senior made the first or second team, and all but three juniors were chosen. Owen recruited a manager from the threesome to keep track of equipment and an aspiring accountant to keep team statistics. The third student withdrew from extracurricular activities when he found an after-school job.

The following week, as drills grew more sophisticated, Owen unknowingly laid the groundwork for the play that would make Frank Koblenz famous in Platteville's league. It happened during infield practice. Owen hit fungo grounders to each of the infielders in turn, to practice throws to first base. He assigned members of the second team to serve as base runners. Then he set up more complicated situations, such as a runner trying to steal second base—with one out, he stipulated, and a two-one count against the batter. Then he proposed a runner on second taking a long lead, and batted out infield fly balls. He hit a line drive to each infielder in turn; they had to throw to second base before the runner could return.

Owen placed a runner leading off third base, eager to run home, and hit a line drive to Koblenz. Frank caught the ball and sidestepped two paces to touch the base. Double play.

"Good play, Koblenz," Owen called. "Now what happens if there is a runner coming from second as well as the guy trying to run home from third?"

Frank thought for three long seconds, then demonstrated his response. "First I catch the fly." He held up his glove and pounded it with his fist. "Then I run over and tag the base." He did so, spun around. "Last, I run like blazes to tag that idiot coming from second."

"You've got the idea," Owen said. "That way you make an unassisted triple play. It's worth practicing." Owen assigned runners to lead off both second and third bases. He hit a hard drive to Koblenz, who dashed to third base before the runner could return, and then ran toward the man coming from second. But that player knew what to expect and had covered half the return distance. Seeing he could not catch up, Koblenz called for the second baseman to receive the ball and lobbed it toward the base, where the second baseman should have been waiting. The second baseman woke up and dashed to the base, managing to catch the ball and touch the base as the runner bore down on it with his arms flailing the air.

Owen called to the runner, "Sweetman, you are out, but that was a good try." Owen then turned toward the third baseman. "If that ever happens in a game, Koblenz, the base runners won't know what's coming. So you'll have the advantage."

* * *

"Morning, Ray. Do you really want a haircut, or did you think I was hiding the *Police Gazette*?"

"The missus says, for a person who spends so much time in the barbershop, there's no excuse for looking shabby." Dodsworth sat in the chair with a sigh of resignation. "Besides, it's already March, and this is only my second haircut this year."

Ollie fastened a strip of white crepe paper around Dodsworth's neck and threw a cloth cape over his shoulders with a flourish. "What'll it be, Ray, the usual?"

"Spring is coming, so make it a little shorter than last time."

Ollie began to ply his scissors. "Yeah, spring is already here. Folks are reseeding their grass and spading their gardens. My better half is going to club meetings again."

"Speaking of meetings," Dodsworth said, "I heard there was an open Klan meeting down at Ft. Lupton. Some kind of recruitment thing."

"Yes, there was. I know all about that one."

"You know all about it? Were you there?"

"Hell, yes. And I was wearing a mask."

"Ollie, are you telling me you belong to the Klan?"

"I am telling you, but don't you advertise it. I joined six months ago, and I'm glad I did. This Platte Valley bunch are good men. The best people have joined—doctors, dentists, lots of preachers, some farmers of course, school board members—"

"You mean somebody from the Platteville school board?"

Ollie concentrated on his work for a moment, carefully snipping hair around his client's left ear. "You know, Ray, I can't say that. If I said yes, with only three members, you'd be trying to figure it out. Besides, who belongs to the Klan isn't as important as what it does."

The barber's comb began raising handfuls of hair from Dodsworth's head for trimming by the scissors. Ollie praised the Klan as the only organization trying seriously to curb young people's wildness. It was taking the Constitution seriously about Prohibition and supported other organizations that did the same, particularly churches.

The shop door opened to admit a man of early middle age, dressed in denim trousers and jacket.

Dodsworth called out, "Hello, George." The farmer returned the greeting. "Ollie, this here is George Lydell. He has the place two miles from my old one. George, meet Ollie Scott. His real name is Oliver."

The barber shifted his tools to shake hands with the new client.

"So George," Dodsworth said, "you came for a professional haircut. Doesn't Susan usually trim your hair at the kitchen table?"

"I'm waiting to pick up some welding that wasn't ready," Lydell said, "so I thought this would be a good way to spend the time."

"You came to the right place. Not only is Ollie the best and only barber in Platteville, he's the best in Weld County. He's nearly done with me, and you're next. So sit down and tell us what you know about the Ku Klux Klan."

Lydell took one of the cane-backed chairs. "Why the Klan?"

"Only because that's what we were talking about."

"Well," Lydell said, "about all I know is what I read in the paper. And the first movie I ever saw was about the Klan."

"I saw that one myself," the barber said, "about ten years ago. *The Birth of a Nation*. It was about the original Klan, commanded by old General Nathan Bedford Forrest. They did such a great job of keeping the niggers down that the Klan was no longer needed. The modern Klan was founded down in Georgia about the time that movie came out."

After a few more snips of the scissors, Ollie Scott continued his discourse. "The Klan has been important in Colorado four or five years now. There aren't any niggers here, except for a few in Denver. But Colorado is a Christian society, so the Klan concentrates on protecting us from Jews and Catholics. Both of them want to take over, and Klan parades show them who's really in charge."

George Lydell sounded puzzled. "Are you saying Catholics aren't Christians?"

"They aren't our kind of Christian. All their priests with their mumbo jumbo, their gold cups, and stuff. Did you know that they believe wine really becomes Christ's blood? And you can't have Christ's blood lying around, so the priest has to drink up all the leftover wine? Guess what. Whatever they drink, it makes the priests just as drunk."

"Where do they get wine," Lydell asked, "with Prohibition?"

Ray Dodsworth answered with relish. "You hit the nail right on the head. There's a saying that answers your question: not all Catholics are bootleggers, but all bootleggers are Catholic. One way or another, they take care of their priests."

As Dodsworth was talking, Ollie Scott lifted the cape from Dodsworth's shoulders and shook the hair clippings onto the floor. The barber picked up a mug, whipped up the suds inside it, and applied them to the back of his customer's neck.

"But the Klan isn't only keeping Catholics in their place," Dodsworth continued. "Ollie says it encourages young people to follow the straight and narrow, by raiding roadhouses and shining lights into cars parked in the dark. Your son Ron is about the age when he could get in with the wrong crowd. Does he ever get hold of bathtub gin?"

Lydell wondered if he really needed to explain his son to these two men. Finally he said, "I don't think gin is a threat. Ron's problem is that he has learned so damn much more in sixteen years than his mother and I have learned in forty."

"Oh," Dodsworth said, "I know all about that problem. Our youngest boy was like that. He knew more than his teachers, he knew more than the preacher, he sure as hell knew more than his folks. Of course, now he's doing real well in medical school." Dodsworth chuckled.

Scott finished shaving the back of Dodsworth's neck, wiped off the excess lather, and shook rosewater into his hand, which he applied to the neck. Dodsworth stood up, and the barber brushed off his clothes with a whisk broom. As the older man reached into his pocket for money, Ollie brushed off the chair and indicated that Lydell should be seated.

Completing his payment, Dodsworth said, "You know, Ollie, you're too damn fast. I can't go home yet. Marjorie will just invent some chore. I'll stay here until lunchtime."

Ollie grinned at him. "Sure thing. I hid the new *Police Gazette* under that stack of old magazines over there."

The barber turned his attention to George Lydell, securing the paper around his neck and adjusting the cape. He determined Lydell's tonsorial preferences and then worked quietly with his scissors. Dodsworth became absorbed in his magazine. Suddenly, George Lydell heard the ticking of the clock on the wall.

As he was preparing to shave Lydell's neck, Ollie told him, "That boy of yours—Ron is his name, right?—sounds like a smart one."

"Well yes, he's pretty bright. The trouble is he knows it."

"Does he show respect for his elders? How about your pastor? Does Ron get along with him?"

"Ron says religion is a myth. He doesn't even want his four-year-old brother to believe in Santa Claus."

"Well, if Ron can't respect religion, I hope he at least respects the law. That's what the Klan is trying to do with young people—get them to show respect for the law."

As Ollie held up a mirror for George to assess his new haircut, the outside door opened. All three men turned to look at the newcomer. He was a portly gentleman with wispy white hair, dressed entirely in black. Beneath his ruddy face, like the headlight of a steam engine, shone the bright white clerical collar. He began to shrug off his black overcoat as he returned the threefold gaze.

"Top o' the morning to you, gentlemen." The newcomer's voice was melodious and cheerful.

Ollie Scott breathed words that George Lydell could barely hear, "I'll be damned." George cranked out four words, "That will be fine," and waved away the mirror.

Turning to put the mirror away, Ollie found his voice. "Good morning, Father. What can I do for you?"

"Why, I've been hoping for a haircut, if you're not too busy."

George nearly leaped from the chair, pulling coins from his pocket as he rose. He pressed the coins into Ollie's hand and lunged to the coat rack, where Ray Dodsworth was already pulling on his coat.

"I've got to go, Ollie," Dodsworth said, "Marjorie is expecting me."

"It was good to meet you. Thanks for the haircut," George Lydell said. Then he followed Dodsworth out the door.

The barber turned to his new customer. "As you can see, Father, you're next."

While the priest climbed into the chair with the deliberation of age, Ollie thought of the two deserters. Wouldn't you know it, they talked a good fight; but when they met the problem in the flesh, they turned tail and ran. That's why the Klan was needed. Klansmen weren't afraid of action.

"Father, I believe I've seen you around town, but you haven't come into the shop before."

"True. I've served at St. Nicholas going on six years now. Our housekeeper usually trims my hair. She even bought proper professional clippers, bless her soul. But the poor woman was suddenly called away to Omaha, where her brother is very ill."

Ollie Scott picked up the cloth cape and gave it an extra shake. Catholic hair was a lot like Protestant hair. And Catholic money was just as good.

* * *

Owen found Ruby in the kitchen peeling potatoes when he came home from baseball practice. She looked up, smiling when she heard his step, so Owen did not sweep her into a surprise embrace.

"Hello, Rube. Were you off teaching the Stark girl this afternoon?"

"Yes, Irene's doing well. She has the ragtime numbers down pat. For a change, we played and sang a couple of show tunes together. She has a lovely clear voice."

"Is she your most talented student?"

"Oh yes."

"Her brother is going great guns too. He'll finish his Vo Ag project early, he looks like a great first baseman, and I may let him try pitching."

"Seems like you've had baseball practice for days and days. When do the games start?"

"We go to Brighton for the opener next week. The first big game here is against Ft. Lupton in two weeks."

Ruby dropped the last peeled and quartered potato into a pot, then added water at the sink. "You know," she said, "I saw the most beautiful baby at the Starks. I wanted to play with her instead of teaching piano."

"Whose baby was it?"

"She's the fourth child of Martha Starks's younger sister, who is visiting with the baby and two of her other children. The baby—her name is Rose—was born just before Thanksgiving. So she isn't five months old yet, but she's so responsive. I had Irene repeat a piano number so I could play with the baby."

Owen grinned. "What did the baby's mother think about that?"

"Oh, she was holding Rose on her lap so I could get acquainted. She finally decided Rose was also distracting Irene, so she took her away for a nap."

"Then did you reduce your fee to make up for playtime with the baby?"

"Owen, don't make fun of me. You know I want our child more than anything."

"I didn't mean any harm, Rube. I want a child too, but we shouldn't worry about it. You're healthy, and so am I, so it's bound to happen."

"Next you'll tell me you're so sure because you were an animal husbandry major and I'm only a home economist."

"Come on, you know every branch of science follows the same method, and any findings can be shared."

Ruby relented, smiling wanly. "You're deliberately missing the point. Meaning no disrespect to animal husbandry, but if my monthlies come as usual, I'm going to see Dr. Sorenson in Ft. Collins."

* * *

The baseball diamond was situated in a corner of the playground shared by the elementary and high schools. The backstop behind home plate was made of sturdy fencing material. Bleachers behind the first and third baselines together seated nearly two hundred spectators. In front of each bleacher were benches for the teams, the home team nearest first base, and the visitors near third.

Matt Stark had shown pitching talent in the tryouts, so Owen made him the starting pitcher, moving Frank Koblenz from third to first base and sending the second team's third baseman to take Koblenz's place.

As the game began, Owen noticed Arthur Stark sitting in the bleachers with Ollie Scott and a man Owen did not recognize. That new hired man was really taking hold, if Stark could spend the afternoon watching Matt play baseball. In his months at the school, Owen received few parental complaints and experienced nothing like Mrs. Gorman's call on Isabel Nelson, but Arthur Stark had a lot of authority. Would he want to help manage the baseball team? To protect team morale, he could not seem to favor Matt. With luck, his teammates realized Matt earned the chance to start as pitcher.

Matt held Ft. Lupton scoreless the first inning despite walking a batter, giving Platteville a chance to move ahead by two runs when their turn came at the plate. In the second inning, Matt walked the first two batters, and the third hit a home run, giving Ft. Lupton the lead. The fourth batter also walked, but an easy grounder by the next man at bat created a double play, shortstop to second to first. Matt walked the fifth batter, and he would have walked the sixth; but that frustrated hero stretched outside the strike zone, hitting a pop fly to the second baseman. Mercifully the inning ended with Platteville only one run behind.

Matt redeemed himself at the plate. He hit a triple with a man on second, driving in the tying run. Soon he dashed home when a wild pitch got away from the catcher, regaining the lead for Platteville. Owen thought it unlikely that Matt would magically regain control on the mound, however, so he began the third inning with a new pitcher and restored Matt and Frank Koblenz to their usual positions. Owen would try two more pitchers before the game was over.

The lead changed five times in the next six innings. The Platteville Bears led by one run at the end of the eighth inning, and the ninth opened inauspiciously. The first Ft. Lupton batter hit a solid single to the outfield. The second batter bunted, laying down a weak grounder along the third baseline that quickly lost its momentum, stopping a third of the way along.

Frank Koblenz raced forward from third base while the catcher threw down his mask and started toward the ball. Intent on reaching the ball, the two players nearly collided. Both reached for the ball, and a tug-of-war was avoided only when Frank yielded. By then the throw to first base was late. No outs, with the tying run on second base and the winning run on first.

The runner at second base sensed that his destiny was to tie the score. He was prepared to accomplish the feat without assistance. He took a long lead off the base. When the next pitch bounced in the dust at the catcher's feet, he ran to third, sliding gloriously into the bag, although the catcher made no attempt to throw him out. The other runner advanced from first to second. A left-handed batter came to the plate, and both runners took long leads. The Ft. Lupton fans yelled advice to the batter and the runners, while the Platteville supporters yelled louder encouragement to the pitcher and catcher.

Into this chaotic noise, the pitcher launched a fast ball, high and a little outside. The batter swung hard and late, lining a drive directly to Frank Koblenz at third base. Frank leaped into the air to make the catch. Owen nearly yelled, Now is your chance!

Frank dashed over to the base, stomped on it authoritatively, and spun around to confront the runner coming from second. Suddenly realizing the situation, the runner tried desperately to contain his momentum and dodge the ball in Frank's outstretched hand. But physics triumphed over desire, and he stumbled. Before he could recover, Frank tagged him, converting the erstwhile winning run into the third out of the inning and final out of the game. Thanks to Frank Koblenz, Platteville's one-run lead held, and there was no need for the bottom half of the ninth inning.

* * *

Ollie Scott closed his shop and hurried to the ball game. He recognized Arthur Stark sitting in the bleachers with Charley Vesser. Scott remembered Vesser from the Klan raid in Big Thompson Canyon. As they jostled to make room, Vesser explained that his nephew played on the Ft. Lupton team, so he stayed on in Platteville for the game after concluding his business.

When the game began, Stark pointed out his son on the pitcher's mound, surprised he was not at first base. He mentioned the varsity third baseman, named Koblenz, now at first base.

"Koblenz." Charley Vesser was puzzled. "You don't mean the kid you saw drinking at the Halfway House."

"No, no. That was his older brother, name of Emil. This one is called Frank."

"So they are Huns," Vesser announced, "and Catholics, too."

Arthur Stark beamed with pride at Matthew's successful first inning on the mound. He was distressed when Matt walked the first two batters in the second inning. Then Vesser's nephew came to the plate, the third Ft. Lupton batter. The first pitch was a ball. The second pitch floated over the center of the plate, and he hit it into left field. The fielder ran back and back, but the fly ball went over his head. Home run.

"That," announced Ollie Scott, "was a hell of a hit."

"I thought he could do that," Vesser said, "if he got the right pitch."

Arthur Stark sounded chagrined. "Matt was afraid he'd walk another batter. He was trying so hard to pitch a strike that he didn't put any steam on it."

The three men watched in silence for a while. When Matt Stark did not take the mound for the next inning, none of them commented. The other Platteville pitchers deliberately walked Charley Vesser's nephew, leading Vesser to mock the pitchers' lack of courage. Matt demonstrated mastery at bat and as first baseman, so his father again felt comfortable. As the lead alternated, the three Klansmen were caught up in the game's excitement.

When the eighth inning ended with Platteville leading by a single run, Vesser offered to bet his companions fifty cents that Ft. Lupton would win. Ollie Scott accepted at once while Arthur Stark, normally opposed to gambling, joined in after his refusal was described as disloyalty to his son.

The ninth inning began with the first two Ft. Lupton batters reaching second and third bases, where they took eager leads. The crowd was frantic. The third batter hit a line drive to Frank Koblenz at third base. Koblenz caught the fly, touched the base, and turned to chase and tag the runner coming from second base.

The bleachers went wild, and fans surged down to the field, but the three Klansmen kept their seats.

Ollie Scott was amazed. "An unassisted triple play. I've never seen that before."

Arthur Stark said, "The kid had his wits about him to do that."

Charley Vesser spoke sharply, his voice tense. "Arthur, and you too, Ollie. Now you see what a problem Platteville has. You already have Catholics telling you how to run the schools. Now that Catholic kid made a great play, and it will encourage their ambitions. We need to show them who is in charge."

* * *

"Excuse me, Mr. Mattison." Owen heard a strange voice behind him. He turned to see a middle-aged man wearing coveralls and extending his right hand. "I'm Frederick Koblenz, Francis's father."

Owen shook the proffered hand with pleasure. "That was a great play your boy made. You must be proud of him."

"Francis would not have known what to do by himself. Thank you for teaching him."

"Oh, you knew about that?"

"Yes. Francis never talks about school unless we pry it out of him. But a couple of weeks ago, we got him to talk about baseball, and he told about practicing the triple play."

"We only spent a few minutes on it. Frank—uh, Francis—is a quick learner."

109

Would the father demand that he use the boy's baptismal name? Seeming not to care, Koblenz moved on to another subject. He lowered his voice, and an expression Owen first labeled as shyness came over his face.

"There's another thing we must thank you for," Koblenz leaned his head closer to Owen's ear. Now his tone seemed conspiratorial. "Thank you for understanding when Francis told you they could not stay for the Bible reading."

Koblenz had thanked him for being on the Catholic side. But Owen was not on either side. Why did everybody insist he choose a side? What would happen to Platteville if everyone had to take sides? Owen finally said, "Frank did a good job of presenting the reasons. I was raised a Baptist, and without his explanation, I would not have realized your problem."

"Well then," Koblenz said, "I thank you for listening to Francis."

* * *

Still not ready to tell why she insisted on a picnic, Ruby watched Owen fasten the top button of his winter coat. "It's a good thing you brought this blanket," he said, "instead of your tablecloth. We're pushing the season to come here before May, even if tomorrow is May first. At least we'll keep our seats warm."

When Ruby finished unpacking the lunch, she looked through the bud-heavy twigs on the limbs of the cottonwoods, across the river to the snowy mountaintops in the far distance. "At least the ice is gone from the roads, and most of it from the river."

She held the fried chicken out to Owen. Owen took a breast and a wing and held the potato salad out to Ruby. She took a spoonful; he took three.

"The weather's going to be all right," he said, "as long as the wind doesn't come up. But I still can't figure why you wanted to come out here today. Are you still refusing to tell?"

"It's not complicated. I have a surprise for you. It's something special, so I thought we should come to this special place."

"When do I find out what it is?"

"When we've finished eating."

Owen attacked his food with such vigor that Ruby said she meant when both of them finished. He smiled and took his second deviled egg.

When Owen finished and was waiting for Ruby, she lifted a pecan pie out of the picnic basket and gave him a knife to cut it. After he took a piece, she took a sliver. Soon their pie was eaten, and Owen turned to her with an expectant look. She opened the top of the picnic basket, reached under a spare napkin, and retrieved a small package, which she handed to Owen.

The little box was wrapped in white tissue paper and enclosed by pink and blue ribbons that came together to form a brilliant bow. Owen untied the bow, pulled the ribbons off, and opened the box. Inside a bed of tissue paper lay a shiny egglike shape with a tiny handle. He took the object out, examined it closely, turned it over, and finally shook it next to his ear.

Owen gave no sign of recognizing the item. "This isn't really for me, is it?"

"No, silly, it's a baby's rattle."

"Ruby!" Owen embraced his wife. "Are you sure? When did you find out?"

"My monthlies didn't come for nearly two months, so I made an appointment with Dr. Sorenson. I left home hours before the Thursday music lesson and drove to Ft. Collins. I told him I planned to ask him why I don't get pregnant, and he assured me that I am."

"Golly." Owen was silent as joy seemed to grow inside him. "When is the baby due?

"You seem pretty calm about it. Just another strong, silent Mattison."

"I told you it was bound to happen. And it's wonderful! Just tell me when I get to brag about being a pa."

"About the middle of December. Certainly in time for a merry Christmas."

"That will give us plenty of time to get ready. What do we do first?"

Ruby laughed at him. "Well, we don't panic. First thing I'm going to do is set up my diet. In Home Ec, we learned about a diet that concentrates nutritional advantage for the baby."

"I don't see how you can benefit one without helping the other."

"See, you didn't learn everything in animal husbandry. You can brag all you want to about scientific farming, while I'll just practice scientific nutrition, growing our own private crop."

Owen renewed his embrace, speaking quietly into her ear. "Now who's being silly? Let's concentrate on having the first one, before we start talking about a crop."

Ruby kissed his cheek and returned his hug. But a chill breeze came off the river just then, and Owen shivered, even within her arms.

Chapter 10

HAROLD HEALY BURST INTO the meeting room, showing unusual urgency as he rushed to sit at the far end of the table.

"Evening, gentlemen," he said, looking directly at Maclean. "I don't know if you want to do anything about it, but I just saw young Mattison's car parked outside the Gorman house."

"Are you sure," Thompson asked, "that it's his car? Model Ts can look a lot alike."

"Well," answered Healy, "it's the only touring model in town that has a rack on the running board for camping gear."

Arthur Stark pulled out his handkerchief and blew his nose to mask his distress. They gave Mattison one of their best jobs, and his wife gave piano lessons to Irene. She got a dollar every week. They needed to show whose side they were on.

Newton Maclean spoke up. "I'd certainly like to know why Mattison, or any faculty member, calls on that woman. She's a ringleader of the walkout, even worse than Fred Koblenz."

"Now I remember," Stark said. "I saw Mattison talking to Fred Koblenz after the baseball game."

Roy Thompson asked, "What should we do about Mattison?"

"We'd better get him in here," Stark said, "and ask him to explain himself. He lives less than a block away."

Maclean asked, "Does anybody know if he has a telephone?"

Healy said, "He does. I've talked to him on it."

"So have I," Arthur Stark said. "Last fall, when he was coming to discuss Matt's Vo Ag project."

"Harold," asked President Maclean, "would you please call Mattison? Don't threaten him or anything, just get him here."

The school superintendent went to his office, which had one of the school's two telephones. Maclean explained that their questioning of Mattison should be outside the regular meeting, so he would not call it to order.

Healy returned quickly. "No answer at the Mattison house. The two of them must be together, and they haven't gotten home yet. I suggest we proceed with the meeting, see if we can thrash out the budget question, and I'll try again in half an hour."

"Very well," said Maclean. "The meeting will come to order."

* * *

Ruby laughed. "I thought sure you would say, 'That standing rib is a pretty good cut of beef.'"

"The meat was way better than just 'pretty good.'" Owen held the choke with his left hand and spun the crank with his right. Then he spun it again. No response from the engine. "When I saw the fuss you made over that little Lucy, I was sure you'd tell the Singletons that we're expecting."

Owen spun the crank hard twice more, then paused to catch his breath.

"I did tell Ardis," Ruby replied, "out in the kitchen, while you and Harry were setting up the card table."

"So she's waiting until we're gone to tell Harry. Good for her. She takes her card playing too seriously to let women's talk get in the way." Owen spun the crank again and gave a grunt of satisfaction when the engine caught. He climbed into the driver's seat and pulled away from the curb, ignoring Ruby's offended silence.

Owen concentrated on driving across town. The amount of current flowing from the magneto to the headlamps depended on the speed of the engine. The car speed required to make the lights adequate was unsafe, in Owen's opinion, while a safe speed for driving in town left the ground ahead of the car dangerously dark, particularly when the moon was obscured by a cloud.

Nevertheless they arrived safely at the door of the little house. As they entered, Owen turned on the electric light. After taking their coats to the closet, he settled at the dining room table. He turned the pages of the Greeley *Tribune*, seeking his recent submission, but he folded the pages away when Ruby came in from the kitchen and sat down.

"Ruby, there's a couple of things I've been wanting to ask about the baby."

"Don't tell me you want to indulge in women's talk!"

"All right, I guess I get your point. I didn't mean to be rude, talking about Ardis Singleton. By that measure, I do want to hear some women's talk. First thing, will you want to have the baby here, in this house?"

"Home deliveries are fine in normal circumstances. If there are complications,

114

the people and equipment to deal with them are at the hospital. And you never know until it happens if there will be complications. Dr. Sorenson says he will meet me at the Greeley hospital."

"I'm glad you're going to the hospital. My mother had all six of us at home, but science has progressed a lot since then. So being in the hospital could make a difference. Second question: How long do you think you can go on teaching piano lessons?"

"Well, I won't begin to show for about two months. That takes us to the summer. Very few students want to take piano lessons during school vacation, so that will be a natural time to stop."

"So after summer comes, you won't need—" Owen was interrupted by the telephone bell. He looked at Ruby silently while they counted the rings, one long and two shorts. "Sit still," he said, "I'll get it." He took three quick steps into the kitchen.

Ruby listened to the tone of Owen's voice. The sound of surprise was followed by what she took to be resistance, which yielded in turn to agreement. He returned from the kitchen shaking his head in wonderment.

"That was Harold Healy, the superintendent. He says that the school board is meeting right now at the high school, and they want to talk to me. Immediately."

"But it's nearly ten o'clock at night!"

"He said he called twice earlier, but we weren't home. He apologized, but he made it plain I'd better go. At least I won't have to change clothes."

Owen retrieved his coat from the closet and walked into the dark night. Passing between budding lilac bushes that flanked his front walk, he turned toward the high school, noting lights in the second-floor windows of the superintendent's office and the nearby classroom. He entered the unlocked front door, found the stair lights on, and climbed toward the darker second floor. With each step upward, his resentment grew. Why call him away from home in the middle of the night?

Entering the open classroom door, Owen saw Harold Healy and the three board members at the table. He had met all four ten months earlier when he interviewed for the position, but Arthur Stark was the only one with whom he felt acquainted.

The four remained seated. President Maclean shuffled some papers in front of him, then addressed Owen. "Thank you for coming, Mattison, particularly at this hour and on such short notice. We won't detain you very long, but please, do have a seat."

Owen saw that there were no other chairs at the table, nor were any detached chairs to be seen in the room. He sat down at a student desk in the front row.

The board president continued with icy formality. "The formal meeting of the Board of Education has been recessed. This is an informal information-gathering session. We think you can help us, but we won't compel you in any way. Your presence here is voluntary, and anything you choose to tell us will be held in the strictest confidence. We are not keeping a record."

Maclean paused. His presence did not feel voluntary to Owen. What in God's name did they want?

Maclean continued. "Do you have any questions about the nature of our inquiry?"

Speechless with resentment, Owen merely shook his head.

"Very well," said Maclean. "Superintendent Healy has an important question for you."

"Mr. Mattison," the superintendent said, "please explain to the board what you were doing in the Gorman home tonight."

"Why, I have never been inside the Gormans' house. I've never even met Mrs. Gorman."

Owen's interrogator was unimpressed. "Your automobile was seen parked outside their home before nightfall."

"Well, we were next door. My wife and I had dinner with the Singletons, followed by an evening of card playing." Owen surveyed the skeptical gazes before him. He swallowed hard and managed to control the volume of his voice. "If you can't take my word for it, then telephone Harry Singleton."

Maclean spoke solemnly. "I'm sorry, but I feel we must do that. I gather that we have your permission. Please wait while we do so. Will the superintendent oblige?"

Harold Healy rose from the table and walked out of the room.

Arthur Stark spoke for the first time. "As long as you are answering questions, Mattison, I've got one. What were you talking about to Fred Koblenz at the baseball game?"

It was true. They were worried about what side Owen was on. He would not tell them that Koblenz talked like he supported the Catholics. No need to lie about it though. "Mr. Stark, I was talking to Mr. Koblenz because he came over and introduced himself. I congratulated him on Frank's triple play, and he thanked me for teaching Frank how to make it."

Stark sounded relieved. "So the Koblenz kid isn't a baseball genius who figured it out on the spot. You taught him. Good for you."

Harold Healy returned through the open classroom door, speaking as he walked back to the table. "Harry Singleton confirms that the Mattisons were with them until twenty-five minutes ago."

Newton Maclean stood up at the table, and the other two board members quickly rose to join him. Maclean spoke as he walked toward Owen with his hand outstretched. "Mr. Mattison," he said, "we apologize for our misunderstanding, which certainly was not your fault. Thank you again for coming out on short notice, and keep up your good work."

Owen stood up to receive Maclean's hearty handshake. Superintendent Healy stepped over to express similar sentiments. Arthur Stark came next, seeming particularly pleased, and Roy Thompson followed. Owen's right hand began to tingle from their gestures. Why couldn't they just apologize?

President Maclean said the board had one more item to consider in their formal meeting, and Mr. Mattison could be excused.

Owen kept himself from running down the dark stairwell and out into the street. Ruby was playing the piano quietly when he returned to the little house. He paused outside the door and strained to hear the tune. He identified it as a lullaby, and his haste suddenly evaporated. He turned the knob quietly and tiptoed into the living room.

But Ruby saw him and yanked her hands away from the piano. "Owen! Whatever did they want?"

"I'd just as soon hear you play another song like that one."

"Oh no. I've been sitting here, going crazy wondering what's going on. You've got to tell me."

Once Owen began, the floodgates opened. He told of the few lights in the darkened building, Maclean's description of the proceedings, Healy's question and departure for the telephone, Stark's question, Healy's return, Maclean's apology, and all the handshakes.

When he finished, Ruby said, "I could learn to hate this town."

* * *

Owen opened the door and entered the shop. Scott laid aside his magazine, sprang to his feet, and waved Owen into the chair. Grinning, Owen pointed out that Mr. Dodsworth had preceded him, and he had no desire to jump ahead of the line. As Owen expected, Dodsworth denied any interest in a haircut; he only was there to get out of the house. Owen was next. The ritual concluded, Owen settled into the chair.

Ollie determined his stylistic preference and began snipping. "I haven't seen you since the Ft. Lupton game," the barber said. "That was a humdinger. People talked about it for days, especially that triple play."

Owen said, "You don't see a triple play very often, let alone one that's unassisted. And that wins the game."

Ray Dodsworth jumped in. "I enjoyed that game. Then I went home and had a hell of a time explaining to the missus how one player can make a triple play all alone. That third baseman is a great ball player. What's his name?"

"It's Frank Koblenz," Owen replied, "and he is a sharp kid." Owen did not claim credit for teaching Frank how to make the play. Would these two men agree that baseball could become more important than religion in Platteville, at least for a few hours?

"Oh, sure," Dodsworth said, "Fred Koblenz's boy, it must be the younger one. They have a nice place west of town, a dairy farm. Fred's grandfather bought the land from the railroad."

Owen's curiosity was piqued. "You mean the Koblenzes are a pioneer family?"

"Yes," Dodsworth said, "they were here before Platteville even had a name. Just like the Stark family."

"I didn't know that. I see Frank every day, but I've only met his father once. He didn't act like a leading citizen."

"That's an interesting idea," the older man said. "How does someone act like a leading citizen? By telling you how to run your business?"

"No," said Owen, "it's not that obvious. It's like the school board. They don't tell, they suggest, but you realize they expect you to follow the suggestion."

Ollie Scott's scissors fell silent as he reentered the conversation. "You can't call Koblenz a leading citizen, because he's Catholic. This is a Protestant town, even if the Koblenz family has been here from the beginning."

"Actually," Dodsworth said, "Fred and his wife are real active in St. Nicholas Church. You could call him a leading Catholic citizen."

"I don't know about that," Ollie said. "Can somebody be both a good Catholic and a good citizen? You can't have allegiance to America and the Pope at the same time." The barber returned to his work.

Owen sat quietly, feeling no desire to pursue the topic. Previous conversations with Scott and Dodsworth had an element of introducing the newcomer to Platteville, but now he had lived there for almost a year.

"There's one Catholic in town," Ray Dodsworth said, "who wants you to see that she's a leader. I mean Mary Gorman. Her husband John is a decent guy, and he's got to stay on the right side of folks coming into his store. But Mary will tell you how to run your business if you give her half a chance—or even if you don't."

Owen remembered Isabel Nelson's tale of Mrs. Gorman's attack on Edgar Allan Poe, but he kept the memory to himself. He was immediately glad.

"I hear folks from other towns saying we have a problem with the Catholics in Platteville." Ollie Scott had turned on the electric clippers, but he turned them off again so his words would have no competition. "And they may be right. The Catholics are telling the school board to stop the Bible readings, and I heard that Mary Gorman is trying to say what stories the literature class can read."

Owen blinked. There really were no secrets in Platteville.

Scott continued, "The Catholic parents' ambition to run things gets encouraged when someone like that Koblenz kid makes a great play. They outshine the Protestants."

Dodsworth had long since put aside his copy of the *Police Gazette*. "Listen, Ollie," he said, "what can you do about it? You've got the baseball coach there in your chair. Are you telling him to only let Protestants play?"

"Hell no," the barber said. "He's got to use the best players he has, to win. But somebody has to let the Catholics know they aren't in charge, and they aren't going to be. It's that kind of thing that gets the Klan to burn a cross."

The barbershop was totally silent. For the first time, Owen heard the ticking of the clock on the wall. He felt embarrassed, as if a friend had used a nasty word in church. But the feeling lasted only as long as the silence, which was destroyed when Scott turned on the electric clippers. Their clatter effectively suspended conversation.

Ray Dodsworth again buried his face in the *Police Gazette*. Scott finished with the clippers and put them aside. Silently he worked up the lather in a shaving cup and applied it to the back of Owen's neck. He stropped the razor and carefully established Owen's hairline on the back of his neck and around his ears. Rosewater applied to the neck, clippings flipped to the floor from the cape, the whisk broom applied to Owen's clothing, and the haircut was complete. Owen paid, added a tip, bade the others farewell, and walked out of the shop.

Dodsworth spoke up soon after the door closed. "By God, Ollie, for a minute there, I thought you were going to say you are a Klansman and invite the kid to join."

"Thanks, Ray, for not letting on that I belong. You're the only person I told, and I don't think you've told anyone else."

"You're welcome. Proves that we aren't a bunch of gossipy women. But why didn't you tell Mattison more about the Klan?"

"There's a lot of misunderstanding around here about the Klan. I could feel him tense up when I mentioned it. I figure it's not up to me to straighten people out. Besides, I saw him talking to Fred Koblenz at the baseball game like they were old buddies."

"Catholic or not, that Koblenz boy is a great baseball player." Ray Dodsworth opened the *Police Gazette* and smoothed out the page he was reading.

Scott retrieved his magazine and settled in the barber's chair to await another customer.

The clock on the wall ticked on.

* * *

"Owen, last night at the Mizpah meeting, some ladies asked about the special class for Catholics. Is that working out?"

"The kids still get teased when they leave homeroom, and it still divides the school. I haven't heard any comments about Mrs. Parker's class. You can't get too get excited about something that lasts only five minutes."

"Doesn't the separate class mostly call attention to religious differences?"

"That's the effect it has on the Protestant kids, and it isn't limited to kids. Today at the barbershop, Ollie Scott started out talking about Frank Koblenz's triple play. Then he said plays like that encourage Catholics to attempt to run everything. He wound up by suggesting the Ku Klux Klan might burn a cross to show them their place."

"How did he get from the triple play to the Klan?"

"He thinks the success of their sons in sports inspires Catholics to think they can take over."

"What did he mean by 'take over'?"

"I don't think he knew himself, but I didn't ask."

"Did anybody react to that?"

"Old Ray Dodsworth was there. He didn't say anything, and I didn't either. I think we were both embarrassed when Ollie brought up the Klan. When Ollie finished, I got out of there." Owen reached for the mashed potatoes.

"You know," Ruby said, "I thought the Klan was fading away. It was just starting up in Illinois when I came to Ft. Collins. The Klan was involved in election campaigns, and my father was running for reelection as county judge. He nearly had to join the Klan to win, but he managed to avoid it."

"Well, I can't imagine the Klan paying attention to a little town like Platteville."

"In Illinois, I think it was stronger in rural areas than in cities."

"Well," Owen said, "I think the Platte Valley group is mostly from Greeley, so it's more a city thing here."

Ruby saw Owen eyeing the vegetable dish and passed him the green beans. "The school year is about to end," she said, "so the hard feelings may die out over the summer."

"That could happen. The kids will have three months without seeing the Catholic students excused every morning. I'm a little jealous. I won't have that long away from the job. I'll have six weeks to visit all the student projects and write reports, and then I'll get a month's vacation. Do you still want to go to the mountains in August?"

"You know I do. Can you really name the dates you want to be gone?"

"That's no problem. Are you starting to wind up your piano teaching?"

"Well, I've run into a couple of problems. Both Irene Stark and Maggie Fitzgerald insist on continuing on into the summer. I talked to Martha Stark privately, told her that I'm pregnant. I remember exactly what she said: 'The idea that women in the family way should not be seen in public is as dead as Queen Victoria, thank the Lord.' She said it would be good for Irene to know someone who is expecting and that I will always be welcome in their home. But she suggested bringing Irene here during the day, since she'll be out of school and won't have the bus to ride."

"I thought you didn't want to give lessons in this little house."

"That was for fear of bothering you. But if you're gone to visit your student projects, you won't be here to be bothered. And when you go away in the car, I can't use it to go to my students. The answer is obvious. Let them come to me."

"You seem to have it all figured out. You're talking about just the two students, Stark and Fitzgerald."

"A couple more indicated interest in summer lessons, but they weren't as determined as Irene. I doubt I'll hear anything more from them."

Owen chose his words carefully. "It will be all right to have one or two or even three students come here for lessons, but only in the early summer. You'll have to cut the lessons off before we take our mountain trip. Then after we get back, we'll concentrate on getting ready for the baby."

Smiling, Ruby reached across the table to grasp Owen's hand. "I think that sounds just right."

Owen was relaxed, warmed, and excited by her touch all at the same time. He mentally labeled the feeling as happiness. Then he remembered what had bothered him about his trouble cranking the Model T after their visit with the Singletons.

"Ruby, I expect you'll want to go on driving, and it's great that you can use the car when I'm at work. But the Model T has gotten stubborn. Women in the family way may be accepted in public now, but they shouldn't have to deal with a car that won't start. New Model Ts have been coming with electric starters for five years, so it shouldn't be hard to find a used one."

"But you'll need money."

"Remember, I just got a raise from the newspaper. And they've been printing every item I send them."

Chapter 11

ON THE EVENING OF Friday, June fourth, Ruby was preparing dinner when their telephone ring came through. A husky male voice asked for Owen. When Ruby said Owen would be home in half an hour, the caller identified himself as the editor of the *Tribune* and left his number.

A faculty meeting to discuss graduation plans delayed Owen. Ruby was quietly playing the piano when he came home, received the editor's message, and strode to the telephone. When Ruby finished the piece she was playing, the telephone call was over. Ruby found Owen sprawled in the kitchen chair, drumming his fingers on the tabletop.

"Whatever did the editor want?"

Owen continued drumming on the table. If only there was some way to avoid telling her. She didn't need more worries. If something went wrong though and she didn't even know where he was, she would never forgive him. His tattoo on the tabletop was no way to inspire confidence, so Owen carefully folded his hands. "He called to tell me the paper got an announcement after the deadline for tomorrow's edition. The Klan is going to march in Platteville tomorrow afternoon, and he asked me to cover it."

"Oh, Owen. You said the Klan won't bother a little town like this."

"Maybe that's what the story will be about—whether Platteville is bothered by the Klan marching through."

Ruby shook her head in disappointment. "So you agreed to take the assignment."

"Yes, I did, with one reservation. I had the editor promise my name won't be connected with the story."

"So you go on being anonymous even for your biggest story. Thank goodness. Where will you go to find out about it?"

"I start by seeing the parade. It's supposed to be from north to south on Main Street, beginning at four o'clock."

"What do you mean by 'start'? Where else can they ask you to go?"

"They want to know if the marchers are local people, where do any others come from, and how did they get to Platteville. And like I said, the impact the march has on the town. The Klan may burn a cross. I'll cover that, if they do. The editor has no advance idea of how long the story should be. I'll be paid by the column inch. I nearly forgot, they're giving me a nickel raise—thirty cents an inch, instead of twenty-five."

"Owen, you told me that we don't need the extra money I earn by teaching piano. We really do not need more money, particularly if you earn it so dangerously."

"The Klan people are not as scary as they look. To notify the paper they're having this parade means that they want publicity, so they aren't going to hurt the reporter who is getting it for them."

"I see. You don't want a byline on the story, but you're going to walk up to those masked Klansmen and introduce yourself."

"Don't be silly. I told you I don't want people to know I'm the reporter."

"So what will keep the Klan from attacking you before they find out who you are?"

"Ruby, I've given my word to the editor, and I can't back out now. I'm sorry it worries you, but I'm going to be all right. You'll see."

* * *

Owen thought the march would focus on the three blocks of the business district, which began a block inside the town's northern boundary, marked by Grand Avenue. Heading north on Main Street, Owen slowed the car as much as traffic allowed. He peered down side streets and into shop windows, but he saw no white robes. There had to be an assembly point where they could gather, put on their sheets, and form ranks.

Soon he was north of the business district among the newer homes where Owen and Ruby had visited Harry and Ardis Singleton, neither knowing nor caring that their hosts were neighbors of the Gormans. On the other side of Grand Avenue, three houses stood beyond the town boundary. Among them was a vacant lot overgrown by a spring crop of weeds.

Among the weeds, Owen saw five automobiles. Two were still in motion, as their drivers decided where to park. Owen shifted into low gear, slowing the Model T to a crawl. He saw a man partially hidden behind one of the cars, pulling a white costume over his head.

Found them! Now what should he do? He couldn't just drive in and start asking questions. Owen shifted back into second gear, picked up speed, and drove to the intersection of the highway with a county road.

He glanced at his wristwatch. Ten minutes until four o'clock. Well, they were planning to march south. He could park down in the business district and let them come to him.

Back on Main Street, Owen considered letting the Klansmen file past, then following them in his car; but that would make it impossible to interview anyone. When they were on foot, he should be too. He drove into the business district, quickly reaching the block where Ollie Scott's modest barbershop stood next to the larger, more elegant Platteville Mercantile. The barbershop seemed closed, unusual for a Saturday afternoon. The Mercantile looked crowded, and Owen thought he recognized Ray Dodsworth sitting on a bench outside the big store window.

Suddenly he understood. The Gormans owned the store. The Gormans were Catholic, and Catholics were a Klan target, so the Gorman store was the marchers' main goal. The best place to see the action was the front of the store. He drove into the next block, where the old livery stable was now the Ford dealership. Beyond the garage was a weed-grown vacant lot. Owen parked next to the lot and walked back toward the Mercantile.

Sure enough, there was Ray Dodsworth, sitting on a bench outside the store and reading a newspaper. Owen walked up to the older man. "Hello, Ray. Seeing you here, the barbershop has to be closed."

"Yup. Hello yourself, Mattison. Are you doin' some shoppin', or would you like to sit a spell?"

"The shopping can wait. Thank you." Owen sat down on the other end of the bench as Dodsworth folded his paper and laid it down.

"Nice warm afternoon," the older man said. "Did your missus give you a long list to buy?"

"No, I'm only after one item," Owen said. "I was interested in a haircut, but it looks like the shop is closed." His mouth closed quickly. Owen just got a haircut the previous week, and Dodsworth had been in the shop. Did he remember? Dodsworth was unperturbed, so Owen continued, "Why would Ollie close up on a Saturday afternoon?"

"He told me he had to go to a meeting. Out of town somewhere."

"I reckon it was important, for him to close the shop."

"I reckon so."

Owen wondered if he should show his interest in the parade. Dodsworth seemed satisfied to sit in silence, so Owen watched the people going in and out of the store until he found a way to ask without revealing his reason. "Ray . . . tell me, have you heard anything about the Ku Klux Klan marching here this afternoon?"

"A Klan march? Where did you hear that?"

"It's just gossip. My wife picked it up from a friend."

125

"Matter of fact, I heard the same rumor in the barbershop. Then my wife heard it over the telephone. Do you know when it's supposed to happen?"

Owen glanced at his watch. Nearly five minutes past four. Should be any minute now. "I heard they would march north to south on Main Street at four o'clock."

Dodsworth stood up, walked toward the street, and peered to the north. "I see 'em coming. Bunch of white up there."

Owen joined Dodsworth at the edge of the street, suspecting that his sight was better than the old man's. The marchers were coming right down the middle of Main Street, just crossing Grand Avenue—white robes, cone-shaped caps, all faces covered except for one man in the front rank. Marching four abreast, they made four files, but Owen could not count the ranks from his vantage point.

There were hooded figures at the intersection to stop automobiles traveling on Grand Avenue. After the marchers passed, these sentinels ran ahead to the next intersection and took up new positions.

Dodsworth resumed his seat, and Owen followed him to the bench.

Owen said, "They look like they're pretty well organized."

"You ever seen a Klan march before?"

"No."

"They put on a good show. I seen 'em in Greeley and once in Denver. They had a big one in Washington DC, last year. Forty thousand men."

Owen wondered how long he could function as a secret reporter. He reached back to feel the small notebook in his hip pocket, but he did not pull it out. Now he could see the advancing parade from his seat.

Shoppers came out to watch. In the block ahead, a mother sat down at the curb, holding a toddler by the hand and balancing a baby on her lap. Owen saw the marcher at each end of the front rank carried a rifle, but the four men in the front rank were not marching in step. Of course, there was no band music to establish a beat. Hard to keep in step unless someone counts cadence. The Klan was not interested in close-order drill.

The marchers were a block away. Word of their arrival had traveled inside the Mercantile, and more customers came out to stand on the walk, obscuring the view from the benches.

"Down in front, there!" Dodsworth growled.

A man wearing coveralls, holding the hand of a girl about five years old, turned around and spoke loudly. "Up in back, Dodsworth, if you want to see."

Owen rose from the bench. "Ray, I guess I'll go down to the street."

"Go ahead. Klan parades are a lot alike. I'll keep my seat."

Owen stood behind a young family at the street's edge. Mother, father, and baby. That would be Ruby and Owen before long.

The advancing Klansmen were now opposite the barbershop, and Owen saw four ranks and four files, sixteen marchers altogether. The masks were simple drapes over the face, stitched to the headband of the conical cap, with holes cut out for the eyes. In the front rank, the only Klansman whose mask was folded away seemed to be the leader. He wore an insignia over his heart, a circle with the red shape of a drop of blood in the center. Owen did not recognize him.

The father of the small family standing in front of Owen spoke sharply. "Look! That's Dr. Ostrum, the dentist from Greeley."

As Owen repeated the name to memorize it, his attention was seized by the masked man marching between Ostrum and the rifleman at the left end of the approaching rank. The way he walked, with the slight suggestion of a limp as his left foot touched the ground, was very familiar. But who was it?

As the marchers reached the Mercantile, the leader raised his hand as high as his ear. The march halted. The leader said a word softly, and the two men with rifles shifted them to the position of port arms, holding the rifles diagonally across their chests with both hands. Another word from the leader, and the two riflemen turned and trotted to the curb, followed by the three men behind each of them. The onlookers hastily made way as the men double-timed around the sides of the store building. They did some close-order drill after all.

There was a moment of silence as the eight men, half of the marchers, tramped around the store. The silence was punctuated by a child's whimpering. Then the two foursomes came back along the sides of the building, completing their circles. As they headed for the street, a woman emerged from the store and burst through the crowd. The mother standing in front of Owen told her husband, "Now you look! It's Mary Gorman."

The files led by the riflemen returned to their original places, and all sixteen men executed a left face to turn them toward the store.

At that instant, Mrs. Gorman stepped into the street and began to berate the Klansmen. "You big cowards! Hiding behind those masks because you don't dare show your faces! Who do you think you are, invading our property, scaring little children, interrupting our trade! You don't even say what you want!"

Mrs. Gorman focused her attention on a tall Klansman in the row facing her. Suddenly he reached up, lifted his mask as high as the tip of his nose, and spat a black stream of tobacco juice toward the woman's skirt. It hit well above the hem and splashed onto her shoes. The leader spoke a few quiet words, and the Klansmen faced to the right and continued marching south on Main Street.

Mary Gorman was speechless as her face turned beet red. She stumbled back into the crowd as her husband appeared, to lead her back toward the store.

Owen pulled his notebook from his hip pocket and a pencil from his shirt pocket, and wrote "Dr. Ostrum" and "Mary Gorman" on the first page. As the Klansmen marched away, he nearly dropped his pencil. He saw the hesitant gait of the third man in the front rank, and the identity flooded his mind. It was Arthur Stark!

Owen stared down the street, not hearing the crowd around him, unaware of customers reentering the store. Arthur Stark, one-third of the school board that employed him. Father of Matt Stark, great first baseman. Dairy farmer, breeder of Jerseys, father too of Irene Stark, Ruby's best piano student. Husband of Martha Stark, their first friend in Platteville. There, marching away from him, was Arthur Stark, member of the Ku Klux Klan, striding along with a slight limp, next to a man carrying a Springfield rifle. What other secrets could the Stark family be hiding? How could he tell Ruby?

The Klansmen passed Owen's Model T parked in the street, then walked onto the vacant lot beyond the former livery stable. Autos waited there, the same cars Owen saw in the vacant lot beyond Grand Avenue. So more Klansmen were involved besides the marchers. Sentinels to guard intersections, drivers staying with the cars—there had to be more than two dozen Klansmen. But only sixteen had marched. What else were they planning?

Owen murmured, "They aren't done. I've got to follow them."

*　*　*

Arthur Stark fumed as he walked onto the vacant lot. That idiot! To spit on Mary Gorman! Sure, she was asking for it, but this klavern could not act like a bunch of rowdies if they were serious about their message. Signing up anyone who came along, just to fill vacancies, was a mistake.

Stark's automobile rolled onto the lot and stopped ten feet from him. Charley Vesser shifted into neutral, set the brake, and climbed out of the driver's seat. The engine idled quietly.

"Thanks, Charlie," Stark said, "you're right on time. Are all the cars here now?"

"One is still coming."

"We'll wait. We can't leave until everybody is on board."

"How did the march go? Did you keep things under control?"

Stark sat down heavily in the driver's seat, feeling his anger drain away. "Everything was fine until we stopped at the Mercantile. It's the only business in town owned by Catholics. The owner's wife came out to read the riot act, and that new guy Jarvis spit on her. He chews."

"Good God. Did she provoke him?"

"Oh yes. She is not a very pleasant woman. Some people in town will be laughing about it, but it's no way to make friends for the Klan. Gerry is telling Jarvis off right now."

"You still want to go to the church, don't you?"

"Yes, I'm committed. But we've got to remind everyone to be dignified. People only have to see us to get our message. We don't need to raise a ruckus."

"Look, Arthur, why don't you drive over there by the street so the other cars can line up behind you. I'll go talk to the drivers, tell them they're responsible for keeping their passengers quiet. Then I'll come back and ride with you." Stark nodded his agreement, and Vesser walked away.

Stark looked around him, his vision constrained by the small eyeholes in his mask. Deciding that townspeople were too far away to recognize him, certain that he purchased the Reo too recently to be identified with it, Stark carefully folded the mask up into his cap and jammed the conical cap back on his head. Then he drove his Reo to the space Charley Vesser indicated and turned off the ignition.

A Klansman walked up to the car and pulled off his cap and mask, announcing, "These damn things get awful hot." Stark recognized Oliver Scott, the barber. "Arthur, it looks like you're leading the way to the church. Do you have room for me?"

"Sure, climb on."

Scott climbed onto the running board, opened the back half-door, and hoisted himself into the backseat of the open automobile. He began to chuckle. "Art, did you see the look on Mary Gorman's face when the tobacco juice hit her skirt? First time I've seen her at a loss for words." Scott laughed loudly.

Stark burst into a grin but kept his voice serious. "Even if she asked for it, Jarvis made a mistake."

"I know we can't approve, but you've got to admit it was funny."

Stark glanced around the lot. The other cars were lining up behind him, and most of the Klansmen had found rides. The lanky rifleman who had marched next to Stark in the front rank approached the car, carrying a Springfield. "Mr. Stark," he said, "can I come with you? Ride shotgun, like?"

Stark's voice was cold. "Don't even dream of it, unless you show me that weapon is not loaded."

"Yes, sir!" The man came to attention, executed port arms, pulled back the bolt, and held out the rifle.

Arthur had no military training, so he felt out of place, sitting at the Reo steering wheel to supervise the manual of arms. He accepted the weapon, peered into its empty breech, and handed the rifle back. "All right. Come around and get in, but you've got to stay quiet. No yelling when we drive around the church."

The rifleman's mask flapped against his face as he dashed around the front of the car. Climbing into the passenger seat, he planted the rifle butt firmly against his right hip with the barrel pointing into the air. Arthur felt encouraged. At least they didn't give rifles to the idiots.

Charley Vesser returned to the car. Seeing the rifleman in the front seat, he climbed into the back and leaned forward to report. "Gerry is riding in the last car. He thinks if people know the Cyclops is watching them, they will behave. Everyone has a ride, so we can go."

Stark pulled the mask down over his face, then ground the starter twice. The engine started. He eased into low gear.

* * *

As soon as he saw cars waiting for the Klansmen, Owen wanted to follow them but avoid recognition. He went into the store, waited his turn, and ordered a pound of coffee beans. When they were measured out into a small brown bag, he took the parcel out the door. He paused by the bench to bid Ray Dodsworth farewell, displaying the parcel. "I got the coffee Ruby wanted, so I'm headed home."

"Well, now you've seen a Klan march. What did you think of it?"

"I think I don't need to see another. One is enough."

Dodsworth's grin flashed pearly false teeth. "This one was different. It had a spittin'. Say hello to your missus for me."

"I sure will. And you remember me to Mrs. Dodsworth. So long."

When Owen reached the vacant lot, the Klan cars were in a line, and the last three marchers were climbing into cars. Feeling conspicuous, Owen crawled behind the steering wheel. The driver of the first Klan auto was no longer wearing a mask; it was clearly Arthur Stark. Just then, Stark lifted his cap and pulled the mask down over his face.

Stark's car pulled out of the vacant lot and turned north on Main Street. It would pass Owen's Ford on the opposite side of the street. Before Stark could look in his direction, Owen ducked his head under the dashboard and held it there while he counted the sounds of five autos passing. Then he hurried to the front of the car and cranked vigorously. The engine caught. Owen remembered then: he had planned to stop in at the gas station to enquire about trading for a Ford with an electric starter. It would have to wait. He climbed behind the steering wheel, made a wide U-turn, and followed the Klansmen up Main Street.

Saturday afternoon traffic in the business district was returning to normal, and Owen's progress was slow. Leaving the district, he sped up. At the corner a block ahead of him, he saw the last two Klan cars turning west onto Marion Street. Owen's left turn was delayed by southbound traffic. When he completed the turn, Klan cars were two blocks ahead, and Stark's Reo was at the corner, leading a turn to the north. Owen drove past the greenery of Lincoln Park, wondering why the Klan was on Marion Street. Then he saw St. Nicholas Church, with its bell tower over the front door. Next was a new solid house, the rectory. These buildings were clearly the goal, but what next? Would they park to parade again? Park to invade the Catholic sanctuary?

Owen turned right at the corner, seeing no trace of the Klan cars. Another right turn and he saw the caravan moving slowly and silently. The white robes topped by conical caps were motionless on the car seats. A label for what was going on popped into his mind: *a show of force. That means the Klan is a like a foreign nation we are at war with. And it's being led by a dentist from Greeley and a member of the school board that employs me. My job could be at risk.*

As the caravan filed around the corner, Owen recognized its goal. *They want to parade around the rectory again.* Acting on a hunch, he drove ahead on Marion Street for half a block, parked at the curb, and killed his engine. This was a block of solid homes, with elm trees arching over the street. Hoping nobody watched from a front window, Owen got down from the Model T and stood in the shadow of an elm. After a few minutes, the Klan cars came back after circling St. Nicholas Church a second time. Owen hid behind the tree as the caravan rolled past. Then he quickly cranked the Ford and followed the Klansmen at a prudent distance. *Ollie Scott said it in the barbershop: a Klan parade shows Jews and Catholics who is really in charge.*

The caravan crossed Main Street, continuing on Marion until Platte Street, which took them past the old railroad station. There the town's only hotel, essentially a large rooming house, struggled to stay in business, next to Platteville's only restaurant. When Owen reached the railroad station, he saw the Klan cars parked in a row. Klansmen were pulling off their costumes. Owen parked the Model T in a lot behind the hotel and waited ten minutes before strolling around the hotel's corner. The cars were empty, and nobody was in sight.

Beyond the railroad tracks stood the most prominent hill east of town. Rising sixty feet above Platteville, the hill seemed ordinary from a distance, but it marked an important boundary. The land below was irrigated from rivers like the South Platte originating in the Rocky Mountains to the west. But the South Platte meandered off to the northeast. Directly east of Platteville lay arid plains that stretched beyond endlessly into Kansas and Nebraska. Below the hill was the town with elm-shaded streets, schools, commerce, and vitality, as well as farms that produced an annual crop. Beyond that hill, farm buildings were far apart; stock was watered from wells, and fields lay drying in the sun. Dry land farmers could only hope for a crop if rain came.

Near the hilltop was a huge water tank filled from the river by pumps. This water tower needed no legs to stand fifty feet above the town and provide pressure for Platteville's water supply. Behind the tank, visible on both sides of it, was the Mizpah Cemetery.

Owen put his hands in his pockets and continued his stroll toward the restaurant's door, wondering if he could simply go in and order dinner. The Klansmen had removed their costumes, so they would look like anyone else. Maybe he could strike up casual conversations without identifying himself. Owen was reaching for the doorknob when he saw the crudely lettered sign.

Closed
Private Party

Owen left his hand on the doorknob, wondering if he could go in and pretend he belonged there. But Arthur Stark would be there. He turned aside and walked back to where the automobiles were lined up behind Stark's Reo.

Could the five automobiles tell him what he wanted to know about more than two dozen Klansmen? All the licenses were from Weld County, but Stark's car was the only one Owen thought he had seen around town. So most of the Klansmen were not from Platteville, but none came from afar. The five autos were a mixture of makes, ages, and conditions, no different from five cars parked on any street. So the Klansmen came from all walks of life.

Had he learned enough? No, he still didn't know why they stayed on. Somewhere recently he had heard talk of the Klan's purpose. Oh yes, Ollie Scott said the Klan might burn a cross to show the Catholics their place.

That was it! Owen glanced up at the hill with its water tank. Every person in Platteville could see that tank. That's where the Klan would burn its cross after dark. Daylight would fade in two hours; complete darkness would come in three. Were they having a banquet to celebrate their march, or were they only eating to use up the time until dark?

Owen hurried back to the lot behind the hotel, cranked the Model T, and drove home to dinner and Ruby.

* * *

Martha Stark was interrupted three times by the telephone as she was preparing a cold Saturday supper. Two callers described the march around the Mercantile and Mary Gorman's humiliation. One thought it hilarious; the other found it outrageous. The third caller believed she had identified Arthur

Stark in the front rank of the Klansmen and demanded if it was true. Martha managed to make fun of the idea but cringed as she hung up the telephone.

Despite the calls, Martha had supper on the table when Matt and the hired man finished milking. As Matt was washing for supper, Martha called Irene away from the piano. When all four were seated around the table, Martha said a quiet grace and passed the platter of cold cuts to Tim Holt, the hired man.

Irene broke the silence. "Mom, where's Daddy tonight?"

"Don't you remember?" Martha said. "He had to stay in town for a dinner meeting."

"He stayed in town? Do you mean Platteville or Greeley?"

Martha bit her lip. "Ft. Lupton, I believe. Something to do with his lodge."

"Do you mean," Matt asked, "that he wasn't in Platteville this afternoon?"

"I believe he was not," his mother replied. She stuffed a large forkful of food into her mouth to avoid biting her lip.

"Well," Irene said, "he missed all the excitement then. Did you know there was a Ku Klux Klan march in Platteville?"

"Yes, three different friends called me on the telephone. Where did you hear about it?"

Irene nodded toward her brother. "Matt told me."

Martha stared at her son.

"I heard about it from Ed Bailey." Matt named the boy near his own age who lived on the neighboring farm. "Ed was shopping at the Mercantile, and he saw it all. When he saw me working on the fence, he came across to tell me about it."

"Did you hear," Irene asked, "that there was almost a fight outside the store? And that somebody spit tobacco juice on Mrs. Gorman?"

"That's enough," Martha said, eyeing Tim Holt. "This is not an appropriate topic for dinner table conversation." She picked up a serving dish. "Tim, have you tried these pickled beets?"

"Thank you, Ma'am. I like them a lot."

* * *

Owen drove back to the old railroad station at dusk. He was shaken by Ruby's reaction to Arthur Stark's Klan membership. She had been physically ill, although she finally dismissed her nausea as "morning sickness in the evening" and recovered to put dinner on the table. She begged him not to go back to the depot. Surely he had seen enough to write his news story. Owen resisted the possibility of a woman—even the woman he loved—vetoing his intentions.

Something about the Klan drew him back. It was beyond a report for the *Tribune*. Could he find out why Arthur Stark joined the secret society?

When Owen parked again in the lot behind the hotel, darkness was nearly complete. He wondered where to leave his car. He peered around the hotel corner, looking across the railroad tracks to the hill beyond. In front of the water tank, in a space that had been vacant, stood a tall wooden cross wrapped in burlap. He was definitely at the right place at the right time.

When it crossed the railroad tracks, Grand Avenue became a county road, not much more than a trail, which ran straight up the hill and over it to the east. The Model T had to climb that road in low gear. There were ditches on each side of the road; they were dry now, and a man could hide in them. The Mizpah Cemetery began to the north of the road, beyond the water tank. Beyond the cemetery, there was no place to conceal an automobile for half a mile. Best leave the Ford where it was.

The Klansmen would not need their autos. The hill rose just beyond the unfenced railroad tracks behind the restaurant. The county road was forty or fifty yards out of their way. It would be easy to climb directly up the hill, but he would not choose his own path until certain of theirs.

Owen strolled around the back of the hotel and across a vacant lot. He saw the dim white figures of two robed Klansmen move across the railroad tracks to the base of the hill, where they thrust the end of a torch into the ground and lit the flame. White-robed figures streamed out of the restaurant. Each carried a torch, which he lit from the torch planted in the ground. Owen was more than sixty yards away, but he believed he could smell the kerosene.

When the nearest Klansmen were busy lighting another torch, Owen crouched low and trotted across the tracks into the ditch beside the county road. He fell to his knees inside the ditch, leaving only his head and shoulders above its edge. A crescent moon drifted in and out of the clouds to break the deepening darkness.

A line of torches zigzagged up the hill, a serpentine line growing longer as each new flame flared at its base. So the Klan was parading up the hill, preparing Platteville for a sight yet to come. They had not climbed high enough for their torchlight to be reflected by the water tank, which was barely visible in the growing darkness. He could no longer see the Mizpah Cemetery, but Owen recalled Stark's description of the hilltop before its renovation: brambles, rats, and rattlesnakes. When driven from the old burial ground, where had the snakes gone?

This sudden vision of serpents propelled Owen out of the ditch and onto the road. He could not see it in the dark, but he remembered the gravel surface. So he was confident of his footing, and increased his pace to reach the hilltop before the Klansmen did.

Owen's climb made his breathing rapid. The sound of his own breath added to the slight sound of his footfalls made him self-conscious, as if the sounds he made could draw the attention of the Klansmen fifty yards away. *A silly thought. The marchers are making a lot more noise, and I can't hear a thing.*

When Owen reached the summit, he sensed the water tank as a darkness of greater density. His climb had raised a sweat, and the breeze sweeping across the hill made him shiver. He crossed the ditch and felt his way through wild grass toward the cemetery. Suddenly, something struck his shin. He had no weapon to dispatch a rattlesnake. No longer looking toward the line of torches, Owen hoped his eyes could bring some images out of the dark.

Reaching down to his leg, he felt the branches of a willow sapling. Oh yes. Ruby had helped plant a line of willows along the cemetery boundary, and he had walked into one. Rattlesnakes became nocturnal when the days were hot, but it was early June. No need to worry about rattlers in the dark until August.

The crescent moon came from behind a cloud. Owen could make out shapes beyond the willows. He identified headstones, bushes, and a few single pine trees planted among the graves. Looking toward the water tank, Owen saw its dark outline against flickering reddish light. The Klan torches were approaching. Walking as quickly as he dared, Owen moved toward the tank. He peered toward the ground, trying to walk between the graves rather than on them.

The light downhill from the water tank grew brighter. As Owen got closer to the tank, the light coming from the other side revealed features of the slope on which the tank rested. As Owen crossed the cemetery boundary, he could hear voices on the other side of the tank but could not make out the words. With torchlight from below, the side of the tank cast a clearly defined shadow across the crest of the hill. Owen stayed well within the shadow as he walked the last few yards down to the tank. Finally he touched the tank, leaned against it, and felt one of the metal bands that bound it together. He had gotten that far; now he had to see the other side.

Owen saw weeds growing at the edge of the shadow. They were at least two feet tall and reached several inches out from the base of the tank. He walked to the edge of the shadow, lowered himself to the ground, held his body close to the tank, and looked out through the weeds.

Forty feet away and ten feet lower on the slope, Owen saw a line of torch-bearing figures in white facing the tank. The row of Klansmen had folded back their masks. Half the distance between Owen and the Klansmen stood the timber cross wrapped in kerosene-soaked burlap.

The base of the cross was easy to see in the torchlight, but the upper part was dim and shadowy. The cross was twelve or fifteen feet tall, and the kerosene odor redoubled the smell of the burning torches. The man Owen now thought of as "Ostrum the dentist" stepped forward and held his torch to the base of the cross. The flames spread quickly up the cross and out along its arms. The breeze made the flames dance, and the assembled Klansmen cheered. Owen curled his body more tightly against the tank and pressed his face close to the ground behind the weeds.

Ostrum planted his torch in the ground and turned to face the Klansmen. Four of them set their caps on the ground and came forward as a man next to Ostrum posed a series of questions. Owen could not hear the questions, but the increasingly enthusiastic affirmations were unmistakable, and stimulated further cheering.

Then the four knelt in a line in front of Ostrum, who walked forward carrying a bowl of liquid. He laid a hand on each of the bared heads in turn, while murmuring an incantation. Then Ostrum approached each man in turn, still reciting some ritual, and sprinkled drops of the liquid on each shoulder and above each head. Finally Ostrum pulled a card from his pocket and read out a sentence in a firm voice. The kneeling men repeated it in unison. The responsive oath continued for four more complete sentences, with each repetition louder than the one before. The kneeling men stood up as the Klansmen cheered even louder.

Owen used his elbows to push back from the weeds. It must have been a Ku Klux Klan initiation. Probably a secret ceremony. Although the cross blazed on the hill for all Platteville to see, surely the Klansmen would not welcome intruders. Owen pushed himself back from the weeds and deeper into the water tank's shadow, scrambled to his feet, and ran into the darkness of the cemetery.

Chapter 12

AS OWEN PARKED THE Model T, he saw the living room light. Too bad, Ruby was still up, probably still angry. Climbing out of the car, Owen looked to the east where, despite the surrounding elm trees, he could see the cross still burning. He walked to the front door and turned the knob. The door was locked. Strange—they had never bothered to lock the door.

He walked around the house to the kitchen window, but it was dark. He returned to the front door and knocked softly. No response. Then he remembered the key ring in his pocket. He inserted the house key into the lock, where it turned easily, and the door swung open.

Ruby was sitting slouched in their one easy chair, chin resting on chest, sound asleep. Owen paused. A book had fallen beside Ruby's ankles. She was wearing one of her low-waisted dresses with a belt that hung low on her hips. The belt buckle was loosened to make room for the bulge of her pregnancy. Her chestnut hair was tousled, curls glistening in the light from the floor lamp behind her shoulder. Her face in the shadow seemed pale.

Owen walked quietly across the floor, bent down, and kissed her forehead. Ruby's eyes fluttered. "Oh, you're back," she mumbled. Then she yawned, her eyes snapped open, and she straightened in the chair. Owen knelt down and aimed his lips for hers.

Ruby turned her head aside. "Owen, I was worried sick. And I actually was sick, but you went anyway. I felt so alone."

Owen sat on the arm of the chair and held his wife tightly. "I'm sorry, so sorry . . . Is that why you locked the door?"

"Yes. I kept thinking about Arthur Stark marching at the head of the Klan. We've had a lot to do with his family, and I thought they were good friends. But I guess we don't know him at all. If we could be wrong about him, how about the rest of Platteville? So I locked the door."

"At first I thought you were locking me out. I even tapped on the door. Then I remembered that I have a key."

"What counts is that you're back, and you're safe. Let me look at you." Owen stood up for inspection. At her request, he turned around to show his back. "Your clothes are awfully dusty, but I don't see any rips. Where have you been?"

"It sounds silly, but I was lying in the dirt, hiding behind the water tank. And I saw the Klan fire up a fifteen-foot cross. It's still burning—you can see it from our yard."

"I'll take your word for it. Owen, you promised to be careful. How did you get that close?"

Owen returned to sit on the chair arm again, quietly laying an arm on Ruby's shoulders. "I wasn't very close. The cross was down the slope from me, and the Klansmen were all on the other side of the cross. I hid my face in some weeds at the edge of the water tank, and then I saw a Klan initiation."

"How did you get up the hill without being seen?"

"That was easy. While the Klansmen climbed up the hill behind the restaurant with their torches, I walked up the county road fifty yards away, in the dark."

"Was Arthur Stark on the hill with the others?"

"I think I saw him carrying a torch up the hill, but I couldn't be sure in the darkness."

"You aren't going to name him in your *Tribune* story, are you?"

"No, no. There's a chance—maybe one in a thousand—that I could be wrong. I did see his face this afternoon with his mask off, and I swear it was him. The Klan leader never wore a mask, and I heard people say that he's a dentist from Greeley named Ostrum, so I will report that name. The editor probably knows about him already. I'd better get started while it's fresh in my mind."

"Fine, if you think you have to." Ruby got to her feet. "Tomorrow is Sunday, and you can work on it all day. I'm going to bed."

Owen turned on his heel, came back to his wife, and kissed her cheek softly. "All right," he said, "I'll work at the kitchen table." He went to the other door, swung out the brass bed, and pulled it down to the floor. "Sleep tight, sweetheart."

* * *

Arthur Stark set the car's brake, climbed down, and walked around to the back door of his home. Passing into the dining room, he saw light coming through the open parlor door. He paused by the stairs, tempted to creep up to their bedroom without talking to Martha—no reason to disturb her, he could argue. But she was disturbed already, and avoiding her would only make matters worse.

No longer trying to soften his footfalls, Arthur marched into the parlor, where Martha sat waiting in one of the two armchairs. He said, "Hello, my dear."

"Arthur, please shut the door. Nobody else needs to hear what I have to say." Martha's voice was cold. Arthur complied, started to walk toward Martha, thought better of it, and sat down in the other chair facing her.

"I lied for you this evening," Martha said, "and I don't intend to do it again, ever. I lied to your own children in front of the hired man. Before that, I let a good friend think I found the idea of you belonging to the Klan ridiculous."

"Well," Arthur began, "I never asked you to lie."

"Perhaps not, but you gave me the lie to use. You said you were going out of town to a dinner meeting. You never told me your Klan was going to meet and march."

Arthur could not remember a time when Martha was so outraged. He let his chin sink to his chest, trying to look contrite while he decided what to say.

"Surely you didn't think your march could be kept a secret from your family. I had three telephone calls before supper, all telling about Mary Gorman being spat on, and one of them demanding to know if you were marching in the Klan's front row. I actually made fun of the idea, and I can't forgive myself for that."

"I'm sorry," Arthur said at last. "I didn't want to worry you. Besides, you led me to believe that you didn't want to hear about Klan activities."

"There's a big difference between something going on in the Big Thompson Canyon and a march in our own town. You aren't being any more honest with yourself than you are with me. You didn't tell me about this march because you were ashamed to be part of it."

"You're wrong, Martha. I am proud to be a member of the Klan. There are a lot of good people in this Platte Valley klavern, and we are actually doing something about young people's indecency and enforcing Prohibition. Those are causes I believe in deeply."

"Don't try to tell me the Ku Klux Klan is a service club. Why did you march around the Gormans' store? And Ardis Singleton told me that you drove your cars around and around St. Nicholas Church. You wanted to intimidate the Catholics."

"You'll have to admit they can use some intimidation. They own the only decent store in town, and we gave them their own program in school. But they still aren't satisfied. When the klavern started talking about coming here, I supported it, and then I had to participate to keep things from getting out of hand."

"Well, you failed. What do you call spitting on Mary Gorman?"

"Martha, I regret that with all my heart, but you know how Mary is. When she came out to give us a piece of her mind, she provoked the wrong man. The result was a terrible mistake, and the young man who did it is being disciplined. It undercuts all the good things we have been doing."

"It certainly does. Now all Platteville knows the Klan as the group that spits on women. And you're still proud of being a member."

"Well, we finished the evening with something spectacular. We burnt a fifteen-foot cross on the hill east of town. All Platteville could see it. You could have seen it from here. I regret what happened to Mary Gorman, but I don't regret belonging to the Klan."

Martha Stark frowned. "If you're so proud of belonging, are you going to tell your children about it? Matt heard about the parade from Ed Bailey, and he told Irene. I told them you were at a dinner in Ft. Lupton, and they were sorry you missed the excitement in Platteville."

"All right, if the topic comes up naturally, I'll tell them. But there's no reason to make a mountain out of a molehill. I'm not going to stand on a chair to make an announcement."

* * *

"Morning, Art," the barber called. "Did you see, our march made the front page of the *Tribune*." Scott got up and waved Stark toward the chair.

"I saw it. In fact, we need to talk about our klavern, if you've got a minute. I don't need a haircut."

"Art, I'll talk with you anytime you want. Have a seat."

Stark took one of the five chairs provided along the wall for waiting customers. Scott sat down two chairs away.

"That newspaper story bothers me," Stark said. "It has details only an insider would know. I don't complain about naming Gerry. His membership is no secret—he never wears his mask any more, and he is making us respectable. Anyone in the crowd could have described Jarvis spitting on Mary Gorman, but there wasn't a crowd to watch us circle St. Nicholas. That was a last-minute idea, and nobody notified the paper about it. Then the story describes the cross burning and says we initiated four new members. Whoever knew that had to be there."

The barber answered abruptly. "Art, I don't see why you're so worried." Stark contained his annoyance at the barber's familiarity. He was the only man in town who shortened "Arthur" to "Art."

"After all," Scott concluded, "the story is favorable."

"What do you mean, favorable?" Stark's voice was sharp.

"Favorable to the cause, because it gets our message across, just by giving the facts. Any Catholic who reads it will wonder what we'll do next. When we drove past the rectory the second time, I saw old Father O'Donnell peeking out the window, and he looked as sick as his own ghost. Isn't that what we want?"

"Of course it is," Stark said. "They'll think twice now before they plot something. But I'm worried about the future. There's a big decision coming up. You and I, as members from Platteville, should have the major say in it. Should the klavern plan more activities around Platteville or not?"

"That is a big decision. We've made the Catholics nervous, wondering what we'll do next. How do we follow that up?"

Stark agreed. "The longer we go without doing more, the more nervous they'll get. They'll imagine worse things than we can even think of. We've done enough for now."

"Maybe so," Scott said. "But I have an idea about how to win us new friends. Let's set up a booth on the Pickle Day fairway, stock it with pamphlets, and bring in some of our best kleagles to recruit new members."

"That won't help our reputation in Platteville. People come from all over, even from Denver, for Pickle Day."

"I know," Scott said. "It's gotten as big as the Weld County Fair. That's why the Klan should be there, to get new recruits from all over northeastern Colorado."

"I don't think that's in the cards. There's been a big negative reaction to our parade, particularly the spitting business. We need to let things calm down." If he couldn't convince Ollie, he wouldn't have a chance with the others.

"Pickle Day will be the first or second week of September," the barber replied. "Everyone should be calm enough by then."

"I don't think so. I can see wiseacre kids challenging our men to a spitting contest. Besides, we don't want people joining just because they don't like Catholics. We should be more interested in closing down bootleggers and booze parties than in scaring Catholics."

"I thought you were mad at them for fighting the Bible reading."

"I'm still mad about that. I'd like to get more people to see it my way, but the Klan isn't going to accomplish that, after Jarvis and his damn tobacco juice."

Ollie chuckled. "Maybe not, but I'll never forget the look—" The barber swallowed the remainder of his sentence. The door opened, and in came Ray Dodsworth.

Stark joined Scott in the chorus. "Hello, Ray!"

* * *

"Hello, Cath—" Martha began, but her voice died as Mrs. Koblenz used her left hand to grasp her skirt at the knee and sweep it aside. The skirt was not quite long enough for the gesture. Mrs. Koblenz marched past them, staring straight ahead.

So Catherine tried to act like Martha was a fallen woman. Catherine had to know about Arthur and the Klan.

Matt bounded ahead and caught the screen door before it could slam. "Gee, Ma," he asked, "what's wrong with her?"

"It's a long story, Matt. We'll talk about it later."

* * *

When Koblenz asked to see him in his capacity as school board member, Arthur suggested they meet in the room used for board meetings. He remembered his fruitless visit to the Koblenz farm and thought it would be easier to stay in charge of the conversation if Koblenz came to the seat of the board's authority.

"Hello, Arthur." Koblenz offered his hand.

Stark gripped it loosely. "Hello, Fred. You're very prompt."

"I didn't want to keep you waiting."

Stark led his guest into the building and up the stairs. In the board's usual classroom, he waved Koblenz toward the other end of the table and took the place usually occupied by Newton Maclean, the board president. Although Koblenz would not know this was the president's place, Arthur felt a sense of entitlement. He smiled when he realized what was missing. Maclean's gavel was locked up in the superintendent's office. "Well, Fred, what's on your mind?"

Koblenz leaned back in his chair. "Arthur, on my way into town, I remembered the devilment you and I got into, some in this very building. Then I thought back to the old story I heard so often I got sick of it, about our grandfathers."

How long would Koblenz beat around the bush? Stark barely managed to curb his impatience. "You mean, about how they gave Platteville its name."

"Yes. I don't know if they told it the same way in your family as they did in mine."

Arthur decided to play along. "The story I heard was, they were the first settlers since the fur trappers to really make it here. Before the town was laid out by the railroad, it was only a watering stop for engines, with a blacksmith shop and a saloon. To get a post office, they had to have a name."

Koblenz took over the narrative. "The town was just north of the ruins of old Ft. Vasquez. But there was already a fistful of towns named after old forts—Ft. Morgan, Ft. Collins, Ft. Lupton. Nobody needed another 'Fort.'"

Stark claimed the next turn. "Particularly not a Ft. Vasquez. The Spanish settlements were all in Southern Colorado, so they didn't need a Spanish name up here. They decided to name the town after the river, although there was a Platteville in Wisconsin already."

"But there's an angle to that story," Koblenz said, "that I never considered before. It occurred to me just the other day. Your grandfather wasn't worried so much because the fur trappers were French and Spanish, as he was unhappy because the French and Spanish were Catholic. And they still are."

"Oh, come on, Fred. If my grandfather felt that way, why would he even work with your grandfather?"

Frederick Koblenz suddenly pounded the table a single time with both fists. His voice was nearly a shout. "If your grandfather did not feel that way, how do you explain his grandson—you—joining the Ku Klux Klan?"

With a supreme effort, Arthur controlled his voice, hiding his suddenly clenched fists in his lap beneath the table. "I joined the Klan because it is doing something to keep our kids from heading straight to hell! It is one organization that is taking Prohibition seriously. When the Constitution says 'Don't drink,' it means you do not drink!"

Koblenz glared for long seconds at the friend of his youth. He folded his hands on top of the table, seeing his fingers grip so hard that his knuckles turned white. His voice shook, but his words were measured. "The Constitution also says something about equal rights. It does not say you can hang people because of their skin color. It says something about freedom of religion. It does not say you can spit on people because of the way they worship God."

"All right, Fred, spitting on Mary Gorman was a mistake. The hothead who did it is being disciplined. But you're talking about Klan mistakes and forgetting the good things it does. Like raiding speakeasies. Like breaking up petting parties in parked cars."

"It sounds like you believe it's a good thing for the Klan to enforce the law."

"Well, it is, when the government can't get the job done." Arthur had his own anger under control, and Fred no longer looked like he was going to crawl down the table to attack him. If they could talk reasonably, there were facts Koblenz ought to recognize. "Listen, Fred, if you are so keen on following the law, why didn't you and your friends recognize the authority of the school board?"

Koblenz shook his head in sorrow. "Arthur, by now you must know what we objected to in your—the board's—decision to make everybody listen to the King James Bible."

"I understand your objections. I'm complaining about what you chose to do about it—encouraging your kids to walk out of the classroom, destroying school harmony. You didn't have to do that. You could have asked the board to hear your side."

"Since the board never held a public meeting on the issue, we never had a chance to make that request. You just had the teachers start reading the Bible selections you picked, and then you sent parents a notice announcing a rule that everybody has to attend. We recognized the board's authority when we appealed to a higher authority, the Colorado courts."

"You still should have talked to us first. But since you went to court, I assume you're willing to abide by the result."

"That depends. If they decide the Colorado Constitution allows your board to make our kids study a Bible that our church prohibits, then, our lawyer says, we'll appeal to the U.S. Supreme Court. The final word on defining the rights of citizens belongs to them."

"So you really want to fight to the end. Meanwhile the board is stuck with paying an extra teacher to handle your kids. We've had to commit our entire contingency fund, so we may have to ask for a tax increase. What will your neighbors think of that?"

"We'll have to tell them that you can't settle questions of faith, or of right and wrong, on the basis of the dollar."

Arthur felt a warm flood engulf his face. "Don't get sanctimonious on me, Fred. All right, faith is not measured by money. But faith doesn't come in a bottle either."

Fred Koblenz glared down the table, his brow furrowed. "Exactly what do you mean by that?"

"I mean that you Catholics fought against Prohibition tooth and nail, and now that it's the law of the land, you do everything you can to undermine it."

"I've heard people say that, but nobody offers evidence to back it up."

"All right, Fred, you asked for it. I have some evidence you can't deny. A year ago, when I was a new member of the Klan, we raided the Halfway House in Big Thompson Canyon. It was the first raid I went on. We broke up the dance and a bathtub gin party, and who was attending that gin party but your son Emil."

Arthur was astonished to see Koblenz's glare turn into half a smile. "I appreciate that you don't claim you saw Emil actually drinking gin. He told me about it the next day, said he didn't drink, and I believe him. He also asked me if you could possibly be a member of the Klan, because he thought he recognized the way you walked. I doubted it. A couple of months later, when you came to the house, he was sure of it."

Arthur was silent as his mind filled with images. Lanky Emil Koblenz with his date, near the kitchen door at the Halfway House, with Arthur unable to remember his name. Emil noisily admiring Arthur's Reo in the twilight. A shorter Emil, two years earlier, accepting his high school diploma.

"So," Koblenz went on, "I knew you were in the Klan long before other people knew. But I never told anyone, and I wouldn't have mentioned it to you, but I got to wondering if your grandfather thought like you do."

"Fred, I joined the Klan because it's doing something about young people, and because it's taking Prohibition seriously. Surely you don't approve of how these flappers dress and how they smoke and drink."

"No, I don't. But I know it's hard to tell young people how to live their lives, because you'll inspire them to do the opposite. I'm willing to grant that you joined the Klan out of good motives, but you picked the wrong organization. What does it take to convince you of that? Surely you read about that Klan leader in Indiana, convicted of rape and murder."

Stark replied as calmly as he could. "You're making a mistake if you judge my group by what happens in Indiana. Real Klansmen expect to defend the purity of womanhood. We renounce the influence of foreign powers, like your Pope, but I certainly didn't join the Klan to harass Catholics. However, you should realize the Klan came to Platteville primarily because of the trouble you caused over Bible reading."

"Well, I suspected that. And that trouble, as you call it, will go on until we get the last word from the Supreme Court. But the main reason I asked to talk with you—believe it or not—was to thank you and the board for providing the morning meeting for our kids. Helena Parker is enthusiastic about it, and I've heard positive comments from students, including my son Francis. It's a short meeting, but I think some real moral instruction is taking place. You can't measure such things in dollars, but I'd say the board is getting its money's worth."

Arthur Stark sat quietly in the president's chair. His hands lay on the tabletop, palms down, fingers slightly curled, relaxed. He suddenly felt very tired. "Fred, I'm glad that you appreciate what the board has been trying to do, and I'm glad it's doing some good. But you have a strange way of expressing your gratitude."

* * *

Feeling awkward, Ruby bent down to dust the piano stool. She had abandoned the flapper's boyish look and folded away her chemises. *In this high-waisted dress, the bulge of expectancy can be more a suspicion than a confirmation.*

She put the duster away and returned to sit in the armchair. She laid back her head and let her mind wander. *It's warmer but still June. July could be really unpleasant. I definitely have less energy and get tired sooner. What a shock when Owen said he recognized Arthur Stark among the Klansmen. I went to the Stark farm three days later for Irene's lesson. Maybe her parents were fighting over Irene continuing her lessons with me. Irene even paid the silver dollar herself.*

Ruby thought she had barely closed her eyes when a gentle knock on the front door made them open wide. She moved quickly to open the door and saw Irene on the doorstep. Beyond the girl, a large automobile was parked beside the lilac bushes. Nobody was in the car.

"Irene! Look at you! You've gotten your hair bobbed, and you drove here all by yourself! Come in."

The smiling girl entered, carrying some sheet music, which she took to the piano.

"I like your hair a lot," Ruby said. "When did you get it cut?"

"Just last Saturday, and I'm still getting used to it. It's a lot less trouble."

"And what about driving the car? How long have you been doing that?"

Irene sat down on the piano stool. Ruby sat in the dining room chair placed next to it.

"Daddy showed me how, and I practiced around the farm for a week. It took a long time to get used to the clutch. Then I drove into town with him two times, but today is the first time I've driven the car all alone."

"Congratulations! Did the car give you any trouble?"

Irene suddenly blushed. "I came down your street a little too fast. I was afraid I would run right into your lilac bushes, but I managed to get stopped."

Ruby laughed. "We have plenty of lilacs. It wouldn't hurt to lose a few. They attract bees."

Irene regarded her teacher solemnly. "That's enough about me. How have you been, Ruby? Are you feeling all right?"

"I'm fine. I haven't had morning sickness for the last two weeks, although I get tired a little easier. But I want to ask about you. I thought your father was dead set against you cutting your hair, and I'm surprised he suddenly taught you to drive."

"I was a little surprised too."

"Well? Don't stop there."

"It's kind of a long story."

"Don't worry. I won't count conversation as part of your lesson hour."

"Well, did you hear about the Ku Klux Klan parade?"

"Yes, and I read about it in the *Tribune*."

"A lot of people recognized my father marching with them, even with his mask on, and they asked Matt and me about it. He didn't tell us the parade was going to happen. I think my mom knew, but he never even told my brother and me that he was in the Klan."

"That must have made things difficult for you."

"It sure did. I think letting me bob my hair and teaching me to drive were his apology."

Ruby asked, "Does he tell you anything about his Klan membership?"

"Daddy doesn't agree with a lot of things they do in other states, like Indiana. And he was really upset by them spitting on Mrs. Gorman. He said he joined because the Klan is one organization that is taking the Constitution seriously—he means Prohibition. I talked it over with Matt. Matt says Daddy doesn't like the twentieth century, and he keeps hoping the Klan will hold it back."

Chapter 13

OWEN PARKED THE MODEL T near the former livery stable, now the Ford garage, Platteville's only automobile dealer. He glanced at the neighboring vacant lot, where Klan cars had gathered to pick up marchers. Its weeds were cut to allow a display of autos for sale. Inside the garage, he saw a lanky young man working on a car engine. Owen recognized Frank Koblenz's brother, Emil, as the mechanic wiped his hands on a cloth and came to greet him.

After the handshake, Emil said, "You got this buggy worked on in the high school shop, didn't you, Mr. Mattison?"

"Yes, that's why it's still running."

"So I reckon you didn't come here for service."

"No, I've decided to trade in this old flivver for something modern. A touring car is fun, but a family needs a closed car. I'm looking for an electric starter and a heater in a dependable car."

"The boss went on some errands, and he left me in charge. Told me to sell as many cars as I can." Koblenz grinned.

"I'd like to see what you have to offer," Owen said, "or at least talk about what cars you think I should be interested in."

"It sounds like you need a two- or four-door sedan. Ford makes the Model T with those bodies, if you're interested."

"Isn't the T underpowered for those heavier cars?"

"A lot of people think so. The T was a great product when it hit the market, but that was in 1908. We hear rumors Ford will put out an entirely new engine and car, maybe next year, but that doesn't help you now."

"I can't afford a new car, so I'm looking for a good used one. Next year I may not be able to buy any car at all." No telling what new expenses the baby would bring.

"For a sedan, you might consider a Hupmobile or a Chevy or a Studebaker. With used cars, the condition is more important than the make. Any of them can be reasonably priced as used cars. Should be less than four hundred dollars."

"Will I have to go into Greeley to find one like that?"

"You'll have to go to Denver to find a wide selection. But you know, we have a car here that you should look at, a four-door sedan. It's a '24 Chevrolet. I'll get the key and show you."

The two men walked to the lot displaying a dozen automobiles in a single row, some with prices marked on cards inside their windshields. Owen wondered if the autos were put there partly to discourage further Klan use of the lot.

Emil walked to the middle of the row and stopped beside a blue-gray car with clean, square lines. "They advertise 'Body by Fisher,' you know. And it's got six cylinders," Emil continued as he unlocked the driver's door and rolled down the window. Then he invited Owen to sit in the driver's seat. Owen saw no sign indicating the price, but he dared not ask, fearing his sudden eagerness would show.

The upholstery was clean. Plenty of space in the back for blankets and picnic baskets and baby equipment. And the baby. Looking around the car, he saw an unfamiliar metal box with three shutters hung beneath the dashboard. Owen nodded toward the box. "Is that what I think it is?"

"Probably. It's the heater."

"That's something we've never had."

Emil Koblenz held out the ignition key. "Like to take her for a drive?"

Owen suppressed a grin. Yield not unto temptation. "Not so fast, Emil. You haven't told me the price."

Emil showed him the tag attached to the key. "It says here we're asking $325. Your Model T would make a good down payment."

Emil could not accompany him because he had to keep the shop open, but everyone in town knew Owen, and his boss would certainly approve the test drive. Owen accepted the key and was pleased when the engine started with the first turn of the starter. He drove onto Main Street and turned south, moving at moderate speed until the sharp turns at the town boundary took him onto the highway. As the car accelerated, Owen missed the Model T's rattles.

He passed the ruins of old Ft. Vasquez and came to the intersection with the road to the bridge over the South Platte. Straight ahead, the highway passed close to the Lydell farm and the picnic spot in the cottonwoods. If Ruby were along, he would head there, since they hadn't been back since Ruby gave him the baby rattle; but that would not be a test of the car. He turned west, drove over the bridge, and climbed over the first of the rolling hills. The Chevrolet conquered the incline in high gear, even gaining speed.

Owen began to enjoy himself. The car had an electric windshield wiper on

150

the driver's side of the windshield. Owen found the control and turned it on. It soon made a scraping noise against the dry glass, so he turned it off. He found the heater control and turned it on, satisfying himself that it worked all too well for a day in July. He pulled into a farmer's yard and turned around.

When Owen returned to the Ford agency, he asked Emil's permission to run a compression test on the engine. The mechanic supplied the tools Owen used to remove the spark plug from each cylinder in turn. Owen inserted the gauge into the plug opening, nodded to Emil behind the driver's seat, then read the gauge when Emil ground the starter. He was pleased by every reading; the piston rings were fine.

The shop's proprietor returned as the testing neared completion. Owen walked out with him to the Model T, which was surveyed with care. Owen restrained a sigh of relief when the engine caught after one spin of the crank. The proprietor offered him $125 for the Ford as a trade-in, only fifty dollars less than Owen had paid fourteen months earlier. Owen decided not to bargain further. *That car doesn't owe us a thing. We drove hard miles for the honeymoon in Wyoming, and then it helped us move to Platteville.*

Owen arranged to pay the remaining two hundred dollars plus interest in twelve monthly installments. Then he headed for home, not quite believing what he had done. He needed a special way to tell Ruby.

When Owen drove up the street to park by the lilac bushes, Ruby was working at her new flowerbed near the front door. She looked around, startled, and pushed herself to her feet. "Owen, what on earth is that?"

Owen walked around the car, bowed low, and gestured toward the car with an exaggerated flourish. "This, my dear princess, is your new royal carriage."

Ruby walked toward him. "Owen Mattison, did you buy a brand-new car? Without even telling me you were looking?"

"It isn't brand-new. In fact, it's two years old. If it looks brand-new, that's a bonus."

"How can we ever afford it?"

"It's not that much—$325. They gave me $125 for the T, and we pay off the $200 over a year."

"But Owen, what made you think we need a new car, when we need so many other things for the baby?"

Owen walked past the lilac bushes to place his hands lightly on Ruby's elbows. "Rube, it is our biggest need. When the baby comes, it will be snowing. I will not take my wife and child in an open car through a snowstorm."

"But that's nearly six months away. Why the hurry?"

"The hurry is because I know my Ruby. You aren't going to stay cooped up at home, and when you go out, you've got no business cranking an old Ford." Owen took Ruby's arm and led her toward the car. "See, this has an electric starter. It has a battery and generator, so the lights will burn even when the motor isn't running. And it has a heater, which will be really important for the baby."

Owen opened the front passenger door for Ruby. His hand on her elbow urged her into the car, but Ruby planted her feet firmly and shook her head. "You claim we need the car with an electric starter so I can drive it. Well, let's just see. I'll drive right now, if you don't mind."

Owen solemnly walked his wife around the front end of the automobile and opened the driver's door for her. "Your Highness," he said, "the horses await your command. Allow me to serve as your footman."

* * *

Ruby sat quietly behind the steering wheel. Her mind was in turmoil. *There are so many things that we need more than a new car, I've got a long list. He could have told me he was interested in trading for a new car. He could have invited me to go shopping with him. And now he wants to play a children's game.* A new thought made her annoyance fade. *Maybe he has the imagination needed to be a great father.*

"You may think you're a footman," she said, "but you're really my Prince Charming."

* * *

When the Starks approached, Rev. Daniel Cobb stepped forward to grasp Martha's hand with both of his. "Good morning, Martha. It's so good to see you. I look forward to it every Sunday."

"That was another fine sermon, Dan. It's given me a great deal to think about."

"Thank you, I'm glad you liked it." As Cobb reached out to take Arthur's hand, his voice became quieter and less cordial. "Arthur, could I see you briefly in my study? Say, five or six minutes from now? That is, if Martha will excuse us."

"Sure, Dan. I'll drop in for a few minutes."

The Starks moved on into the warm July sunlight, where groups stood on the walk talking quietly.

"I'm not invited to the study," Martha said. "If it's about that boring finance committee, I'm delighted to miss it. I'll talk to people for a while. Then I'll wait for you in the car."

"Thank you, dear, for being so understanding."

Arthur examined the spines of shelved books in the pastor's study, noting the titles but feeling little interest in their contents. He was beginning on his second circuit of the room when Cobb came in, apologizing for Arthur's wait.

The two men sat down, and the minister plunged into his topic. "I'm sure you know, Arthur, it has been common knowledge since you marched down Main Street that you belong to the Klan. We've never talked about it, you and I, because I never discuss activities outside the church with members unless they ask for advice."

"I appreciate that, Dan."

"I had a telephone call Friday from Dr. Gerald Ostrum, who identified himself as the Exalted Cyclops of the Platte Valley Klan. I didn't tell him I recognized his name from newspaper stories."

"Gerry told me he planned to call you. I didn't encourage him—in fact, I tried to discourage him. I guess I was too subtle, since he called you anyway."

"I was astonished when he asked permission to come to the service next Sunday and present two hundred dollars to First Methodist. He was clearly not interested in just mailing us a check."

"I'll bet he specified some conditions."

"He wanted to lead a group up to the pulpit to make the presentation, say a few words, and offer a prayer. He said he called well in advance so I could plan the worship program and let him know at what point they should enter the sanctuary. He said they would wear robes and caps but no masks, and he suggested I talk to you if I had questions about the organization. I said I had some reservations, but I would consider his offer."

"It's appropriate to have reservations. Tell me what they are."

"Frankly, I don't want to build a worship service around the very men who marched into town and demonstrated how—excuse me for saying it—how vicious they can be."

"That doesn't offend me, Dan. Some vicious things went on that day that damaged the Klan's reputation. You know, we build a reputation for decency partly by making donations to Protestant churches."

"I believe the Presbyterians got a donation from the Klan last fall. I never spoke to Jed Rollins about it, but he must have made some arrangement like the one Ostrum proposed."

"I'm sure," Stark said, "that there was such an arrangement. But I'm upset that Gerry Ostrum thinks what worked back in October is all right now, after the klavern showed such a dark side to the town."

"Arthur, I'm beginning to understand your feelings on the question, but I should ask you point-blank. You belong to the finance committee, so you have an idea of the good things we could accomplish in this church with two hundred dollars. Should I accept the offer?"

"No, you should not. Some people would say you were making a bargain with the devil."

"Not to be overdramatic," the minister said, "but you seem to say this church should not sell its soul for two hundred dollars."

"Not for two hundred or any other number of dollars, but ideas about souls and salvation are more in your line of work than they are in mine. See, I joined the Klan because it has the same enemies as the church and the schools—things like bathtub gin and crazy dancing and the whole flapper outlook on life. I'm beginning to see that when goals are the same, methods can be different. The right goal doesn't always make the method right."

"That's an important realization." The minister glanced at his wristwatch. "I gather you won't object if I tell Dr. Ostrum to keep his two hundred dollars."

"Not at all. I'll tell him for you, if you want."

"I promised to call him tomorrow, so I'll tell him. And I'm sure you have a status to maintain there, so I won't tell him that we talked. Now I think we've kept Martha waiting long enough." Cobb rose to his feet.

Arthur stood up. He grasped his pastor's hand and shook it heartily. *Not only a good preacher, this Dan Cobb, but a fine man.*

Chapter 14

"I CAN'T BELIEVE WE'VE never been to a carnival together," Ruby said.

Owen and Ruby strolled arm in arm along the Pickle Day midway. The event's organizers called on Owen, as on previous Vo Ag teachers, to help judge the harvest displays. Their camping trip was delayed, which disappointed Ruby, but she said she would make up for it by enjoying the fair. Ruby's pregnancy was obvious then, the second week of August, and Owen haltingly asked if she would be comfortable, going out in public. Ruby laughed at him. She wasn't going to miss the fun just because people might suspect she was expecting.

The second booth in the row gave the event its name. The Kuner Company offered free dill pickles, their main product, to all comers. Susan Lydell stood behind the counter, using tongs to lift pickles from a barrel of brine onto two plates. Each plate was next to a stack of paper napkins.

Owen greeted Mrs. Lydell, who looked up from her work and laid her tongs on the counter. "Well, hello yourself, Owen and Ruby. Ruby, you look wonderful."

"Thank you, Mrs. Lydell. How are your boys?"

"Please call me Susan. The boys are fine. Ronald is happy with his Vo Ag project, and Robbie is all excited because our mare is going to foal again." Suddenly Susan Lydell blushed. "I'm s-sorry. I didn't mean that seeing you made me think of the mare."

Ruby's laughter rang through the fairway. "It's all right. I do feel some kinship with your mare."

Owen picked up a paper napkin and wrapped it around a pickle, which he presented to Ruby. "I'll bet you could use one of these."

"You aren't limited to one," Susan said. "Eat as many as you like. I went on regular pickle binges when I was expecting Ronald."

Owen wrapped a pickle for himself. "I don't think Ruby has those cravings."

"How fortunate," Susan said. "Thanks to the good Lord."

Ruby finished her mouthful of pickle before she responded. "More thanks to nutritional science, I think. I've been on a diet that focuses nourishment on the baby but provides the essentials for me."

A young mother followed three children to the counter, insisting they take only one pickle each. Another family approached from the opposite direction, so Mrs. Lydell began lifting more pickles from the barrel. Ruby and Owen bade her farewell and wandered on along the midway.

Two booths farther, they came upon the baseball toss. Two youths stood at the counter, throwing fierce pitches at metal objects shaped like pint milk bottles. Half a dozen stacks of three bottles each stood on a long table at the back of the tent. Owen recognized his baseball team members, Matt Stark and Terry Sweetman.

Owen was guiding Ruby past the baseball toss when Matt saw him. "Hey, Coach," the youth called. "Come try your luck. See if you can win a prize!"

Owen saw the prizes, ranging from glass ashtrays and garish painted plates to assorted stuffed animals, on a table at the side of the tent. He greeted the boys but expected to walk on past.

Ruby stopped. "Owen, that looks like fun. Can you win one of those teddy bears? We'll want one when the baby comes."

"Probably make a fool of myself," Owen muttered. He remembered his embarrassment when he needed three tries to sink a free throw, showing basketball basics to the girls.

"Come on, Coach," Matt said, "I'm ahead of Terry, three to two. See if you can get ahead of me."

Owen introduced Ruby to the boys, who responded shyly to her inquiries about their families. Then he walked to the counterman and asked, "How do I win one of those big teddy bears?"

"Knock three bottles entirely off the table, you win a coupon. Fifteen coupons get you the bear."

"How much do the balls cost?"

"One ball is a nickel. You get eleven balls for four bits, twenty-four for a dollar."

Owen turned toward the boys. "Don't wait for me," he said, "go ahead."

"We're resting now," Matt said. "Right, Terry?"

"Yeah. And Matt is trying to borrow money to get more balls."

Owen tossed a dollar bill onto the counter. "I'll take twenty-four," he said. "Give me fourteen, and give five each to these characters."

The counterman set down two dozen dirty, scarred, and misshapen baseballs on the counter and gave ten of them to the boys. Owen glanced at Ruby standing quietly beside him. He wondered if she understood what a sleazy operation it was. Balls that would not take a straight path through the air, bottles weighted heavily to stay upright. Or understand how easy it would be for their coach to look foolish before his athletes.

He seized a ball, thrust it toward her nose, and demanded, "Would you like to throw the opening pitch?"

Ruby shook her head firmly. Ashamed of letting his annoyance show, Owen faced the stacks consisting of two bottles an inch apart with the third bottle balanced on top of them. Ideally the ball should go to the center of that space between the lower bottles, knocking them both off the table and causing the top bottle to tumble. The pitch should be fast and hard and direct; nothing could be gained by falling down from above. He stepped back to make room for a windup and threw as hard as he could at one of the stacks. The ball hit high on the top bottle, knocking it over, and smashed against the canvas backdrop. Three more throws were needed to dispatch the two lower bottles.

Owen called on the boys to take a turn. Matt swept away one stack with two throws; Terry missed entirely with one throw and refused to throw again. Owen shut off every sensation but the line stretching fourteen feet from the counter to the bottles. He controlled his breathing carefully and whipped the ball across the space. All three bottles tumbled off the table, and cheers sounded behind him.

Owen heard "way to go, Coach" and "hit 'em again!" He turned to see six familiar Platteville High students in a semicircle behind him. Other people, total strangers, were pausing to watch. His struggle with the battered baseballs was none of their business. Then a new thought showed the way to ignore them. *I'm just a kid again, showing off for my girl.*

After the attendant replaced the bottles, Owen knocked down four stacks with a total of six throws. He called on the boys again. Matt got one stack with his three remaining balls, while Terry recovered his poise to knock off two stacks with his four. Owen then used his remaining four balls to vanquish two more bottle trios.

The attendant slapped down eight coupons in front of Owen. "You're doin' great, buddy," he said. "Buy another buck's worth to win that big bear for your missus." He doled out coupons to Matt and Terry.

Matt pulled three coupons out of his shirt pocket, added them to the two just given him, and placed the five on top of Owen's eight. "Mr. Mattison, I don't want any of this guy's junk. You better use my coupons."

"Me either," Terry pronounced, adding four more to the pile. "Does that give you enough for the bear?"

"Too many, I think, thank you." Owen counted out fifteen coupons, returning leftovers to each boy. Handing coupons to the attendant, he said, "Give us that big brown bear, the one with the blue ribbon."

The man did as requested, handing the two-feet-tall bear to Owen, who spun around and placed it in Ruby's arms. There was a cheer from the assembled crowd that grew louder when Owen planted a kiss on Ruby's cheek. Ruby's face turned pink, but it was easy for Owen to believe her smile.

Ruby hugged the bear to her bosom with her left arm and reached out with her right hand to Terry and Matt. "Thank you, Matt, and thank you, Terry. I'm honored you gave up your souvenirs to give our baby this wonderful bear. And Matt, please say hello to Irene for me."

Owen and Ruby left the midway to attend the harvest exhibit prize ceremonies. Owen and the other judges were introduced to the crowd in the exhibit tent. Any complaints about their work were to be made on the spot, "or forever hold your peace." No complaints were voiced. Then the Mattisons walked to the Methodist Church, where the ladies' auxiliary sold buffet dinners.

After their meal, Owen expressed mild interest in the movie showing at the Rex Theater, but Ruby knew she would only fall asleep in a dark room. They returned home, and Ruby went to bed while Owen packed camping equipment into the Chevrolet.

* * *

Owen dismantled the three sections of his fishing pole, gathered up his gear, and followed the path up through the aspens to their camp. In full daylight, the tree trunks were starkly white; and although Owen felt no breeze, the golden aspen leaves were quivering. They were called quaking aspen because their small leaves waved from side to side if the air moved at all. The bright gold of the aspen leaves complemented equally brilliant red and orange vegetation to make a symphony of fall colors. It seemed remarkable for the third week of August.

In five minutes, Owen reached the Chevrolet, where he stored his fishing gear. He went on to the tent and quietly pulled the entrance flap aside. Ruby was still asleep on her cot. Owen poured water from the water bag hanging on a car bumper into the coffeepot. He lit the one-burner coal oil stove, turned up the flame, measured ground coffee into the percolator, closed the top basket, and put the pot on the burner.

Then he gathered twigs and branches to lay a fire in the circle of rocks that made a fireplace. He touched a match to the pyramid of twigs. When the square of branches surrounding the pyramid burned nicely, he got the kitchen box from the car's backseat to take out the frying pan, tin plates, and tableware.

He set the frying pan over three rocks of equal size placed several inches apart and pushed most of the fire between the rocks. As the frying pan was heating, he placed a spoonful of lard in it to melt. He poured flour onto a plate, stirred in some salt, made a pass with the pepper shaker, and rolled the four trout in the mixture.

"Good morning. It looks like you had some luck." Ruby stood in the tent opening, dressed in her usual jodhpurs, stretching and yawning.

"It is a good morning, I caught four nice ones. They aren't giants, but they are legal. Can you stand a couple of fresh trout for breakfast?"

"Oh yes." Ruby looked around and out through the aspens toward the mountain peaks. "It's so lovely here, and this cool air makes me hungry. I'm glad we came."

"You know I always keep my promises." Owen set the frying pan down carefully and walked toward Ruby.

She shook her finger at him, smiling. "No, you don't. I need to brush my teeth." Ruby went back into the tent, to return carrying a hairbrush and a small bag of toiletries. "I'll bet," she told Owen, "you have breakfast ready when I get back."

Owen saw that the coffeepot was perking rhythmically. Then he set the frying pan back on the campfire, gave it a moment to heat up, and pulled it back to receive the four trout.

Next Owen retrieved a wooden crate from the Chevy. He opened a folding campstool and set it near the upended crate: Ruby's breakfast table. He went to the fire to turn the trout over, found the tomato juice can, punctured it, and poured juice into two tin tumblers. He removed the frying pan from the fire, tested the trout for doneness with a fork, and turned the two smaller fish onto Ruby's tin plate and the other two onto his own.

As he poured coffee, Ruby walked out of the aspens. "Owen, that fish smells great, but I don't need a table. I'm happy eating on the ground."

"Maybe you're happy, but it's a bad idea. It is getting hard for you to get down that low and harder yet to get up."

"I can still bend over. If this crate is going to be a table, it should be a table for two." Ruby placed her juice glass on the plate next to the trout. "I'll hold everything up while you turn this thing on its side." She held her plate in the air with one hand and lifted the tin coffee cup with the other. "Now lay this down and bring the other campstool."

Owen did her bidding. Their plates were near each other on the makeshift table, and he was seated across from her, twisting his body to keep his knees out of the way, but able to look into her eyes. "You know," Owen said, "you're pretty smart."

Ruby smiled at him. She lifted her plate from the crate to her lap and lifted a forkful of trout to her mouth. After murmuring approval, she said, "You kept your cooking talent completely hidden until I got pregnant. I'll have lots of babies, if you'll go on cooking. I'll just plan the menus."

"Sorry, I'm only an outdoor cook. Nothing comes out right when I work in the kitchen." Owen felt his face form a grin. "But that was a nice try."

The sun was well up in the sky, and the day was becoming warm. His attention drawn by the flash of a bird in the woods, Owen turned to look. The bird was gone, but the golden aspen leaves trembled before his eyes. He could not feel a breeze, but Owen suddenly shivered. He wanted to reach for Ruby's hand, but she was busy with her trout.

* * *

"Hello, stranger," Isabel said to Owen. "You look brown as a berry. Did you get away for a vacation?"

"Yes, we had nearly a week in the mountains. Chilly at night, but we had a fine time, and the fishing was great."

"Did the travel cause any problems for Ruby?"

"No, the whole trip was really her idea."

"I was with Ruby at Mizpah Cemetery work sessions and learned that congratulations are in order. You'll soon be a father."

"Not too soon. About mid-December, we think."

"I'm happy for you both. Ruby is very happy about it."

Conversation died as Ms. Banbury entered the room and took her seat, calling the meeting to order. Owen took out his small notebook, ready to record any new policies. The principal quickly covered several routine items, including the reaffirmation of faculty sponsorship for each of the four classes.

Counting the principal, there were six regular faculty members. Since Superintendent Healy taught one class, he could be counted as number seven; and Mrs. Parker, who led the special instruction for Catholics, made eight. As part-time teachers, the last two were excused from the meeting, and Ms. Banbury wanted to take advantage of their absence.

She drew some notes out of a folder, and her tone suddenly was anything but routine. "I would now like to initiate a confidential discussion of the separate moral instruction for Protestant and Catholic students. We have this chance to talk among ourselves, without students or parents or administrators listening, so I invite your candid opinions."

Owen smiled to himself. Although she taught barely half time, Ms. Banbury identified herself as a faculty member, not an administrator.

The principal continued. "I've been discussing this matter with the grade school principal, to the end that we may approach the school board on behalf of the two faculties to ask them for a reconsideration of the policy. So I'd like to go around the table and invite your reactions."

Ms. Banbury turned to face the colleague on her right. "Would you care to begin, Mrs. Nelson?"

Isabel folded her hands on the tabletop. "It's too early to say for sure, but in the last two days, I haven't noticed any difference from last year. The separation by religion has not become a routine part of the day. There is a disturbance every morning when the Catholic students leave their homerooms. The Protestant students harass them verbally this fall, same as they did last spring.

"I don't know what the board hopes the Bible reading will eventually accomplish. I don't think student behavior has improved any, if that was their intention. And I resent their prohibition of discussion. I teach literature classes, and many Bible passages could be springboards into fruitful discussions.

"I appreciate the court's ruling that Catholic students can't be forced to attend the Bible readings. Maybe they are getting benefits from their separate instruction. I hope so. On balance, if the board regards the Bible-reading requirement as an experiment, I'd have to say that it's been a failure."

Ms. Banbury thanked Mrs. Nelson for her candid comments, and then she nodded her head at Owen as the next in line.

Owen spoke quietly but forcefully. "I would endorse everything Mrs. Nelson has said. The Bible-reading requirement divides the school. The Catholic students hate being marked as different, and the Protestant kids love to remind them of it. And this carries on even outside the classroom. It destroys school unity, and it threatens the spirit of our athletic teams. The baseball team got over it last spring because a couple of its best players were Catholic, and they showed they deserved their positions. But it was a problem for both the speedball team and the men's basketball squad.

"I don't know where Mrs. Nelson got the idea that the Bible-reading requirement could be an experiment, but I hope it's true. If something is undertaken in an experimental mood, it should be easy to judge it a failure and end it. In my opinion, the Bible-reading requirement tears the school apart without providing any measurable benefit. I'd like to see it closed down."

Ms. Banbury elicited the opinions of the other four faculty members, as she had promised. All four elaborated on the points that Isabel and Owen had made but added no new arguments. Ms. Banbury expressed gratitude for their opinions and promised to join the grade school principal in seeking a hearing with the school board. Owen went home feeling that at least one faculty meeting had not been a waste of time.

* * *

161

"Keep away!" Billy shouted. "That's a mad dog. If you get close, he'll bite you!"

Owen grabbed the spaniel's collar and tugged on it mightily. Gus looked at him for an instant. Owen looked into the dog's deep brown eyes, and the snarl began to fade. "Come on, boy," Owen urged. "Let's go home."

Billy advanced again, threatening with the stick. Gus shook his head, nearly loosening Owen's grasp, bared his teeth, and barked frantically. Owen worked around in front of the dog, in between Gus and Billy. The dog calmed down gradually, and Owen led Gus away.

Hours passed without Owen knowing it. He lit the parlor lamp against the dusk and began his homework.

His father came into the parlor, looking grave. "Owen, I've just been talking to McCaffrey. He claims Gus has gone mad, his kids are afraid of the dog, and he says that Gus should be put down."

"But Pa! Billy teases him with sticks! No wonder Gus snarls at them."

"This is serious, Owen. McCaffrey says he saw Gus himself. Claims he knows what mad dogs are like. He says if we don't take care of the dog, he'll get the sheriff to do it. Now Gus is your dog, and he's your responsibility. I'm sorry."

Gus came when Owen called and did not protest when the rope was tied around his neck. Holding the rifle in one hand, Owen led the dog into the pasture and tied him to a fence post. Owen backed away a few feet. Gus followed him, until stopped by the rope. In the fading light, Owen aimed carefully between the dark brown eyes and began to squeeze the trigger. But he could not fire. The brown eyes he was looking into had changed. They were no longer Gus's eyes. They were Ruby's soft brown eyes, regarding him steadily.

Owen stirred, in between sleep and consciousness. The sweaty pillow seemed less real than the dream. He felt Ruby beside him, breathing softly. It had been years since Owen recalled having to shoot Gus. He didn't even know Ruby then. Awake, Owen turned to lie on his back and stared into the darkness.

Chapter 15

OWEN QUIETLY OPENED THE front door. Ruby sat in their lone easy chair, her head sunk onto her chest, sound asleep, with a booklet resting on the chair arm. Owen shook his head. She needed more rest, but that wasn't a healthy position for sleep. When the cool air of late October had no effect, he closed the door with measured force. She looked up with bleary eyes.

"Hello, Rube. You'll get a stiff neck, sleeping like that."

"I guess I dozed off." She yawned and rubbed her eyes. "It surprises me, because I wasn't bored or sleepy."

Owen walked to the chair, bent down, and kissed her cheek. "What's in that booklet that's so fascinating?"

Ruby pulled a stubby pencil and a scrap of paper from the publication. "It's supposed to help name the baby. It gives lots of names with their meanings."

Owen sat down on the sofa. "You mean, like Rex is Latin for 'king.'"

Ruby smiled. "You know, I always thought Rex was a dog's name until I saw the Rex Theater here."

"You aren't thinking of Rex for our son's name, are you?"

"No, no. I was mostly using this booklet to write on. I've been writing down various names to see how they look."

"How they look is more important than what they mean?"

"No, I've been writing them down and then reading them out loud. I really mean how they sound, not how they look."

"I don't like the sound of Rex," Owen declared, "no matter what it means."

"How you react to a name depends a lot on experience. If you know someone with the same name, it influences how you think of them. The only Rex I ever knew was a dog. But there's another thing to consider. In some families, a few names get used again and again to bind the family together."

"Well, I'm not thrilled with families that use the same name time after time and have Charley the Second and Charley the Third. When they use Roman numerals, that's plain pretentious."

"Can't you imagine an Owen James Mattison, Junior?"

"No, I can't. There aren't any Juniors in our family. I don't respect fathers who name sons after themselves."

"How about naming a baby after a grandfather or a grandmother? Remember, the baby may surprise you by being a girl."

"Well, grandfathers would be all right, so we should consider grandmothers too."

"Our two families live so far apart, maybe we can bring them together a little by using names from both families."

"There's nothing wrong with that, but I would have to hear the name to decide. Like you said, a lot depends on how it sounds."

"How would you like to name a daughter after her two grandmothers, your mother and mine? That would be Rebecca Kate Mattison."

"That would be fine, if we have to name a girl. As long as we can call her Becky around the house . . . but suppose it's a boy?"

Ruby grinned at him. "I was teasing you. We should be ready for a girl, but the way I've been growing in the last few weeks, I'm sure it will be a boy. And he'll be playing baseball. It feels like he's having batting practice already."

Owen grinned. "Well, I don't want to name him Babe Ruth. How about Ty Cobb?"

"I've got two family names that are better. Let's name a boy after your youngest brother and my youngest brother. Peter Glenn Mattison."

"That sounds good," Owen said. He picked the paper scrap out of Ruby's lap and examined it. "And it looks all right too. But we've got at least two months, so we don't have to decide right away. To start with, we can talk about it over dinner." Owen directed a look of mock pleading at his wife. "You are planning on dinner this evening, aren't you?"

"You poor starving man! We're having cold cuts with potato salad and fresh fruit. Come on, help me set the table."

Ruby rose up awkwardly from the easy chair, grasping Owen's hand.

* * *

Stark threw down his pen and hurried out the back door.

"Surprise, Pop!" Matt called. "It was finished, so Mr. Mattison said I could bring it home if I could get it loaded. Hope you don't mind, I took the team and wagon."

"We'll talk about your poor judgment later. Who owns that other team?"

"They are the Baileys'. They just got them last month. Ed talked his Pa into letting us take them."

"Hello, Mr. Stark!" The neighbor boy, who had been sitting down out of sight, stood up in the wagon as Matt halted the horses.

Arthur acknowledged Ed Bailey's greeting and nodded as Matt called out the names of his other three classmates as they stood up. Arthur walked around the wagon, inspecting the brooder house. It was a solid piece of construction. And Matt got it done ahead of schedule. Proved he could stick to a major project and finish it.

Arthur asked, "How much does this thing weigh?"

"We figure," Matt answered, "between a quarter and half a ton."

"How did you get it loaded?"

"We dragged it up two ramps with a block and tackle fastened to a ceiling rafter." Matt began to climb down from the wagon seat. "Everybody in the class helped. Then we just barely cleared the shop door getting it out."

"I hope you have a plan for unloading it." Arthur addressed his son eye to eye as Matt had jumped down from the wagon.

"Yes, sir, but first we have to get it to exactly the right place. You can help me be sure about that. We'll lead the horses now."

Arthur recognized a new self-confidence in Matt. Some serious carpentry could work wonders, and it didn't hurt to win a few baseball games.

Matt led the horses slowly through the cottonwoods, steering carefully to avoid low-hanging branches, and finally turning into a space between the granary and the equipment shed. Remembering the tour of possible sites with Owen Mattison a year earlier with a less mature Matt, Arthur confirmed Matt's choice of site.

Matt jockeyed the wagon until the brooder house windows faced south. Then he asked his father to hold the horses steady during the unloading. Arthur reminded Matt to set the wagon's brake.

The boys took down the stakes that formed one side of the wagon and carefully placed two beams against the wagon bed, which became ramps. Then with great effort, they pried and pushed the brooder house onto the top of the ramps. Next they pried and heaved, lifting the side of the structure until it slid nearly five feet down the ramps and touched the ground. It rested at an extreme angle, with one side on the ground and the other high up on the ramps.

"Now comes the hard part," Matt told his father. "The five of us will go to the high side and support as much of the weight as we can. When I give the signal, you walk the horses forward to pull away the ramps. We'll try to slow the fall so that nothing gets broken."

"I can see," Arthur said, "that's the only thing to do. But you all be careful!

Keep your hands out of the way." Arthur walked to the front of the wagon and reached up to release the brake.

The boys found places, three between the two ramps and one outside of each ramp. Arthur went to the bridles of the lead team. When all muscles were tensed, Matt nodded, Arthur led the horses away, and the brooder house landed on solid ground with a crash and clatter.

Arthur stopped the horses, reset the brake, and joined the boys looking over the building. Its slanted roof was six feet off the ground at its high point. The row of windows facing south promised natural warmth. Fastened at the bottom, they could easily be opened when the heat grew excessive. Arthur Stark confirmed the small miracle the boys had already discovered. No windows were broken.

"Thank you, boys," Arthur said, "Matt couldn't have done it without your help. There's no way you can catch the school bus, so I'll give you a ride home in the Reo."

"Not just yet," a new voice said. Martha Stark walked up to the group from beside a cottonwood trunk, where she had watched the unloading. "I didn't know you were coming, so there's nothing special. But come into the kitchen for cold milk and cookies from the jar."

* * *

The classroom door opened. Owen got to his feet, for out of the room marched the dumpy form of Ms. Banbury, the principal. "Good evening, ma'am."

Owen glanced at his wristwatch and then held out Ms. Banbury's coat.

Ms. Banbury's voice diminished nearly to a whisper. "Apparently Harold Healy dropped some hints, and they agreed to reconsider the Bible reading. So we don't have to request a review. The best thing is, they're in a reasonable mood." Then she shifted to her normal volume. "Please say hello to Mrs. Mattison for me. Farewell." Her shoes tapped away down the hall.

Owen glanced at his watch. Still half a minute to go. The classroom door opened again, and Arthur Stark walked out. Owen scrambled to his feet again. "Hello, Mattison. Change of signals. We've decided to take a break. Come on in." Owen entered the classroom, seeing the familiar table, with a single chair in the space between the table and the first row of student desks. He saw the open door leading to the administrative offices. "The other members have gone to the men's room. It gives us a chance to talk for a minute. Please take a seat."

To Owen's surprise, Stark did not go to a chair behind the long table but sat at a student desk. So Stark was not speaking as a school board member. Man to man, not employer to employee. Owen sat down two desks away.

"I'm sure you know," Stark said, "that Matthew brought the brooder house home last week."

"Yes, sir. It took the whole class to load it onto your wagon. I'm relieved that it got there safely."

"It was a shock to see that house coming down my driveway."

Owen stifled a grin. "You didn't know that Matt was bringing it home?"

"He hadn't even told us it was finished. I gather you didn't ask him if we knew about it."

"Why, no. When he showed up with the wagon and two teams, I assumed he had your permission."

Arthur Stark shook his head. "It was his idea of a joke. Maybe I can laugh about it years from now."

"He did a remarkable job on the brooder house," Owen said. "I'm giving him the highest possible grade for the project."

"Yes, it's a good solid structure. It should last a hundred years unless the termites get to it. Or dry rot."

"The stringers it rests on were treated with creosote, which should help."

"That was one of the ideas you came up with that didn't occur to Matt. You did a good job teaching him, and the brooder house shows it."

"Matt is all right. He has the sense to realize when he's made a mistake and knows where to find out about fixing it."

The other members of the school board came through the door, followed by Superintendent Healy. Stark took his seat at the long table, and Owen moved to the lonesome chair provided for the faculty member.

Board President Newton Maclean tapped the table lightly with a small gavel. "The recess has expired, and the meeting remains in order."

Maclean turned in his chair to face Owen. "Mr. Mattison, thank you for coming. We are talking to several faculty members about the Bible-reading policy and the separate Catholic instruction, so we can understand their impact on the school. We are doing this in closed session to encourage your frankness. Platteville's citizens have strong opinions on the subject that we've been hearing for more than a year. We want to have a quiet talk with faculty members, who should know more about how the policy is working, than the public can ever learn through gossip. Does this procedure meet with your approval?"

Owen curbed an impulse to simply shrug his shoulders. "It sounds good to me, sir."

"First," Maclean continued, "we want you to think back to when the Bible readings began. Did you have advance warning that the walkout would occur?"

"That was the first day of school last fall. A student came up to me before school began to explain why Catholic students could not remain for the Bible reading, so I had a few minutes' warning."

"Who was that student?"

Owen hesitated. Did he have to take sides? "I believe he spoke to me in confidence, Mr. Maclean."

Maclean seemed taken aback. "Well, uh, did you make some kind of promise? Of confidentiality? And, uh, do you think it still applies?"

It was a point worth making; there had to be limits to the board's intrusions. But it was time to give in. "No, I made no such promise, and I was not asked to. That student was, and is, willing to take responsibility for his actions. It was Francis Koblenz. He goes by Frank."

"And just what did you say to young Koblenz?"

"I said that I would have to discuss the matter with Ms. Banbury, but they could go that morning if they came back in five minutes."

Treasurer Thompson spoke up. "We've heard from Ms. Banbury about the emergency faculty meeting, when the faculty decided to tolerate the walkout. Did you support that policy?"

"Yes, I did. But only until your board reversed it."

Maclean waved a dismissive hand at Thompson and regained control of the questioning. "And two other students, Nathan Gorman and Margaret Fitzgerald, walked out with Koblenz?"

If he already knew, why did he ask? But Owen answered, "That is correct."

"How did the Protestant students react to the walkout?"

"They were taken by surprise that first day, but even then, they resented it. They felt the others should not be excused when they were required to listen to the Bible selection."

"Did this resentment continue after the Catholic students were given religious instruction of their own?"

"Resentment may not be the right word, but the bad feelings certainly continued. At that age, students can't stand to be different. They want to belong, to be part of the herd. And they can be very mean to those who don't belong. As it is now, the school is torn apart every morning for separate versions of the opening ceremonies. That destroys the unity of the school, and that disunity carries over into athletic endeavors. It damages the team spirit needed to win games."

Arthur Stark spoke emphatically. "Are you trying to say we should give up the idea? Have the school day open with no moral instruction?"

"Well, Mr. Stark, you have to weigh instructional methods according to their effectiveness. In vocational agriculture, we find the best learning comes from experience, so we require a major experimental project from each student. And look at the athletic program. We expect it to teach things through experience, like teamwork, taking the initiative, and striving to win but not quitting when you lose."

Stark's own son had benefited from both programs. Would he acknowledge that? Owen fell silent, fearing that he had said too much. His feeling seemed confirmed when silence engulfed the room.

After a long minute, Roy Thompson broke the silence. "Of course, there is an important role for learning by experience. You teach automobile repairing that way, and Vo Ag that way, and cooking and sewing that way, for the girls. But everyone should learn to deal with the abstract as well as the concrete. They should learn to deal with ideas of right and wrong. Over time, that will build student character."

Superintendent Healy stirred for the first time since taking his seat. "Gentlemen," he said, "I wish to support Mr. Thompson's statement. Consider the humanities. My own training has been mostly in science, and I sometimes regret it. You have taken the approach that moral ideas must be presented directly, through precepts found in the Bible. Maybe the best way for students to confront moral ideas is to study them indirectly, when they are found in great works of drama, or art, or literature."

Newton Maclean picked up his gavel with his right hand. Rather than tapping the table, he merely let it fall into his left palm. "We can't hope to solve the great questions of educational philosophy tonight. And I have to close off this discussion with Mr. Mattison because our next faculty member will be waiting in the hall. But I want to thank you, Mr. Mattison, for bringing up some points I want to think about very carefully."

"He's right, Mattison," Arthur Stark said. "You have given us food for thought. Your remarks about learning through experience are particularly important, and I join in expressing our gratitude. Unfortunately we must move on. Please ask your colleague to come right in."

* * *

When Owen reached home, he gave Ruby a weather report. "There's a chill wind out there tonight. It feels like snow, and it's so overcast you can't see any stars." He took his coat to the closet, then came over to the stove that warmed the little house, rubbing his hands together.

"The first big snow came just after Thanksgiving last year," Ruby said. "And that's only a week away, so we may be in for it. But tell me about the school board. Were they friendlier than last time?"

Owen sat down across the table from Ruby. "Oh yes. Ms. Banbury was going out as I went in. She whispered that they were in a reasonable mood tonight. The board took a break then, and Arthur Stark asked me in for a private chat."

When Owen described Stark's pleasure with Matt's brooder house, Ruby again questioned how Stark's attitudes as father and school board member could avoid conflict with Klan beliefs. She recalled Irene Stark's comment that her brother claimed their father disliked the twentieth century.

Owen said, "I'm sure he doesn't want to keep nineteenth-century methods. He practices scientific farming and wants it taught in Vo Ag. But he is upset about young people's behavior and deplores the failure to enforce Prohibition. I think he is the strongest supporter of Bible reading, but when I spoke out against it for dividing the school, he thanked me and said I gave them a lot to think about. When the other board members came back in, President Maclean started out with a nosy question, asking what student warned me about the walkout. When I suggested it might not be any of his business, he got kind of confused."

"Good for you!"

"In the end I had to confirm it was Frank Koblenz. The best news is, Superintendent Healy hinted that listening to the Bible may not be the best way to teach morals. And Mr. Thompson, the treasurer, agreed with me that learning through experience is important. Even Arthur Stark agreed with that."

"Do you think they might give up the Bible readings?"

"I think there is some chance of it. They did listen to what I had to say, and the fact they were even asking for faculty opinion is a good sign."

"What you say about Mr. Stark makes me think he is a nicer man than I realized. It makes his Klan membership even more mysterious."

Owen Mattison smiled at his wife. She was sitting calmly, sideways in her chair, so that her bulk would not collide with the tabletop. The baby would come in less than a month, but for now there was just the two of them. The little house was cozy, despite the storm gathering outside. More than he had for months, Owen felt at peace.

Chapter 16

OWEN HURRIED HOME AFTER Friday classes, mindful that Ruby's doctor said the baby could come at any time. Although the last snow was cleared only three days before, a strong wind drove clouds to block out the sun, threatening another storm. Owen hoped Ruby would not insist on attending that evening's school Christmas program to hear Irene Stark sing with the chorus and play a piano solo. Ruby had given her two additional lessons to perfect her number and polish a possible encore. Owen did not want Ruby to walk the few dozen yards to the high school entrance, because there would be snow and ice on the way home.

Owen entered their home through the unlocked front door. He half expected to see Ruby playing among the baby clothing and toys they brought home from the lavish shower given her by the Mizpah Club, but he did not see her in either the living or dining areas.

"Hey, Rube," he called, "I'm home." There was no answer. Owen hurried into the kitchen. Ruby was sitting in a chair by the kitchen table, using both arms to clasp her midsection. Her face was contorted, but she smiled wanly when she saw Owen. He dashed to her side. "It's started! You promised to call me."

Ruby inhaled a deep breath, and her shoulders slumped. "I don't need you yet—but I'm glad you're home." Owen took her hand, squeezed it firmly, and carried it to his lips.

"It started just after breakfast," Ruby said, "but I'm only having contractions every ten or eleven minutes. And I'm sure they're real—no more false labor. It will be hours before the baby comes."

"I'll feel better when we get you to the hospital."

"I don't want to go there just to wait. I was so embarrassed, getting everybody excited over false labor. If I get to the hospital early, they'll just say, 'Oh, it's her again.'"

"Next you'll want to stay here for the Christmas program because it starts in only five hours."

Ruby's ghostlike smile reappeared. "I have given up on that. Irene will be just fine without me there. We can go to the hospital after supper if the pains are closer together."

Owen shook his head. "Rube, we aren't having supper here. Clouds have hidden the sun, and the wind is rising. Every sign says another blizzard is coming. We are going to be in Greeley by supper time, while it is still daylight."

They argued for a few more minutes. Owen thought Ruby would be grateful to have the decision made for her, and he proved to be correct. They called Dr. Sorenson at his office in Ft. Collins. Most of his practice was in the college town, but he had stipulated that the birth take place in the Greeley hospital, half the distance between Ft. Collins and Platteville.

Ruby described her symptoms, and after Ruby introduced him, Owen asked the doctor about weather conditions north of Platteville. Dr. Sorenson said they should come to Greeley as soon as they were ready, and he would meet them at the hospital after Ft. Collins office hours.

Ruby made Owen eat some lunch leftovers before she would agree to leave. Then Owen loaded Ruby's suitcase into the Chevy, tucked a blanket around her when the coat would not button, and drove north through the first flakes of snow. In ten miles, the snow thickened and began to stick to the road, making Owen slow down. He squeezed Ruby's hand when the pains came.

When they reached the hospital, Ruby was taken to a labor room. Owen was shown into a room for expectant fathers, which was supplied with battered furniture, ashtrays, and old magazines. After half an hour, he was admitted to the labor room. The contractions were still about ten minutes apart, and Ruby was growing tired. Eventually Owen stopped trying to carry on a conversation between pains, so Ruby could doze. He returned to the waiting room to find a magazine.

When he carried it back toward the labor room, a nurse stopped him, saying that Dr. Sorenson had arrived and was examining Ruby. After another half hour, the doctor came into the fathers' room, shook Owen's hand, and reported his findings.

"Things are proceeding normally, but the cervix is not much dilated yet, so it will be several hours. Our main problem is, it is quite a large baby. I've taken an X-ray to be sure of what we have. Happily the presentation is the normal headfirst position. There is adequate room to effect the delivery, but I anticipate having to assist with forceps. For now, we must wait, and it's time for supper. I'm headed for the restaurant across the street. Would you care to join me?"

"Thank you, but I think my place is with my wife."

"Actually it was Ruby's suggestion. She's worried you haven't gotten adequate nourishment. Tell you what. You go see her. I'll be at the nurses' desk to catch up on paperwork. If you don't come in five minutes, I'll go on, but I expect Ruby will send you out."

The doctor's prediction was valid. Ruby said she liked Owen's company, but there was nothing he could do to help, so Owen should join Sorenson. When the storm was over, he could drive back home to bed. Owen said that they would see about that.

The restaurant was of the greasy spoon variety, but Dr. Sorenson was a gracious dinner companion. He was interested in the religious conflict in Platteville and in the Mattisons' reactions to the community, as well as the circumstances of their romance as students in Ft. Collins. Owen responded to the doctor's questions, but he brought the conversation back to Ruby and their baby. Since Sorenson had said the baby was unusually large, Owen told him of Ruby's special diet intended to focus nourishment on the child. Could that be the reason for the large baby?

The doctor answered thoughtfully. "A baby is considered to be abnormally large—a condition called macrosomia—when it weighs more than ten pounds at birth. This usually results from the mother developing diabetes during pregnancy. Well, I don't think your child will weigh more than ten pounds, and Ruby is not diabetic. She may have eaten foods that transferred more sugars through the placenta than other foods would have, but any result would be hard to measure. Don't forget heredity. Big parents tend to have big babies. You look six feet tall, and you weigh around two hundred, right?"

Owen nodded. He pushed his cherry pie away half-eaten, which made the doctor chuckle.

Outside, they found the blizzard had intensified. The driving wind was forming snowdrifts, and the street was slippery. There was no automobile traffic. Back inside the hospital, they stamped their feet to shake off the snow.

"That's a mean storm," Sorenson said. "We can't count on the roads being passable tomorrow morning, so I'm going to spend the night here. There's a resident's lounge I can sleep in. You won't return to Platteville, will you?"

"Tomorrow is Saturday," Owen replied. "I don't need to be there. Even if I did, I still belong here."

"This staff sees fathers as a nuisance, but I can get them to set up a cot for you in Ruby's room. She'll be happy to have you around."

* * *

Owen talked softly when Ruby's eyes were open, but she began to keep them closed between contractions. Late in the evening, Dr. Sorenson appeared again. He told Owen the dilation of the cervix was progressing well, and he made sure that the night duty nurse knew where to find him. He encouraged Ruby to rest whenever she could.

After the doctor left, Owen sat beside the bed and watched over her. Sometime after midnight, he became aware of Ruby stirring, then crying out sharply, and realized he had fallen asleep himself. He saw that Ruby did not really open her eyes during the contraction. When it ended, she was sound asleep. Owen went to the cot in the corner of the room, stretched out on it, and sank into fitful sleep.

Owen became aware of a commotion. He opened his eyes, blinking against the harsh light of every electric bulb in the room, and sat up on the cot. He saw Ruby was awake, but she did not return the "Good morning!" that he tried to make cheerful.

Dr. Sorenson came bustling into the room, followed by a nurse. "Morning, Mr. Mattison," the doctor said. "It looks like we have some action. If you'll go back to the waiting room, I'll come in to tell you about my exam."

Ruby was seized by a contraction that made her cry out. Owen wanted to stay, to reassure her, but the doctor had dismissed him. Going out of the room, he smiled the brightest smile he could muster, but Ruby's eyes were closed in pain.

In the waiting room, Owen looked at his wristwatch. Five minutes until five. He walked to the window, where an incompletely drawn shade left a glass area uncovered. Expecting to see restaurant lights across the street, he pulled aside the shade, but there were no lights. Apart from the faint glow of a distant street lamp, he saw nothing but a profound darkness. Staring into it, he realized all was silence beyond the window. The blizzard was over. Owen sank into a chair.

When Dr. Sorenson hurried into the room, Owen snapped awake. The doctor's air of urgency made Owen clamber to his feet.

"Things have speeded up," Sorenson announced. "The waters broke long ago, the cervix is completely dilated, and the contractions are less than five minutes apart. Ruby is being taken to the delivery room. It's Sunday morning, and anybody I called to assist would get here too late since streets are blocked by snowdrifts."

Owen wondered what point the doctor was making. The answer came when Sorenson continued. "You will have to administer the ether. I'll show you what to do. Come on now, let's get changed. We'll talk more about it on the way."

Sorenson marched away down the hall. Owen ran a hand through his hair, as if he could brush the cobwebs from his mind, and hurried to walk beside the physician.

"Ruby is worn out," the doctor said. "We need to take the edge off her pain these final minutes, but we need her to keep pushing, so she has to stay conscious. You'll be tempted to give her too much, but I'll keep an eye on you. For God's sake, let me know if you start to feel faint."

Owen believed he had never in his life felt faint. He trailed the doctor into an antechamber of the delivery room, containing three sinks and shelves stocked with linens. Sorenson scrubbed his hands thoroughly, giving Owen an example to follow. A nurse pulled white gowns over their arms and tied them behind their backs. He followed Sorenson into the delivery room and saw Ruby lying on her back, legs spread apart, with a white cloth draped over her knees. Sorenson paused while the nurse held rubber gloves for each of his plunging hands, another example for Owen. Then he walked to Ruby's head and motioned Owen to take a position on the other side.

"Ruby," Sorenson said, "I've brought a friend to help you out."

Owen stepped forward. "Hello, Rube. It won't be long now."

Ruby's eyes shifted from Sorenson to Owen. "Owen, who let you—" she began, but her face was contorted by another pain. Sorenson used the occasion to show Owen how to apply the ether cone and pour the ether. The result was apparent when a suddenly relaxed Ruby attempted to repeat her sentence, which came out, "Oo led chew in ear."

"It's all right, I'm learning how to do this. We'll do it at home next time and save money." Ruby grimaced, and Owen felt foolish. Not the right time for a joke.

"Listen, Ruby," Sorenson said. "When the next pain comes, I want you to push, push with all your might. Can you do that for me?"

Ruby answered with a word. "Hurts."

"Your husband is here to help, to see that it doesn't hurt so much." Sorenson pulled the white mask up over his nose and stationed himself at the foot of the table.

When the next contraction came, Sorenson urged Ruby to push, and Ruby's groan escalated into a scream. He nodded to Owen, who poured ether, smelling its sharp sweetness, and then remembered to stop. Ruby relaxed, but she remained awake. She even smiled back when Owen smiled at her.

"It will take a couple more," Sorenson said. He picked the forceps up from their resting place. Owen gripped the ether bottle more tightly. God forbid that Ruby should see the forbidding instrument. When the next pain came, Sorenson shouted, "Now push!"

Ruby cried again, and Owen poured, but no child appeared. Ruby's breath came in desperate pants until Dr. Sorenson repeated his command. Ruby screamed sharply, Owen poured more ether, and the room was suddenly filled by the baby's first cry.

"It's a boy," Sorenson announced, handing the baby to the nurse, who held him while the doctor tied and cut the cord.

The nurse carried the baby to a station in the corner of the room. She placed him on a scale, adjusted the counterweights along the metal arm, and announced loudly to the room, "Nine pounds, ten ounces!"

Later, when the baby was washed, dressed, and wrapped in a blanket, he seemed in a happy frame of mind and was placed in Ruby's arms for the first time. "Welcome to the family," she said softly, "Peter Glenn Mattison. I'd like to introduce your father."

* * *

After Peter was settled in the hospital nursery, Owen returned to Ruby's room and found her drifting into exhausted sleep. Dr. Sorenson helped him convince the head nurse that Owen should be admitted to the hospital office to make long-distance calls charged to his Platteville number.

Owen called his mother at the farm to announce the birth of her first grandchild. Kate Mattison's voice sounded tinny and distant, but she was thrilled by the news and renewed her offer to come and help when Ruby and baby returned to Platteville.

Owen had not responded to the initial offer because Ruby believed she would not require help in their tiny house after five lazy days in the hospital. Owen thought she might change her mind. "Ma, we haven't made plans for going home yet. The doctor wants her to stay in the hospital for five or six days to get her strength back. Can I call you back? How much warning would you need?"

"I can come on two or three hours' notice. I'll get one of your brothers to drive me."

"It should be Peter. We agreed on a boy's name a month ago. It's Peter Glenn Mattison. Glenn, you know, is Ruby's younger brother."

"That is a fine-sounding name. I will tell Peter about it right away, but I should get back to my work before you have to buy the telephone company."

"All right, Ma, I'll call again soon."

Next, Owen gave the operator the number for Ruby's parents in Illinois, saying he would speak to either one. As he expected, the operator required some time to establish the necessary connections, so Owen hung up and awaited a ring.

When the ring came, the connection was faint and full of static, and Owen had a difficult time establishing his identity with Ruby's mother. They had met only once, and she had never heard his voice on the telephone. When the light dawned, however, he heard something like a shriek. "Oh, you're Owen. The baby came! What is it? How is Ruby?"

"It's a boy, born this morning just before six a.m. He weighs nine pounds, ten ounces."

"Oh my goodness!"

"The baby is very healthy. Ruby had a hard time, but she's sleeping soundly right now."

The woman's voice faded. Owen strained to hear and as the voice grew stronger, realized that Ruby's mother was speaking about Ruby, "—was the baby of the family. So this is our eighth grandchild, and he has the highest birth weight. Have you given him a name?"

"Yes, that's one reason I called. We're naming him after my youngest brother and Ruby's. Peter Glenn Mattison."

"That's marvelous! I'll call Glenn right away with the news."

"Is there any other family member you want me to call?"

"No, you've got enough on your mind. I'll call Ruby's oldest brother, in Oklahoma. He may be a little peeved that Ruby chooses to honor Glenn. And I'll call her other brother and sisters, who will be amused by his peevishness. Now Owen, I'll let you go, but promise to give Ruby a big hug for me and for her father. And kiss the baby for us too."

"Oh, I certainly will."

Owen returned to Ruby's room, finding her still asleep. As Owen prepared to drag a chair over to the bed, a nurse appeared in the doorway, holding her left forefinger over her lips in a "stay quiet" gesture and motioning Owen out into the hallway with her right hand.

The nurse led Owen halfway down the hall before she spoke. "Mr. Mattison, we've been very lenient with you. But now your baby has arrived safely, and we must insist you adhere to the hospital rules. You may see your wife and child only during visiting hours. They are Monday through Friday, three p.m. to nine p.m., and noon to nine p.m. on the weekends."

Why did they allow him to make long distance calls on their telephone if they were sending him away? Owen wondered if he could ask Sorenson for another intercession but remembered the doctor had gone home. It was not yet ten o'clock on Saturday morning. If he returned to Platteville and came back by noon, he would barely have time to turn around. Oh, but he would have time for a bath.

Owen visited the nursery on his way out of the hospital. Peter was in the middle of the row of just three babies, sleeping soundly, although his companions seemed restless. All were covered by blankets up to their chins; but Owen saw Peter as the largest, healthiest, and happiest of the group. Despite his fatigue, Owen stood a little taller before the nursery window. He regretted the absence of other parents, but in five days there would be many chances to meet other families and compare babies. Time to go.

Owen emerged from the hospital, smiling into bright sunlight.

Snow was being cleared from sidewalks even as it melted around the edges, and the Chevrolet started without complaint. On the way back to Platteville, Owen decided to share his news with someone outside the family. He wondered briefly who would be happy to pass the word along. The answer was obvious: Martha Stark, particularly if she would answer the telephone, rather than her husband.

* * *

Owen began his visits at the nursery window. Although he remembered the birth of his brother Peter, Owen had forgotten how tiny yet perfect a baby's hands could be. He spent whole minutes in fascinated staring at Peter Glenn Mattison. Then he would go to Ruby's room and describe Peter's state and compare him—very favorably—with the two or three other babies in residence. A nurse would bring Peter in for breast-feeding, which Ruby and baby both seemed to enjoy. When Peter was returned to the nursery, Ruby's supper arrived. The small hospital did not maintain a cafeteria, so Ruby sent Owen to the restaurant across the street. He returned to stay with Ruby until visiting hours ended.

Ruby's return home would depend on how well she regained her strength. Owen spent most of his time on Saturday watching her nap, and she was still fatigued on Sunday. By Monday, she claimed that she was "all slept out"; and on Tuesday, Owen helped her walk in the hallway.

On Wednesday, Owen expected to learn when he could take his wife and child home. He got to Ruby's room at four o'clock, expecting she would be eager for another walk. But she lay in bed, still in the hospital gown, and Owen thought her face seemed flushed.

Her eyes fluttered open when he entered the room, and Owen went to plant a kiss on her cheek. "Hey, Rube, how are you feeling?" Ruby grasped Owen's hand on the sheet, and she did not reach up to embrace him, but she smiled. Owen pulled up a chair beside the bed. "Do you have any word on when I can take you both home?"

"When Dr. Sorenson came in this morning, I felt fine, and he was glad that I've done some walking. But I still have a slight fever, and he wants to wait 'til tomorrow to decide. He asked if I will have help with the baby when I get home."

"Did you say yes? My ma is ready to come."

"I said I wasn't sure. I still can't see four people staying in that tiny house, even if one is a baby. There is only one bed."

"You and Ma can have the bed. I'll set up one of the camp cots."

"There's no room for that in the kitchen. Everybody would still be sleeping in one room."

"There would be three people on hand to take care of Peter. We might even spoil him."

"Owen, I still want to do this by myself, if I can."

"Well, Ma says she can come on short notice. So we can wait and see how it goes."

Later that evening when Owen was taking his leave, he kissed Ruby good-bye; and this time she embraced him. When he left the room, leaving the door open as she requested, he heard a sharp, quick cough. He stopped, wondering if it came from a neighboring room, but he heard two more coughs and was sure they came from Ruby. He turned back toward her room to see a nurse entering it. Best to let well enough alone.

The echo of those few coughs stayed in his mind as he started the Chevrolet, and he wished he had gone back into Ruby's room. When he reached the highway, the drone of the engine accentuated his sudden fatigue, and he fought to stay awake for the trip home.

Chapter 17

OWEN'S WORRIES ABOUT RUBY returned the next day and threatened to overwhelm his teaching. He administered an announced quiz in the biology class. After collecting papers, he reviewed Mendel's laws of inheritance. His voice struck his ear as a strange, distant sound. By early afternoon, he yearned to dismiss the students and drive to the hospital. When the sixth period finally ended, Owen made sure Superintendent Healy would again take charge of the basketball practice, climbed into the Chevy, and headed north to Greeley.

Entering the maternity ward, Owen paused at the nursery window, seeing Peter in a crib. Despite the glass partition, he could hear heartbreaking cries coming from Peter, with help from the other two babies. A nurse was folding small clothing, oblivious to the babies' demands. Owen stifled an urge to tap on the widow, and walked on.

In the hall outside Ruby's room, Owen heard a sharp, extended coughing fit. When Owen started to push the door open, a nurse appeared, shaking her head.

She came out into the hall, pulling the door shut behind her. "Mr. Mattison, I'm sorry, but your wife is not well. You can go in to see her, but do not get close to her because there is a risk of infection. Dr. Sorenson wants to talk to you. I will tell him you are here."

Owen practically burst the door open, but he quieted when he saw Ruby. She was lying back against two pillows, with the bed cranked up to raise her head and shoulders. An apparatus of bottles and tubing hung near her bedside, dripping fluid into a vein. She was very pale, and her breathing was shallow and rapid.

"Ruby! What's wrong?" Owen rushed to the bedside.

Ruby grimaced in pain, coughed, and held a cup to her lips. Her sputum was stained a reddish brown, and tears streaked her face.

"They won't let me see Peter." Her sob turned into a cough, and she fought to gain a breath. "I could infect him."

Dr. Sorenson came into the room, nodded to Owen, and went to Ruby's bed. He picked up her hand, feeling her pulse. "Ruby, I've ordered some things that will help. We're going to rub you down with alcohol to bring down your temperature, and then we'll bring in an oxygen tank so your lungs won't have to work so hard. The nurse will show you how to put the mask on and take it off. Now is there anything else you need?"

Ruby's voice was faint. "My baby. How is he?"

"He's getting excellent care in the nursery. Don't worry, we'll bring him to you as soon as it's safe. Now I'm going to borrow your husband for a minute." Sorenson led Owen to the familiar fathers' waiting room, which was empty. They sat in adjoining chairs. "I'm sorry to tell you that your wife has developed double pneumonia. Both lungs are infected. We have confirmed the diagnosis with an X-ray. Her temperature was below one hundred yesterday afternoon. It has gone up to 104.9."

It was the highest human temperature reading Owen had ever heard.

Sorenson continued, "Her lungs are filling with fluid, making it increasingly difficult to breathe. There is no cure for this disease. All we can do is treat the symptoms, as we are by giving her oxygen, to make it easier for the body's natural defenses to do their job. That usually suffices with people of Ruby's age. But Ruby had an exhausting labor, and her natural defenses are nearly used up."

Owen heard the misery in his own voice. "Do you mean her life is in danger?"

The doctor laid a hand on Owen's shoulder. "We are doing everything we can. If we can pull her through tonight, her chances are at least fifty-fifty."

"Where did this pneumonia come from? What caused it?'

"Lung infections have various causes. We have taken cultures of her blood and sputum in hopes of answering that question. But we won't have the lab report for two days."

After the doctor took his leave, Owen made a quick trip to the nursery window, where he saw Peter being fed. So the hospital could do something right: the noisiest baby got the bottle. He returned to the fathers' room and waited half an hour, his mind spinning with images he dared not examine closely.

When he was invited into Ruby's room, the sheets had been changed, the pillows fluffed up, and Ruby was wearing a rubber oxygen mask that covered most of her face. Her eyes, peering over the top of the mask, were lively and seemed to have lost their dullness. Owen saw she could not talk with the mask on, so he drew a chair up to the side of the bed.

He told her about peeping through the nursery window. He praised Peter's vigorous cry that rattled the window that afternoon. Ruby pulled aside the mask to cough, but then she managed a slight smile. Owen said he was just back from a second trip to the window, where he saw Peter being fed, proof that his earlier demands brought action. Peter's eyes still looked blue, but Owen was sure they would soon find their son blessed with Ruby's clear brown eyes. Owen looked at her eyes. Yes, eyes could smile.

Wondering what Ruby would most like to hear, he recalled their honeymoon trip to Yellowstone and their August stay in Rocky Mountain National Park. He reminded her of rushing mountain streams with still pools behind boulders and the thrill when the trout took the fly. She still seemed attentive, so he talked of the South Platte and their favorite picnic spot on the Lydell place. He repeated laudatory reports he had heard of Irene Stark's performance in the Christmas program. He talked of Ruby's piano playing and some of his favorite tunes and the remarkable progress of her students. He laughed, recalling her efforts to play the untuned piano after his brothers delivered it.

Owen realized that Ruby had not coughed for some time. She was asleep, and her breathing was deeper and more regular. Owen tiptoed out of the room.

The nurse in charge of the ward refused his request for a cot in Ruby's room. It didn't matter that he had a cot there during her labor. The situation was different; they would be in and out of the room all night, providing procedures she desperately needed. His presence could only make their work harder and its success less likely. Yes, the waiting room was empty, and a cot there would be possible.

For the next seven hours, Owen haunted the hallway outside Ruby's door. When the nurses were leaving the room, they admitted him to sit with her. They would hurry back in with another injection, or to stimulate her circulation by massaging her feet and legs, or to administer another alcohol rub. He would be banished again. Around midnight, Dr. Sorenson visited Ruby's room, conferred with the nurses, and came to tell Owen there was no change in her condition. Well after two a.m., Owen went to the waiting room and stumbled into the cot. The next thing he recognized was the faint light before dawn outside the window. The shade had not even been drawn. Half past six.

Owen performed his morning ablutions hastily, combed his hair, and reentered the ward. He stopped by the nursery window to see Peter sleeping soundly. There were no staff members in the hall, so Owen quietly entered Ruby's room. Ruby was wearing the oxygen mask with her eyes closed, but Owen guessed she was awake. The chair he pulled up to the bedside scraped slightly, and Ruby's eyelids fluttered open. Owen smiled, but her eyes did not seem to greet him. Just then Ruby coughed, pulled the mask aside, and put the cup to her lips. She was racked by repeated coughs. Owen saw her drop the oxygen mask. He leaped to her side, grasped the mask, and held it to her face.

He was trying to refasten the straps when a new voice came from behind him. "That will do, Mr. Mattison. Thank you for helping, but we'll take over now." The nurse's shift had changed, and this was the new head nurse. "We're changing the bed linen, so please step outside. We'll let you know when you can return."

Owen fidgeted in the waiting room for nearly an hour. The nurses had to be giving Ruby the best possible care. Their training included the latest scientific knowledge, and Dr. Sorenson supervised them carefully. The doctor's dedication to proper hygiene was impressive. The equipment they might need was all at hand in the hospital.

Yet if Ruby had delivered the baby at home, she would not have been exposed to pneumonia. Were the microbes in the hospital air, waiting for a vulnerable victim? Exhaustion made Ruby susceptible to infection. Without following the diet she labeled scientific, she would have had an easier delivery. Peter would have had a lesser birth weight but would probably be just as vigorous. Had science betrayed them? He did not ask the nurse who told him to go back in.

Ruby's arms were pale against the fresh white sheets, but she seemed calmer, and her breathing was somewhat relaxed. Her eyes above the mask looked dull, but they got brighter when they focused on Owen. He pulled a chair up to the bedside and told of seeing Peter that morning; the baby's appetite was clearly stronger than those of his fellow patients, and his cries were more impatient. Owen thought he saw Ruby's eyes twinkle with amusement. Realizing Ruby had never seen the nursery, he described its dimensions and activities.

Ruby reached up slowly and pulled aside the mask. Rather than coughing, she wanted to talk. But her voice was barely a whisper. Owen sat beside her on the bed and put his arm around her shoulders.

"You have to take Peter to the mountains," she said. Each word was a great effort, and her voice got no stronger. "Teach him to camp, to fish."

"Of course I'll do that."

Ruby's lips moved again. She seemed to gather her strength. "He'll be a better fisherman than I ever was. Better company . . . for . . . you."

"Don't talk like that. We'll go together, all three of us."

Ruby's hand holding the mask fell down to the bed. Owen reached across to grasp the mask. Before holding it to her face, he reached his arm, mask and all, around her other shoulder and bent over to kiss her lightly on the lips. Ruby did not return his embrace, and her lips beneath his were still.

Slowly, Owen understood. He straightened up, looking into the suddenly vacant eyes. Carefully, he reached up with his thumb and forefinger, and closed Ruby's brown eyes for the last time.

* * *

Owen heard an unusually kind tone in the head nurse's voice. He was sitting in an office; it had to belong to the head nurse, because she sat behind the desk. He tried to remember entering the office, but earlier events flooded his mind. The vacant look in Ruby's eyes. Closing her eyes. Finding this very nurse on the ward and asking her to come to Ruby's room. Watching her feel for a pulse, search with a stethoscope for a heartbeat, and finally pull the sheet up over Ruby's face. The confirmation of what he already knew was like a blow to the heart. He wanted to yank back the sheet, embrace his wife, and implore her not to leave.

But the head nurse took his hand. Owen clamped his jaw shut and let her lead him out of Ruby's room. Now she wanted something, and Owen did not understand what she expected.

"I'm sorry," he said, "I don't follow. What did you ask?"

"I was speaking of what will become of Mrs. Mattison's remains." The voice no longer seemed so kind. "I understand there are no mortuaries in Platteville. We have three here in Greeley. Unless you try to call in someone from Denver or Ft. Collins, which would be very expensive, you need to choose one of the three."

"Oh. Does it make any difference?"

"All three are competent, but you may have a religious preference. The Fitzmaurice establishment mainly serves Catholics, while the Parker and Barrett firms are Protestant."

A vision of masked men marching in white robes flashed across Owen's mind. No way to escape religion. But funerals are religious rituals, so Owen would let religion guide his decision. "Tell me," he asked, "do you happen to be Protestant?"

"Yes, as a matter of fact."

"If you had to bury your husband, which undertaker would you pick?"

"I would call in the Parker people, and I'll tell you the reason. From what I've seen right on this ward, the Parker staff handles the remains with more respect."

Remains. An awful word. But Owen had to go on. "That's an important distinction. Thank you. Shall I call Parker now?"

"If you wish, I will call them to come for Mrs. Mattison. Then you can go to the Parker office later today to discuss arrangements."

Later today. Owen looked at his watch. Friday morning classes would start at Platteville High in fifteen minutes. He explained his problem to the head nurse, who used a passkey to admit Owen to the hospital office. The operator connected him with Harold Healy's office after Healy agreed to pay the charges.

Owen did not express his surprise at finding Healy in his office that early. He told Healy of Ruby's death and said he would be in Greeley all morning. Healy reminded Owen that it was the last day of school before Christmas vacation. Healy himself would meet Owen's classes, send some of them to the library, and dismiss others early. Owen should not hurry back for afternoon classes. Owen expressed gratitude, Healy expressed condolences, and the call was complete.

Owen found a sheet of notepaper and began a list of things he should do. Should he call his parents and Ruby's family now, or wait until funeral arrangements were clear? He heard a light tapping on the office door and called, "Come in!" But he remembered that he had let the door lock behind him. He walked to the door and yanked it open.

Outside was a man dressed in a dark suit and necktie. Owen recognized someone from Platteville but could not call up the name. "Mr. Mattison, I'm Dan Cobb of First Methodist. Calling on a parishioner who is ill and heard of your loss. The nurse said I'd find you here. I'm so sorry. Such a tragedy. What can I do to help?"

"Thank you, Reverend." Of course. They had met at the potluck for new faculty, a year and a half before, when Ruby found the women so pushy about religion. Apparently preachers could enter the hospital at will, not constrained by visiting hours. Couldn't he send the preacher away and get time alone to sort things out?

Daniel Cobb shifted from one foot to the other in the hallway. "My wife got to know Mrs. Mattison in the Mizpah Club. Eleanor admired her hard work in the cemetery and enjoyed her musical talent. Eleanor will want to join in doing whatever we can for you."

What were preachers for, if not to help at such times? Owen made his second crucial decision. "Please come in. We can talk for a minute before the hospital needs this office."

The two men found chairs.

"I believe that you folks have not joined a church in Platteville."

"That's right. We were raised as Baptists, so we go—went—to church with Ruby's aunt in Longmont or with my parents in Windsor."

"Owen, please regard First Methodist as your church in Platteville. Use us like any member would. I'm sure you know that Methodists and Baptists have a lot in common."

"Thank you, that's a very kind offer."

"I believe Mrs. Mattison's home church is quite distant."

"Yes, in Illinois."

"So I assume you aren't planning on a funeral back East."

"No. Ruby loves—" Owen took time to swallow hard, "loved her work in the Mizpah Cemetery, and she loved its view of the mountains. I will see about a plot there."

"I would be honored to conduct Ruby's funeral service in our church."

"Thank you. That's very generous, but I don't know when it will be."

"We can be ready whenever you are. The only time to rule out is Sunday's eleven o'clock worship. However, the two of us should meet in advance to plan the service."

When hospital staff came to claim their office space, Owen asked to board Peter in the nursery until after Ruby's funeral. A modest daily charge was mentioned. Owen wanted to shout that the hospital should make no charge at all, for they had failed to protect his wife, but he swallowed hard and signed the form set before him.

Owen realized that it was after nine o'clock on Friday morning, and he had eaten nothing since Thursday lunch. Maybe he could think more clearly with some food. He crossed the street to the all-too-familiar restaurant and ordered coffee, tomato juice, fried potatoes, poached eggs, and pancakes. When the food came, it seemed repulsive, and the act of eating seemed somehow to betray Ruby. After the first tentative mouthfuls, he devoured all that was before him and added a glass of milk, and the world seemed a more livable place.

On his way out of the restaurant, Owen saw a black Packard hearse driving away from the hospital. A small sign in the windshield read "Parker." Ruby was on her way to the mortuary. The clouds of despondency came crashing back. He curbed an impulse to run after the hearse, went back into the restaurant, and obtained directions to the Parker Mortuary.

* * *

A discussion of cost came inevitably, and Owen agreed to the figure of nearly three hundred dollars, mindful of their savings account. He remembered with sharp pain that half the savings came from Ruby's music lessons.

Before leaving the mortuary, Owen placed a call to Martha Stark, who began talking when she recognized his voice.

"Oh, Owen, what a shock! We're devastated, and Irene will be terribly upset too. We want to do whatever we can to help."

Of course, Martha would have heard from Pastor Cobb or from people at the school. Thank God he didn't have to dredge up the words to tell about Ruby. Martha's voice continued through the wire. "We can take care of the baby as long as you will let us. Irene will want to help, and we'll take good care of him. We'll even spoil him, but you really can't spoil a child that young."

How could Owen cut off the gusher? "Thank you, Mrs. Stark—Martha—but I've made arrangements for the baby to stay in the hospital nursery for the time being. I'm calling from the Parker Mortuary in Greeley. They said I could talk to you about choosing a gravesite in the Mizpah Cemetery."

"I've had good experiences with the Parkers, and I think you will be pleased with them. For choosing a gravesite, the new chairman of that committee is Isabel Nelson. She has all the drawings and records, and is the best person to show you around. Would you like me to call the high school, arrange a meeting, and call you back? With Arthur on the school board, they've been good at doing what I ask."

"Thank you, but I know the staff pretty well, and I don't expect any problem."

As they were saying farewells, Martha pressed her offer of help until Owen promised to call on her if he found a way she could serve. Then he waited until the five minutes between high school classes and asked the school secretary, who expressed condolences, to call Mrs. Nelson to the phone. Owen knew Nelson's classroom was three doors away from the office. Isabel came at once, immediately expressing her sorrow, and told Owen that she would send her sixth period class home for Christmas, go home to pick up her records, and meet Owen at the Mizpah gate at two thirty.

Owen arranged for Parker to add the telephone charges to his bill and returned to the hospital. At the nursery window, he saw Peter asleep. A nurse recognized him through the window and came into the hallway to express sadness about Ruby. Owen asked for an exception to the hospital rule that only babies and medical staff could be admitted to the nursery. That rule protected the babies; he would have to apply to the head nurse or the attending physician. Owen grimaced and was told that Dr. Sorenson had gone to Ft. Collins but would return for rounds Saturday afternoon.

* * *

Returning to Platteville, Owen drove directly out Grant Avenue and up the county road to the cemetery. The Chevrolet ground up the hill easily in second gear, following tracks made by previous vehicles churning through snow into gravel. More gravel had been added since he had walked up in darkness to see the blazing cross and the Klan initiation.

Owen stopped opposite the cemetery gate. The weather was clear and cold, but not quite freezing; direct sunlight was softening the frozen ground. Walking to the open gate, Owen looked to the west to see white-capped Longs

Peak rising above the other snow-covered mountains. Growing up not far away, Owen first appreciated the grandeur of the mountains when he saw them through Ruby's eyes. He discovered his arm held out, as if it were possible for her to materialize beside him. *God help me.*

Hearing a car labor up the hill, Owen saw Isabel Nelson's Mercer runabout park behind his Chevy. Isabel climbed out of her car, carrying a large folded paper that had to be the official cemetery map. Owen walked back to her.

"Isabel, thank you for coming on such short notice."

"It's my job to see anyone interested in a plot, but this is so different. Ruby and I worked side by side here last spring, and we planned next year's improvements together. It breaks my heart to think we may have worked on her own gravesite."

Isabel led Owen through the open gate onto a narrow automobile track. "This is a one-way road," she said. "It turns to go back to the gate."

Owen felt no need to respond.

"The cemetery is an iffy thing this time of year," Isabel continued. "If the ground is completely thawed, this road turns to mud, and people get stuck. If the ground is frozen too deeply, we can't break through to dig a grave. Have you settled on a day for the funeral?"

"Yes. Monday afternoon."

"If you select a site, I'll have the caretaker and his boys dig the grave this afternoon. It will be ready in case of a hard freeze over the weekend."

Owen nodded to indicate approval, and they walked on. Isabel stopped, opened up her map, pinpointed the fur trappers' graves from a century before, and indicated later additions. She assured Owen he could acquire any unoccupied space.

Owen wished he could be alone. No need to share his feelings with Isabel Nelson. Or anyone else. "Where I'd like to look," he said, "is up there by the western boundary, a place where the view isn't blocked by the water tank."

Isabel consulted her map and led Owen to an area with few headstones in the northwest corner of the cemetery. She stopped by a two-foot-tall pine tree.

"Owen, this plot has four gravesites, and the view is magnificent. I know the mountains were important to Ruby."

Owen resented Isabel knowing of Ruby's love for the mountains. It was an intrusion on their privacy. He gazed across the rooftops of Platteville and the cottonwoods lining the river to the rolling hills, and finally the mountains in the far distance. All was silent, and he wished he were alone.

Then Isabel broke the silence, indicating the small tree beside them. "This tree will shade the two headstones at this end of the plot, but it won't interfere with the view. See, it is taking hold nicely. I think Ruby helped plant it here last June."

Silence again, then broken this time by Owen. "This is the plot I want."

* * *

Owen called the two families from his home. Learning of the Monday funeral, Owen's mother spoke through tears to say she would come on Sunday to help him get ready. She would spend the night; the rest of the family would come for the funeral, and they would be ready to take the baby back to the farm.

"Maybe that's what we should do, Ma, but I haven't really sorted things out. Peter hasn't been released from the hospital nursery."

Talking to his mother was easy compared to Ruby's parents. When he told her of Ruby's death, her mother was overcome and turned the call over to Ruby's father, the judge. His questioning drew more details from Owen than he had planned to convey. The judge said they would not be able to come by Monday, but he believed that Ruby's brother would be able to come from Oklahoma to represent the family.

Owen folded down the brass bed frame and tumbled in, then spent the night missing Ruby. He awoke to daylight, feeling tired. He let the kitchen range lie cold, using the camp stove to make coffee and scramble eggs. He called the Parker Mortuary as promised, to confirm his selection of a gravesite and report the grave would be dug. Reminded of the need to name pallbearers, he spent half an hour resolving his internal debate over the wisdom of asking Arthur Stark, despite his Klan membership.

When Stark agreed at once, Owen felt a slight sense of justice in asking Roy Thompson and Newton Maclean, the other two school board members. He could not blame the board for Ruby's death; but the board did bring the Mattisons to Platteville, and all three had suspected him of joining their enemies in the Bible-reading dispute. With the board members committed, he called on Superintendent Healy, but this was more a question of friendship, as was the case with the final two pallbearers, Harry Singleton the banker and George Lydell, owner of their favorite picnic spot.

Owen walked to the Methodist Church for his appointment with Cobb, who asked about selecting pallbearers, and Owen answered with their names. Cobb murmured something about how busy Owen had been. Then they discussed Ruby, with the pastor taking notes: birthplace, family, schooling, the Chicago Music Conservatory, study at college, love of the mountains, teaching home economics, teaching piano lessons, gardening at the Mizpah Cemetery, and eagerness for motherhood.

The pastor said, "Since Ruby was a serious musician, the best way to honor her memory is with music, some the congregation can sing and more they can listen to."

"Yes," Owen said, "but she didn't consider a lot of her favorites—ragtime and jazz—appropriate for playing in a church."

"How about more spiritual music? Did she have some favorite hymns?"

"Oh yes. 'This Is My Father's World,' 'The Old Rugged Cross,' and even 'Swing Low, Sweet Chariot.' She loved Christmas music. Her favorite carol was 'O Holy Night.'"

Owen saw Cobb writing furiously. "I think her two favorite hymns were ones that I also learned growing up—'Shall We Gather at the River' and 'Amazing Grace.'"

"I'm afraid neither one of those is in the Methodist hymnal."

"Gosh, I thought they were universal." Both men lapsed into silence until Owen suggested a solution. "I can find Ruby's old Baptist hymnal. If I get find someone to sing those, could your organist accompany? Would that be appropriate?"

"That would be very appropriate."

* * *

When Owen got home, he found Ruby's dog-eared hymnal and called the Stark farm once more. Martha was surprised when he asked for Irene, but she called her daughter to the telephone. Owen explained the situation and described each hymn. Irene said she would be honored to take part in the ceremony. Owen promised to bring her the hymnal that afternoon and suggested practicing with the organist after the Sunday worship service.

Owen went into the kitchen to make a cheese sandwich, which he washed down with milk, and ate an apple. He would get to the Stark farm at the noon meal hour and wanted to tell them truthfully he had already eaten.

When Owen came to their door, the Starks were about to sit down at the table. Irene took the hymnal and began leafing through it, while Martha turned to Owen. "Now, Owen, your place is set. You must join us for lunch."

"Thank you, but I really can't. I've had my lunch, and I'm on my way to Greeley. Visiting hours start at noon on Saturday, and I'm going to see the baby."

"I certainly wouldn't want to delay that, but there is something I'd like to ask you about. I understand from Arthur that the funeral is Monday at one thirty. Will there also be a service at the cemetery?"

"Yes, the reverend thinks we should commemorate Ruby's love for that place, almost among the mountains. It will be brief because the weather will not be friendly."

"Then after that, are you planning a reception? It's often done that way, you know."

Owen was silent. He thought of the few funerals he had attended. Yes, there had been some kind of gathering afterward. Things to eat. Conversation. Did there have to be something like that? He had heard of something called a wake, but it was Catholic. Before Owen could grow depressed at his lack of foresight, Martha continued.

"I didn't think you would have anything planned—you've had so much else to be concerned with. The Mizpah Club would like to provide the reception as a tribute to Ruby. Several members have already called me, wondering what they can do to help. We'll hold it at the school, which should be available during Christmas vacation. Arthur can see to that. Say the word, and I'll start organizing it."

Owen wondered if he was feeling faint. "I . . . I hardly know what to say."

"It could be held in the Methodist basement, but going to the school, nobody will have to enter a strange church. And people from all the churches will be there. And the school is close to your home, so it will be easy for any of your relatives to come to the reception."

Owen was awed by the insistence of Mrs. Stark's generosity.

"Owen, you won't have to do a thing but show up and talk to some people. We'll provide all the food plus good Methodist coffee, tea, and lemonade. And we'll do the cleaning up afterward. All you have to do is say yes. Will you say it?"

"Yes," Owen said. He said nothing more, afraid of bursting into tears.

* * *

Returning to the nursery, he saw Dr. Sorenson holding his stethoscope against the back of a baby lying on an examining table. Staring through the window, Owen was sure the baby was Peter. Sorenson signaled to a nurse, who came with a clean nightshirt for the baby, speaking a few words and pointing toward Owen in the window.

Sorenson glanced at Owen, stripped off his rubber gloves, and came out into the hall.

"Hello, Mattison, I've been wanting to talk to you."

"That's why I'm here, Doctor. Can you arrange my admission to the nursery, so I can get acquainted with our son?"

Sorenson lead Owen down the hall. "Yes," he said, "I'll leave word that you are permitted to enter and care for your child, provided you wash your hands before handling him."

"That's a good requirement. Thank you."

They came again to the fathers' waiting room. Sorenson sat down and motioned Owen into the facing chair. "First, I want to say how terribly sorry I am. In fifteen years' practice, I've lost only five mothers. It was a terrible combination of circumstances. Ruby's pregnancy did not cause the pneumonia, but her difficult labor so weakened her that the infection had a fatal impact. We really did everything known to medical science, but it was not enough."

Owen nodded silently. The doctor could have kept Ruby at home in Platteville.

"However, I'm happy to tell you," Sorenson said, "that your son has escaped his mother's illness. His lungs are clear as a bell, and he tolerates well the formula we prescribed for him. He can be released from the hospital as soon as you have arranged for his care."

Owen nodded again. Good to have Peter's health confirmed, but he wanted to hear about Ruby.

"The other thing I wanted to tell you is the result of the cultures we took of Ruby's blood and sputum. After forty-eight hours of incubation, the results were essentially negative."

Startled, Owen sat up straight in his chair.

Sorenson continued, "That means we did not find the microbes commonly associated with pneumonia. There is a second type of pneumonia that is not, at its onset, associated with any microbe, although they invade soon afterward. There are other ailments, including the common cold, which apparently are not caused by microorganisms. The causative agent is submicroscopic, so small it passes through a ceramic filter. I read an article that proposes a name for this thing—*virus*, which is Latin for 'poison.'"

Owen remembered the science he taught. "Poisons are usually chemicals. Is this virus thing a living organism?"

"Nobody knows. It has never been seen."

Owen resisted the impulse to shout. "Never been seen, but you believe it exists."

"Its presence anywhere can only be inferred, not proven. It could have been dormant in Ruby and turned active when she became exhausted."

Owen resented the doctor's detached tone. "How do you know it wasn't hiding in the hospital before she even came here?"

"That is possible, even likely. Pneumonia is a common cause of death, particularly among the elderly, and this hospital has its share of such deaths."

A nurse burst into the room, calling Sorenson to attend another patient. Owen walked back to the nursery, wondering if Sorenson would remember to tell them of giving him permission to enter it. He saw through the window that a nurse was changing Peter's diaper. It was not the right time for a confrontation to test the rules. He turned toward the outside door, and despondency returned, making the words echo in his mind in time with the sound of his own footfalls.

Everything known to medical science, but it was not enough.
Everything known to medical science, but it was not enough.
Everything . . .

Chapter 18

ON SUNDAY MORNING, OWEN'S brother Norman drove their mother and sister, Ruth, to Platteville in the family's Dodge sedan. When they arrived at the little house, Owen had the stove warmed up and was beginning to wash several days' worth of dishes. Kate and Ruth embraced Owen in turn, murmuring condolences, and Norman shook his hand. Owen was glad they sensed he did not want to talk about Ruby.

Owen hoped they would understand he had been too busy for housekeeping. His mother said they expected as much and had come to help catch up. Ruth criticized his kitchen technique and shooed him away from the sink. Owen planned to take them to Greeley to meet the baby during afternoon visiting hours. Kate and Ruth approved of the plan, but Norman listed the farm duties he had to perform, so Owen walked his brother back to the Dodge.

"We'll all be back tomorrow," Norman said, "for the funeral and to help out. But the kind of help you need right now is mostly women's work." After opening the Dodge's door, Norman turned back to his brother. "I guess you know how sorry we are about it—about Ruby."

"I know. Thank you, and thanks for bringing them. I don't think Ma will ever learn to drive."

"Pa will drive the car back here tomorrow, probably with Pete," Norman said, "and I'll come a little later with Lew in the truck. Have anything you want to send home with us ready to load. Maybe we can do that before the funeral."

Owen returned to the kitchen and found a towel to help his mother dry the clean dishes Ruth was producing. Kate Mattison reviewed her understanding of the funeral arrangements and wondered if some kind of reception was planned. Owen explained Martha Stark's offer and described Ruby's activities in the Mizpah Club. Kate was relieved others had taken on the responsibility and looked forward to meeting Mrs. Stark.

With his mother's help, Owen scraped together a lunch from the little food he had left in the kitchen, and then he drove them to the Greeley hospital. He resented the ease with which his mother and sister were admitted to the nursery, but the resentment vanished when he held his son and calmed the fussy baby by walking around the room while talking to him. Then Owen watched with pride as Kate and Ruth fed Peter and changed him and succumbed to his charm.

On the way back to Platteville, Owen agreed to send Peter home with them after the funeral, to stay until he could make arrangements for baby care that would fit with his professional responsibilities. He worried silently. Could he find the right person? Could he afford the cost?

Kate and Ruth Mattison worked together to tidy the little house. While Kate ironed Owen's suit for the funeral, Ruth began laundering his ten-day accumulation of clothes. Owen eventually folded down the brass bed for Kate and Ruth, and set up a camp cot for himself. Sleep came easily this time, and soon Monday dawned, cold and overcast.

Owen awakened early to the realization that the time for saying farewell to Ruby was at hand. He detested the idea of a final good-bye and plunged into activity as a way of preventing thought. He folded his cot and packed baby clothing and equipment into boxes very quietly, for Kate and Ruth were sleeping in the corner of the room. When they stirred, he greeted them, then retreated to the kitchen and prepared oatmeal, scrambled eggs, and toast for breakfast, emptying his larder. By the time breakfast was completed, the Mercantile was open, so Owen took Kate to help shop while Ruth again cleared up the kitchen.

Soon after they returned, Owen's father and brothers arrived in their two vehicles. Owen packed everything Peter would not need that day into the truck bed. One item nearly overwhelmed him: the teddy bear won on the Pickle Day midway. At that moment, all of his family was involved in other tasks, so he tucked the bear away without needing to explain his sudden surge of emotion.

* * *

When the reverend spread his arms, Irene bowed her head for the opening prayer, and she managed to look toward the far wall, where Maggie Fitzgerald and her parents were sitting. Irene saw them make the sign of the cross. That settled one question: Catholics could attend Protestant funerals.

After the amen, Cobb stated that Ruby had been a superb musician and the best way to celebrate her life was through music. They were asked to join in singing her favorite sacred numbers, beginning with the Negro spiritual, "Swing Low, Sweet Chariot." Two of Ruby's favorite songs not in the Methodist hymnal would be sung for them by one of Ruby's music students, Irene Stark.

Irene smiled to herself. Not in the Methodist hymnal. When Mr. Mattison delivered Ruby's own Baptist hymnal, Irene memorized the tunes by playing them on her piano, then copied the words and turned the hymnal over to the organist. Irene remained after the Sunday service, and they practiced each hymn until satisfied with the result. The most bothersome problem with unfamiliar music was the tempo.

Irene barely joined in singing the first three hymns, and she hardly listened to the bits of scripture interspersed with them. Then it was her turn. She walked past the casket up to the organ and turned to face the congregation, which she thought was much larger than that attending a Sunday service. She saw Frank Koblenz and Bruno Gorman sitting with their families behind the Fitzgeralds. The Catholics were sticking together. They probably didn't feel comfortable there. Did anyone feel comfortable at a funeral?

The organist finished an introduction. Irene glanced at the sheet clutched in her hand and began to sing in the slightly lilting rhythm they had worked out.

Shall we gather at the river, where bright angel feet have trod?
With its crystal tide forever flowing by the throne of God?
Yes, we'll gather at the river, the beautiful, the beautiful river;
Gather with the saints at the river that flows by the throne of God.

Ruby and the organists had agreed to offer only the first verse. The silence seemed profound until it was shattered by two coughs and a sneeze from the congregation. Ruby nodded to the organist and began singing with the first organ chord.

Amazing grace! How sweet the sound, that saved a wretch like me!
I once was lost, but now am found, was blind but now I see.

The pace was deliberate, the emotions overpowering, and each verse added testimony to a profound faith. Irene's voice was both led and echoed by stately tones of the organ. She sang the four short verses. When she sang "Amen," tears welled up in Irene's eyes. When she found a seat in the first row with her own family despite blurred vision, Cobb launched his eulogy. No longer concerned about controlling her voice, changing from performer to member of the congregation, Irene's sense of loss was renewed. The tears ran untended down her cheeks.

197

Cobb neared the end of his talk. "Ruby Mattison's time here below was tragically short, but that time was spent in the service of the Lord through serving her fellowman. In the few brief months she lived among us in Platteville, she touched many lives. She brought the joy of music to the ladies of the Mizpah Club, sometimes to their surprise, for many did not know they could enjoy the music of today. She taught several students, including Irene Stark, who has paid eloquent tribute to Ruby with her beautiful voice. Ruby showed students and friends alike how music can be an important part of life, and she leaves this great legacy with them. But this is in fact the smaller part of her legacy.

"Ruby looked forward eagerly to motherhood, and she gave up her own life after giving birth to her son, when God chose to call her to His side. So her greatest legacy will live on. Right now, he is staying at County Hospital in Greeley. His name is Peter Glenn Mattison. By the grace of Almighty God, Ruby Mattison lives on in each of us, as she does in her son. Let us pray."

When the prayer was finished, two of the pallbearers strode to the casket and raised the front part of its cover.

Irene's mother whispered urgently, "I didn't know they were going to do this. We go up and say our good-byes to Mrs. Mattison. Go ahead. Her family goes up last."

Irene stepped into the middle aisle, reluctant leader of the respectful and the curious, walking slowly toward the pulpit. Looking down into the casket, she saw Ruby with her bobbed hair perfectly combed, wearing her usual trace of makeup. She wore a bright dress with a necklace of shiny beads. Ruby seemed likely to wake up at any moment and take over the organ playing.

For an instant, Irene hoped someone had made a terrible mistake. Then she shuddered to realize she could imagine such a thing. She hovered over the casket, reluctant to leave Ruby, but she felt the pressure of people behind her. Looking back at the church through tears, she sensed the entire congregation crowding into the center aisle, ready to walk forward, and concluded she should return to her seat.

Back in the first row, Irene began to resent sharing Ruby with all those filling the center aisle. She counted the entire high school faculty and was amazed by the number of students from both high and grade schools who filed past with their families. *Oh. It's the first day of Christmas vacation.*

Finally the casket lid was closed, and her father brushed past Irene and Martha to join the other pallbearers. They lifted the casket onto a kind of cart and wheeled it slowly up the center aisle, followed by the families and then the congregation. By the time Irene came out of the church, her father had helped load the casket into the hearse.

The cold air cleared Irene's mind. The pallbearers rode together as planned in one of the limousines; so Irene, the second family member to master driving an automobile, drove her mother and brother to the cemetery in the Reo. Arriving early at the funeral, the Starks had gotten a fortuitous parking space. When Irene had pulled back onto Main Street, they were the fifth car behind the hearse.

The sky was gray, and the air was bitterly cold. As the vehicles climbed the hill to the cemetery, a breeze cut through Irene's warmest winter coat. Open cars like the Reo were not the answer for Colorado winters. The procession passed through the gate and along the one-lane cemetery road. When the hearse stopped at the point closest to the gravesite, every car halted. Climbing down from the Reo, Irene glanced back along the line of vehicles, which wound back to the gate. The cars' occupants deserted them, to walk forward along the edge of the narrow road.

The pallbearers pulled the coffin from the hearse and started toward the grave. One and then another slipped on the icy ground, remaining upright with the greatest effort. Two of Owen Mattison's brothers came over to help with the burden. When the casket was safely lowered onto staves spanning the grave, the brothers joined Mr. Mattison and their parents on the folding chairs provided for the family.

Irene resisted an impulse to stamp her feet against the cold. She looked out, past the rooftops and the river, but the overcast hid the mountain peaks beyond. When the congregation re-formed around the grave, Cobb spoke briefly of Ruby's love of the mountains and her joy in aiding the restoration of the old burying ground. Then he prayed at moderate length on the theme of resurrection and asked all there assembled to join in reciting the Twenty-third Psalm.

On her way back to the Reo, Irene found herself walking next to a man she recognized as Owen's oldest brother. People behind them were talking quietly. Irene made no effort to follow the conversation until she heard one unmistakable sentence. "Owen seems to be bearing up well."

Norman Mattison turned in his tracks to face the speaker. "Of course," Norman said. "He is a Mattison."

* * *

The Mattisons rode to the reception in the undertaker's limousine. Owen stationed himself near the classroom's door to welcome a far larger group than he had anticipated and receive their condolences. Those to whom he was a stranger identified themselves and described their associations with Ruby, praising her role. He introduced many to members of his own family, who led them out of the doorway. The crowd soon spilled across the hallway into another classroom. Owen eventually guessed the equivalent of a third of Platteville's population of seven hundred was present, including the families of most of his students and the athletes he coached.

His father drew Owen aside to comment on how quickly he and Ruby had established respected positions in the community. Owen merely nodded, giving no voice to his torment. How could he continue without Ruby?

After an hour in the crowded classroom, Owen found himself near the long table. So he took one of the small plates, spooned food onto it, and resumed his station near the classroom door. He greeted new arrivals there, but he hoped none would come while he ate.

When his food was only half-consumed, George and Susan Lydell appeared with their two sons. Owen murmured his practiced responses to their solicitude and learned a flat tire had delayed them. He thanked George Lydell for serving as pallbearer. The members of his own family were involved with other guests, so he directed the Lydells to the food table. George, Susan, and young Robbie were absorbed into the crowd; but Ronald hung back, wanting to talk.

"Mr. Mattison, I'm really sorry about your wife."

"Thank you, Ron."

Ronald stared down at the floor, overcome by sudden shyness or working up his courage to say something outrageous, as he often did in class.

Owen said, "I heard that your mare is going to foal again."

"Yeah, my little brother is real excited, and we're clearing all the places where the botulism microbe can hide . . . Mr. Mattison, may I ask you one question? Just tell me if it's none of my business."

"All right."

"I haven't been to a lot of funerals, but one thing really seemed out of place to me. You had a member of the Ku Klux Klan help carry the casket. You did know about Mr. Stark, didn't you?"

"Yes, I knew." Owen wondered if he should describe conquering his own revulsion at Stark's Klan membership. His answer had to have exactly the right tone. Ron's certainty about the world needed to give way to curiosity. He was Owen's brightest student, but his dogmatism threatened to become a handicap.

Owen lowered his voice in the crowded room. "Ron, the important things you need to know about Mr. Stark are what he does when he isn't marching with the Klan. One of those things is to encourage Irene's music, and another is to practice scientific agriculture. As a school board member, he supports the Vo Ag classes, and you've benefited from them. I sure don't favor the Klan, but you can't judge all its members by the organization's worst actions. If you make simple assumptions about people and things when the reality is a lot more complicated, you can reach false conclusions."

Ronald's expression was one Owen had seen before, when the boy was pondering something. Owen used the lull to set his plate on an empty chair.

"Maybe so," Ron said, "but if you observe people and things scientifically, you have a good basis for your conclusions."

"Don't count too much on scientific observation. For example, one kind of pneumonia is caused by an agent so small it cannot be seen with a microscope. It has never been seen. But I know it exists, because . . . because it killed my wife."

Owen clamped his jaw shut. Ron muttered a farewell and joined his family selecting food.

* * *

Owen seated his mother in the Chevy for the trip to the Greeley hospital, with his father and sister following in their Dodge. At that same hour in the late afternoon, Owen had taken Ruby to the hospital ten days before, clasping her hand during contractions. When Owen thought of the change ten days had wrought in his life, he dared not talk about it. Kate Mattison sensed his distress and recognized his reluctance to speak. The miles passed in silence.

When the four Mattisons reached the nursery, Peter's few possessions had been gathered together, and the baby was just finishing a bottle. Owen carried baby clothing to the Dodge and got the bassinet with folding legs from his Chevy, placing it in the rear seat where Ruth could tend her nephew. Returning to the nursery, he found the drowsy baby bundled into a bunting and asked to carry the child himself. A few yards down the hall, a few more yards outside to the car, and all the way, Owen watched his son's chubby face but saw Ruby's.

When they got to the Dodge, Owen opened the back door for Ruth to enter and seat herself next to the bassinet. Time to hand her the baby, and Ruth was already smiling a welcome, but Owen saw their son as part of Ruby and did not want to give her up.

Ruth asked, "Owen, is something wrong?"

Owen shook his head and, with a marked effort, handed the baby to Ruth. He opened the front passenger door for his mother, who paused by the running board and held up her arms for Owen's embrace.

"I know it's hard to give him up," Kate Mattison said softly, "but you will have him back again before long."

"I hope so, Ma. I'll be able to get to the farm on Thursday or Friday and stay through New Year's, but I may not have things ready to bring him back."

"All in good time, my son." Kate sat in the front seat, Owen closed the door, and his father started the motor. Ruth carefully tucked the baby into the bassinet. Owen returned the waves of his mother and sister as the Dodge pulled out. They would reach the farm in thirty or forty minutes, if the snow held off.

Owen climbed into his Chevy and drove south to Platteville. The somber afternoon was changing into a gloomy evening, but he reached the little house before the light faded. Inside, he stirred up the fire in the living room stove; and soon he could take off his coat. He set a stack of quiz papers on the table but did not feel like grading them. He had resented greeting so many people at the reception, but now he missed human contact.

He set the papers aside, went into the kitchen, and discovered the icebox and pantry overflowing with food from the reception. It seemed far more than he could consume by himself before time to join his family for Christmas. He remembered the plate that he had set down when talking to Ron Lydell was never finished. Perhaps he should start on the leftovers.

Unsure whether he felt hunger or nausea, Owen surveyed the food. He rejected salads and casseroles, settling tentatively on dessert. When he discovered three uneaten portions of mincemeat pie, his stomach turned over. Swallowing hard, he pulled on his coat and cap and fled the house.

Not thinking of a destination, Owen went back to the Chevy, started it, and headed south on Main Street. The car had gotten chilly, but the heater was still turned on, and he no longer noticed the chill after two blocks.

Soon he was out of town and past the ruins of old Ft. Vasquez. Occasional snowflakes promised more to come, but he paid them little attention. When an oncoming car vigorously flashed its lights, he realized daylight was nearly gone. As he turned on his own lights, the intersection approached where the highway turned toward the bridge over the South Platte.

Owen let the car slow down and choose its own direction. The Chevy carried him straight ahead, onto the narrow county road, which soon led him to the boundary fence of the Lydell property. He braked when his headlights picked out the gate that was merely a removable section of barbed wire strands. He crossed the ditch and stopped with his headlights inches from the fence.

Owen could see the shadowy form of the cottonwood trees surrounding the meadow where he had picnicked with Ruby. Snowdrifts choked the trail leading to them. A faint light lingered on from the sunset beyond the far mountains, but the peaks' silhouette was lost in the overcast sky. It was not fair, returning to Ruby's favorite place and finding her mountains invisible. He switched off the lights and the engine, which also turned off the heater.

The snowfall became lighter. Feathery flakes drifted down. A breeze off the river drove them against the warm windshield, where the flakes melted, and tiny streams ran down the glass. Owen sat hunched over the steering wheel, wishing he could hold Ruby in his arms, and feeling cold enter his feet and begin to creep up his legs. His eyes filled, and wetness streamed down his cheeks. He made no effort to restrain the sobs.

When they finally trailed off, he wiped the cold tears from his cheeks and gave his full attention to organizing the thoughts pouring through his mind. *I don't see how I can go on without Ruby. Maybe I don't have to go on. When I had to put Gus down, I shot him between the eyes. Death was instant, and life caused no further pain. Hoping for a similar end, men fire guns through their mouths into their brains. I could do that.*

But then, I wouldn't be with Peter. Ruby expected me to be with Peter. She wanted me to teach her love for the mountains to him. She had asked me to take him to the mountains, teach him to hunt and to fish. Somehow she knew her own life was ending—it was her last request. The preacher said Ruby lives on in Peter. Whatever I can do with my son, I will be doing also with his mother. God give me the wisdom to be a father worthy of his son's mother.

A long time later, Owen started the engine, turned on the heater and the headlights, backed into the dark road, and drove home.

THE END

Acknowledgments

MORE THAN A DECADE has passed since I first wrote a draft of this novel. Several of the people mentioned herein have now passed away. But my gratitude for their assistance has continued.

Owen and Ruby Mattison are fictionalized versions of my father, Lawrence Lamb, and Opal Underwood Lamb, his first wife. Family members will realize their story has been severely condensed by excluding their time in Worland, Wyoming, where Opal died of pneumonia after giving birth to their second child in 1930. There is no grave for Opal in Platteville's Mizpah Cemetery.

The author of any story based on real persons and past public events owes readers an indication of points where the story diverges from the historical record and a list of sources that establish that record. First, please remember all names and characters are fictitious, and characters based on actual persons are few.

My father had dictated a twelve-page oral history paper about his experiences in Platteville, which was supplemented by several conversations. The back issues of the *Greeley Daily Tribune* are indispensable documents for Platteville's social and athletic history in the 1920s, as for all the communities of the Platte Valley. The paper had a network of local correspondents, including my father, but never gave them a byline. I learned of the Klan breakup of a dance at the Halfway House in Big Thompson Canyon from the *Tribune*. The actual raid occurred on Sunday, April 12, 1925, rather than early September, where I have placed it.

A crucial document was the "Kloran [Handbook] of the Invisible Empire of the Knights of the Ku Klux Klan," published in Atlanta, Georgia, no date, kept in the Senter Collection of the Denver Public Library. The ritual minutely prescribed therein provided the two Klan initiations that are part of this story.

The school board's letter to parents of October 9, 1925, which ended chapter three, was copied from the District Court of Weld County, number 6774, *People of Colorado on the relation of Charles L. Vollmar v. George R. Stanley et al* filed for record on December 7, 1925. I copied the letter verbatim, except for fictionalizing the names of board members and the plaintiff. The place of religion in the public schools, entwined with the difficulty of defining the "liberty" secured against state power by the Fourteenth Amendment of the U.S. Constitution, is an issue that stirs conflict in the twenty-first century as it did in the twentieth. The narrow question of whether public schools can require the reading of biblical passages was at last decided by the U.S. Supreme Court in 1963 in *School District of Abington Township v. Schempp*, 374 U.S. 203. (They can't.)

The Colorado Supreme Court settled the question differently for Platteville in 1927, when *People ex rel. Vollmar v. Stanley et al*, 81 Col. 276 declared:

> The conclusion is that the Bible may be read without comment in
> the public schools and that children whose parents or guardians
> so desire may absent themselves from such reading.

With Harold Healy's help, Maclean, Thompson, and Stark got it right, although their reasons were less sophisticated than the court's.

The list of author's debts accumulated in preparing this manuscript is very long. Mrs. Barbara Breeden of the Nimitz Library, U.S. Naval Academy, helped my early research in subnational constitutional law and downloaded the key decisions. Ms. Colleen Nunn and Ms. Christen Satriano of the Denver Public Library were hospitable and helpful. My cousin Mrs. Beth Lomkin showed me around Platteville and arranged for me to interview two of my father's former students, John Briggs and Jerry Wardell. They explained the rules of speedball, among other matters. Beth took me to Mrs. Sally Miller of the Platteville Historical Society and the Society's museum, which has many records and photographs of Platteville's vanished high school. Economies of scale and the quality of modern school busses led to consolidating the high school with a nearby town several years ago. The grade school remains in Platteville.

A number of people with specialized knowledge helped with aspects of the story, usually reading parts of it. Judge John A. Criswell of Colorado's Appeals Court helped with legal points. Deacon Leroy Moore of St. Mary's parish, Annapolis, helped me understand Catholic attitudes of the 1920s, calling on the memories of retired priests. Emily Rocks, RN, validated my treatment of medical and veterinary details. Mrs. Joyce Bryson drew my attention to the former rules of women's basketball.

Persons who read preliminary versions with a friendly critical eye are Tom

Blackburn, Beverly and Norbert Cochran, John Criswell, Edna Donar, Julie Doughty, Allen B. Lamb, Amy K. L. Heckel, Sally A. Lamb (my wife, who passed away in 2007), Donald S. Lamm (no relation), Beth Lomkin, Sally Miller, and Emily Rocks.

Margaret Pearce has helped enormously in preparing this final version.

The book owes a lot to all these folks, but they are not responsible for its flaws.

Edwards Brothers Malloy
Thorofare, NJ USA
June 13, 2013